RODNEY STONE

RODNEY STONE

A Novel

Sir Arthur Conan Doyle

Foreword by Gabriel Chrisman

Skyhorse Publishing

First published in 1896

First Skyhorse Publishing edition 2015

Foreword copyright © 2015 by Gabriel Chrisman

Skyhorse Publishing books may be purchased in bulk at special discounts for sales promotion, corporate gifts, fund-raising, or educational purposes. Special editions can also be created to specifications. For details, contact the Special Sales Department, Skyhorse Publishing, 307 West 36th Street, 11th Floor, New York, NY 10018 or info@skyhorsepublishing.com.

Skyhorse® and Skyhorse Publishing® are registered trademarks of Skyhorse Publishing, Inc.®, a Delaware corporation.

Visit our website at www.skyhorsepublishing.com.

10 9 8 7 6 5 4 3 2 1

Library of Congress Cataloging-in-Publication Data is available on file.

Cover design by Brian Peterson

Print ISBN: 978-1-63220-588-9

Ebook ISBN: 978-1-63450-015-9

Printed in the United States of America

RODNEY STONE

FOREWORD

Sir Arthur Conan Doyle is best known for his Sherlock Holmes stories, but this is not the legacy he would have chosen. His other writings have often been over-shadowed by the famous detective he created, and in some cases entire books have been nearly forgotten. Such is the case with *Rodney Stone*. At this point in his writing career, Doyle had tried to kill off Sherlock Holmes and was choosing instead to write stories and characters that presented ideals he admired and supported, rather than the uncomfortable cynicism of Holmes: he wrote about the traditional masculine ideals of strength, honesty, intelligence, and loyalty. The characters in *Rodney Stone* are heroes Doyle created for readers to look up to, and many of the historical characters that make brief appearances in the book are exemplars a reader will understand that Doyle wished he could have met. On the face of it, this is a sensation novel and an exciting boxing story, but there is much more to be found within its pages by an inquisitive reader.

In *Rodney Stone*, Doyle weaves together several plotlines: the coming-of-age of a middle-class English boy searching for direction in his life, a classic gothic mystery centering on the inheritance of an estate, and a sports story with detailed descriptions of epic, semi-legal bare-knuckle boxing matches and the complex intrigues of the gamblers who organized them. Of these plots, the mystery is almost forgotten through most of the book, as the reader is caught up in the exciting story of the boxing world and the journey of our young narrator as he is presented with a variety of possible models for British manhood.

Doyle's choice of boxing as the theme of this novel reflects the sport's growing popularity in middle-class society during the 1890s. However, the story is set in the past—and it is not just our past, but also the past as Doyle imagined it in 1896. His vision of the early days of the nineteenth century reveals much to modern readers of the interests, worries, and preoccupations of the time in which he wrote. The increasing interest of middle-class late nineteenth-century men in athletic pursuits has been linked with growing male insecurities in a rapidly changing world. With many of the old models of masculine achievement in society, such as the apprentice system fading away or being replaced, and a new male ideal based on youthful strength rather than mature wisdom, Doyle's book offered a reassuring blend of old and new masculine characters. Having his fictitious narrator tell the story fondly from the perspective of his old age in 1851 helps to build the layers of nostalgia that serve to transport the story into the realm of nationalist myth. Clearly, Doyle saw the time of the Napoleonic wars as a high point in the history of the British Empire, and most especially as a high point in the character of the men who lived through it. He holds up several very different men in this book as role models, not just for Rodney Stone, but also for himself, for his readers at the turn of the twentieth century—and now for you.

—Gabriel Chrisman
Port Townsend, WA
November 2014

PREFACE

Amongst the books to which I am indebted for my material in my endeavour to draw various phases of life and character in England at the beginning of the century, I would particularly mention Ashton's "Dawn of the Nineteenth Century;" Gronow's "Reminiscences;" Fitzgerald's "Life and Times of George IV.;" Jesse's "Life of Brummell;" "Boxiana;" "Pugilistica;" Harper's "Brighton Road;" Robinson's "Last Earl of Barrymore" and "Old Q.;" Rice's "History of the Turf;" Tristram's "Coaching Days;" James's "Naval History;" Clark Russell's "Collingwood" and "Nelson."

I am also much indebted to my friends Mr. J. C. Parkinson and Robert Barr for information upon the subject of the ring.

A. CONAN DOYLE
HASLEMERE,
September 1, 1896

CHAPTER I—FRIAR'S OAK

On this, the first of January of the year 1851, the nineteenth century has reached its midway term, and many of us who shared its youth have already warnings which tell us that it has outworn us. We put our grizzled heads together, we older ones, and we talk of the great days that we have known; but we find that when it is with our children that we talk, it is a hard matter to make them understand. We and our fathers before us lived much the same life, but they with their railway trains and their steamboats belong to a different age. It is true that we can put history-books into their hands, and they can read from them of our weary struggle of two and twenty years with that great and evil man. They can learn how Freedom fled from the whole broad continent, and how Nelson's blood was shed, and Pitt's noble heart was broken in striving that she should not pass us for ever to take refuge with our brothers across the Atlantic. All this they can read, with the date of this treaty or that battle, but I do not know where they are to read of ourselves, of the folk we were, and the lives we led, and how the world seemed to our eyes when they were young as theirs are now.

If I take up my pen to tell you about this, you must not look for any story at my hands, for I was only in my earliest manhood when these things befell; and although I saw something of the stories of other lives, I could scarce claim one of my own. It is the love of a woman that makes the story of a man, and many a year was to pass before I first looked into the eyes of the mother of my children. To us it seems but an affair of yesterday, and yet those children can now reach the plums in the garden whilst we are seeking for a ladder, and where we once walked with their little hands in ours, we arc glad now to lean upon their arms. But I shall speak of a time when the love of a mother was the only love I knew, and if you seek for something more, then it is not for you that I write. But if you would come out with me into that forgotten world; if you would know Boy Jim and Champion Harrison; if you would meet my father, one of Nelson's own men; if you would catch a glimpse of that great seaman himself, and of George, after-wards the unworthy King of England; if, above all, you would see my famous uncle, Sir Charles Tregellis, the King of the Bucks, and the great fighting men whose names are still household words amongst you, then give me your hand and let us start.

But I must warn you also that, if you think you will find much that is of interest in your guide, you are destined to disappointment. When I look over my bookshelves, I can see that it is only the wise and witty and valiant who have ventured to write down their experiences. For my own part, if I were only assured that I was as clever and brave as the average man about me, I should be well satisfied. Men of their hands have thought well of my brains, and men of brains of my hands, and that is the best that I can say of myself. Save in the one matter of having an inborn readiness for music, so that the mastery of any instrument comes very easily and naturally to me, I cannot recall any single advantage which I can boast over my fellows. In all things I have been a half-way man, for I am of middle height, my eyes are neither blue nor grey, and my hair, before Nature dusted it with her powder, was betwixt flaxen and brown. I may, perhaps, claim this: that through life I have never felt a touch of jealousy as I have admired a better man than myself, and that I have always seen all things as they are, myself included, which should count in my favour now that I sit down in my mature age to write my memories. With your permission, then, we will push my own personality as far as possible out of the picture. If you can conceive me as a thin and colourless cord upon which my would-be pearls are strung, you will be accepting me upon the terms which I should wish.

Our family, the Stones, have for many generations belonged to the navy, and it has been a custom among us for the eldest son to take the name of his father's favourite commander. Thus we can trace our lineage back to old Vernon Stone, who commanded a high-sterned, peak-nosed, fifty-gun ship against the Dutch. Through Hawke Stone and Benbow Stone we came down to my father, Anson Stone, who in his turn christened me Rodney, at the parish church of St. Thomas at Portsmouth in the year of grace 1786.

Out of my window as I write I can see my own great lad in the garden, and if I were to call out "Nelson!" you would see that I have been true to the traditions of our family.

My dear mother, the best that ever a man had, was the second daughter of the Reverend John Tregellis, Vicar of Milton, which is a small parish upon the borders of the marshes of Langstone. She came of a poor family, but one of some position, for her elder brother was the famous Sir Charles Tregellis, who, having inherited the money of a wealthy East Indian merchant, became in time the talk of the town and the very particular friend of the Prince of Wales. Of him I shall have more to say hereafter; but you will note now that he was my own uncle, and brother to my mother.

I can remember her all through her beautiful life for she was but a girl when she married, and little more when I can first recall her busy fingers and her gentle voice. I see her as a lovely woman with kind, dove's eyes, somewhat short of stature it is true, but carrying herself very bravely. In my memories of those days she is clad always in some purple shimmering stuff, with a white kerchief round her long white neck, and I see her fingers turning and darting as she works at her knitting. I see her again in her middle years, sweet and loving, planning, contriving, achieving, with the few shillings a day of a lieutenant's pay on which to support the cottage at Friar's Oak, and to keep a fair face to the world. And now, if I do but step into the parlour, I can see her once more, with over eighty years of saintly life behind her, silver-haired, placid-faced, with her dainty ribboned cap, her gold-rimmed glasses, and her woolly shawl with the blue border. I loved her young and I love her old, and when she goes she will take something with her which nothing in the world can ever make good to me again. You may have many friends, you who read this, and you may chance to marry more than once, but your mother is your first and your last. Cherish her, then, whilst you may, for the day will come when every hasty deed or heedless word will come back with its sting to hive in your own heart.

Such, then, was my mother; and as to my father, I can describe him best when I come to the time when he returned to us from the Mediterranean. During all my childhood he was only a name to me, and a face in a miniature hung round my mother's neck. At first they told me he was fighting the French, and then after some years one heard less about the French and more about General Buonaparte. I remember the awe with which one day in Thomas Street, Portsmouth, I saw a print of the great Corsican in a bookseller's window. This, then, was the arch enemy with whom my father spent his life in terrible and ceaseless contest. To my childish imagination it was a personal affair, and I for ever saw my father and this clean-shaven, thin-lipped man swaying and reeling in a deadly, year-long grapple. It was not until I went to the Grammar School that I understood how many other little boys there were whose fathers were in the same case.

Only once in those long years did my father return home, which will show you what it meant to be the wife of a sailor in those days. It was just after we had moved from Portsmouth to Friar's Oak, whither he came for a week before he set sail with Admiral Jervis to help him to turn his name into Lord St. Vincent. I remember that he frightened as well as fascinated me with his talk of battles, and I can recall as if it were yesterday the horror with which I gazed upon a spot of blood upon his shirt ruffle, which had come, as I have no doubt, from a mischance in shaving. At the time I never questioned that it had spurted from some stricken Frenchman or Spaniard, and I shrank from him in terror when he laid his horny hand upon my head. My mother wept bitterly when he was gone, but for my own part I was not sorry to see his blue back and white shorts going down the garden walk, for I felt, with the heedless selfishness of a child, that we were closer together, she and I, when we were alone.

I was in my eleventh year when we moved from Portsmouth to Friar's Oak, a little Sussex village to the north of Brighton, which was recommended to us by my uncle, Sir Charles Tregellis, one of whose grand friends, Lord Avon, had had his seat near there. The reason of our moving was that living was cheaper in the country, and that it was easier for my mother to keep up the appearance of a gentlewoman when away from the circle of those to whom she could not refuse hospitality. They were trying times those to all save the farmers, who made such profits that they could, as I have heard, afford to let half their land lie fallow, while living like gentlemen upon the rest. Wheat was at a hundred and ten shillings a quarter, and the quartern loaf at one and ninepence. Even in the quiet of the cottage of Friar's Oak we could scarce have lived, were it not that in the blockading squadron in which my father was stationed there was the occasional chance of a little prize-money. The line-of-battle ships themselves, tacking on and off outside Brest, could earn nothing save honour; but the frigates in attendance made prizes of many coasters, and these, as is the rule of the service, were counted as belonging to the fleet, and their produce divided into head-money. In this manner my father was able to send home enough to keep the cottage and to pay for me at the day school of Mr. Joshua Allen, where for four years I learned all that he had to teach. It was at Allen's school that I first knew Jim Harrison, Boy Jim as he has always been called, the nephew of Champion Harrison of the village smithy. I can see him as he was in those days with great, floundering, half-formed limbs like a Newfoundland puppy, and a face that set every woman's head round as he passed her. It was in those days that we began our lifelong friendship, a friendship which still in our waning years binds us closely as two brothers. I taught him his exercises, for he never loved the sight of a book, and he in turn made me box and wrestle, tickle trout on the Adur, and snare rabbits on Ditching Down, for his hands were as active as his brain was slow. He was two years my elder, however, so that, long before I had finished my schooling, he had gone to help his uncle at the smithy.

Friar's Oak is in a dip of the Downs, and the forty-third milestone between London and Brighton lies on the skirt of the village. It is but a small place, with an ivied church, a fine vicarage, and a row of red-brick cottages each in its own little garden. At one end was the forge of Champion Harrison, with his house behind it, and at the other was Mr. Allen's school. The yellow cottage, standing back a little from the road, with its upper story bulging forward and a crisscross of black woodwork let into the plaster, is the one in which we lived. I do not know if it is still standing, but I should think it likely, for it was not a place much given to change.

Just opposite to us, at the other side of the broad, white road, was the Friar's Oak Inn, which was kept in my day by John Cummings, a man of excellent repute at home, but liable to strange outbreaks when he travelled, as will afterwards become apparent. Though there was a stream of traffic upon the road, the coaches from Brighton were too fresh to stop, and those from London too eager to reach their journey's end, so that if it had not been for an occasional broken trace or loosened wheel, the landlord would have had only the thirsty throats of the village to trust to. Those were the days when the Prince of Wales had just built his singular palace by the sea, and so from May to September, which was the Brighton season, there was never a day that from one to two hundred curricles, chaises, and phaetons did not rattle past our doors. Many a summer evening have Boy Jim and I lain upon the grass, watching all these grand folk, and cheering the London coaches as they came roaring through the dust clouds, leaders and wheelers stretched to their work, the bugles screaming and the coachmen with their low-crowned, curly-brimmed hats, and their faces as scarlet as their coats. The passengers used to laugh when Boy Jim shouted at them, but if they could have read his big, half-set limbs and his loose shoulders aright, they would have looked a little harder at him, perhaps, and given him back his cheer.

Boy Jim had never known a father or a mother, and his whole life had been spent with his uncle, Champion Harrison. Harrison was the Friar's Oak blacksmith, and he had his nickname because he fought Tom Johnson when he held the English belt, and would most certainly have beaten him had the Bedfordshire magistrates not appeared to break up the fight. For years there was no such glutton to take punishment and no more finishing hitter than Harrison, though he was always, as I understand, a slow one upon his feet. At last, in a fight with Black Baruk the Jew, he finished the battle with such a lashing hit that he not only knocked his opponent over the inner ropes, but he left him betwixt life and death for long three weeks. During all this time Harrison lived half demented, expecting every hour to feel the hand of a Bow Street runner upon his collar, and to be tried for his life. This experience, with the prayers of his wife, made him forswear the ring for ever, and carry his great muscles into the one trade in which they seemed to give him an advantage. There was a good business to be done at Friar's Oak from the passing traffic and the Sussex farmers, so that he soon became the richest of the villagers; and he came to church on a Sunday with his wife and his nephew, looking as respectable a family man as one would wish to see.

He was not a tall man, not more than five feet seven inches, and it was often said that if he had had an extra inch of reach he would have been a match for Jackson or Belcher at their best. His chest was like a barrel, and his forearms were the most powerful that I have ever seen, with deep groves between the smooth-swelling muscles like a piece of water-worn rock. In spite of his strength, however, he was of a slow, orderly, and kindly disposition, so that there was no man more beloved over the whole country side. His heavy, placid, clean-shaven face could set very sternly, as I have seen upon occasion; but for me and every child in the village there was ever a smile upon his lips and a greeting in his eyes. There was not a beggar upon the country side who did not know that his heart was as soft as his muscles were hard.

There was nothing that he liked to talk of more than his old battles, but he would stop if he saw his little wife coming, for the one great shadow in her life was the ever-present fear that some day he would throw down sledge and rasp and be off to the ring once more. And you must be reminded here once for all that that former calling of his was by no means at that time in the debased condition to which it afterwards fell. Public opinion has gradually become opposed to it, for the reason that it came largely into the hands of rogues, and because it fostered ringside ruffianism. Even the honest and brave pugilist was found to draw villainy round him, just as the pure and noble racehorse does. For this reason the Ring is dying in England, and we may hope that when Caunt and Bendigo have passed away, they may have none to succeed them. But it was different in the days of which I speak. Public opinion was then largely in its favour, and there were good reasons why it should be so. It was a time of war, when England with an army and navy composed only of those who volunteered to fight because they had fighting blood in them, had to encounter, as they would now have to encounter, a power which could by despotic law turn every citizen into a soldier. If the people had not been full of this lust for combat, it is certain that England must have been overborne. And it was thought, and is, on the face of it, reasonable, that a struggle between two indomitable men, with thirty thousand to view it and three million to discuss it, did help to set a standard of hardihood and endurance. Brutal it was, no doubt, and its brutality is the end of it; but it is not so brutal as war, which will survive it. Whether it is logical now to teach the people to be peaceful in an age when their very existence may come to depend upon their being warlike, is a question for wiser heads than mine. But that was what we thought of it in the days of your grandfathers, and that is why you might find statesmen and philanthropists like Windham, Fox, and Althorp at the side of the Ring.

The mere fact that solid men should patronize it was enough in itself to prevent the villainy which afterwards crept in. For over twenty years, in the days of Jackson, Brain, Cribb, the Belchers, Pearce, Gully, and the rest, the leaders of the Ring were men whose honesty was above suspicion; and those were just the twenty years when the Ring may, as I have said, have served a national purpose. You have heard how Pearce saved the Bristol girl from the burning house, how Jackson won the respect and friendship of the best men of his age, and how Gully rose to a seat in the first Reformed Parliament. These were the men who set the standard, and their trade carried with it this obvious recommendation, that it is one in which no drunken or foul-living man could long succeed. There were exceptions among them, no doubt—bullies like Hickman and brutes like Berks; in the main, I say again that they were honest men, brave and enduring to an incredible degree, and a credit to the country which produced them. It was, as you will see, my fate to see something of them, and I speak of what I know.

In our own village, I can assure you that we were very proud of the presence of such a man as Champion Harrison, and if folks stayed at the inn, they would walk down as far as the smithy just to have the sight of him. And he was worth seeing, too, especially on a winter's night when the red glare of the forge would beat upon his great muscles and upon the proud, hawk-face of Boy Jim as they heaved and swayed over some glowing plough coulter, framing themselves in sparks with every blow. He would strike once with his thirty-pound swing sledge, and Jim twice with his hand hammer; and the *Clunk— clink, clink! clunk—clink, clink!* would bring me flying down the village street, on the chance that, since they were both at the anvil, there might be a place for me at the bellows.

Only once during those village years can I remember Champion Harrison showing me for an instant the sort of man that he had been. It chanced one summer morning, when Boy Jim and I were standing by the smithy door, that there came a private coach from Brighton, with its four fresh horses, and its brass-work shining, flying along with such a merry rattle and jingling, that the Champion came running out with a half-fullered shoe in his tongs to have a look at it. A gentleman in a white coachman's cape—a Corinthian, as we would call him in those days—was driving, and half a dozen of his fellows, laughing and shouting, were on the top behind him. It may have been that the bulk of the smith caught his eye, and that he acted in pure wantonness, or it may possibly have been an accident, but, as he swung past, the twenty-foot thong of the driver's whip hissed round, and we heard the sharp snap of it across Harrison's leather apron.

"Halloa, master!" shouted the smith, looking after him. "You're not to be trusted on the box until you can handle your whip better'n that."

"What's that?" cried the driver, pulling up his team.

"I bid you have a care, master, or there will be some one-eyed folk along the road you drive."

"Oh, you say that, do you?" said the driver, putting his whip into its socket and pulling off his driving-gloves. "I'll have a little talk with you, my fine fellow."

The sporting gentlemen of those days were very fine boxers for the most part, for it was the mode to take a course of Mendoza, just as a few years afterwards there was no man about town who had not had the mufflers on with Jackson. Knowing their own prowess, they never refused the chance of a wayside adventure, and it was seldom indeed that the bargee or the navigator had much to boast of after a young blood had taken off his coat to him.

This one swung himself off the box-seat with the alacrity of a man who has no doubts about the upshot of the quarrel, and after hanging his caped coat upon the swingle-bar, he daintily turned up the ruffled cuffs of his white cambric shirt.

"I'll pay you for your advice, my man," said he.

I am sure that the men upon the coach knew who the burly smith was, and looked upon it as a prime joke to see their companion walk into such a trap. They roared with delight, and bellowed out scraps of advice to him.

"Knock some of the soot off him, Lord Frederick!" they shouted. "Give the Johnny Raw his breakfast. Chuck him in among his own cinders! Sharp's the word, or you'll see the back of him."

Encouraged by these cries, the young aristocrat advanced upon his man. The smith never moved, but his mouth set grim and hard, while his tufted brows came down over his keen, grey eyes. The tongs had fallen, and his hands were hanging free.

"Have a care, master," said he. "You'll get pepper if you don't."

Something in the assured voice, and something also in the quiet pose, warned the young lord of his danger. I saw him look hard at his antagonist, and as he did so, his hands and his jaw dropped together.

"By Gad!" he cried, "it's Jack Harrison!"

"My name, master!"

"And I thought you were some Essex chaw-bacon! Why, man, I haven't seen you since the day you nearly killed Black Baruk, and cost me a cool hundred by doing it."

How they roared on the coach.

"Smoked! Smoked, by Gad!" they yelled. "It's Jack Harrison the bruiser! Lord Frederick was going to take on the ex-champion. Give him one on the apron, Fred, and see what happens."

But the driver had already climbed back into his perch, laughing as loudly as any of his companions.

"We'll let you off this time, Harrison," said he. "Are those your sons down there?"

"This is my nephew, master."

"Here's a guinea for him! He shall never say I robbed him of his uncle." And so, having turned the laugh in his favour by his merry way of taking it, he cracked his whip, and away they flew to make London under the five hours; while Jack Harrison, with his half-fullered shoe in his hand, went whistling back to the forge.

CHAPTER II—THE WALKER OF CLIFFE ROYAL

So much for Champion Harrison! Now, I wish to say something more about Boy Jim, not only because he was the comrade of my youth, but because you will find as you go on that this book is his story rather than mine, and that there came a time when his name and his fame were in the mouths of all England. You will bear with me, therefore, while I tell you of his character as it was in those days, and especially of one very singular adventure which neither of us are likely to forget.

It was strange to see Jim with his uncle and his aunt, for he seemed to be of another race and breed to them. Often I have watched them come up the aisle upon a Sunday, first the square, thick-set man, and then the little, worn, anxious-eyed woman, and last this glorious lad with his clear-cut face, his black curls, and his step so springy and light that it seemed as if he were bound to earth by some lesser tie than the heavy-footed villagers round him. He had not yet attained his full six foot of stature, but no judge of a man (and every woman, at least, is one) could look at his perfect shoulders, his narrow loins, and his proud head that sat upon his neck like an eagle upon its perch, without feeling that sober joy which all that is beautiful in Nature gives to us—a vague self-content, as though in some way we also had a hand in the making of it.

But we are used to associate beauty with softness in a man. I do not know why they should be so coupled, and they never were with Jim. Of all men that I have known, he was the most iron-hard in body and in mind. Who was there among us who could walk with him, or run with him, or swim with him? Who on all the country side, save only Boy Jim, would have swung himself over Wolstonbury Cliff, and clambered down a hundred feet with the mother hawk flapping at his ears in the vain struggle to hold him from her nest? He was but six-teen, with his gristle not yet all set into bone, when he fought and beat Gipsy Lee, of Burgess Hill, who called himself the "Cock of the South Downs." It was after this that Champion Harrison took his training as a boxer in hand.

"I'd rather you left millin' alone, Boy Jim," said he, "and so had the missus; but if mill you must, it will not be my fault if you cannot hold up your hands to anything in the south country."

And it was not long before he made good his promise.

I have said already that Boy Jim had no love for his books, but by that I meant school-books, for when it came to the reading of romances or of anything which had a touch of gallantry or adventure, there was no tearing him away from it until it was finished. When such a book came into his hands, Friar's Oak and the smithy became a dream to him, and his life was spent out upon the ocean or wander-ing over the broad continents with his heroes. And he would draw me into his enthusiasms also, so that I was glad to play Friday to his Crusoe when he proclaimed that the Clump at Clayton was a desert island, and that we were cast upon it for a week. But when I found that we were actually to sleep out there without covering every night, and that he proposed that our food should be the sheep of the Downs (wild goats he called them) cooked upon a fire, which was to be made by the rubbing together of two sticks, my heart failed me, and on the very first night I crept away to my mother. But Jim stayed out there for the whole weary week—a wet week it was, too!—and came back at the end of it looking a deal wilder and dirtier than his hero does in the picture-books. It is well that he had only promised to stay a week, for, if it had been a month, he would have died of cold and hunger before his pride would have let him come home.

His pride!—that was the deepest thing in all Jim's nature. It is a mixed quality to my mind, half a virtue and half a vice: a virtue in holding a man out of the dirt; a vice in making it hard for him to rise when once he has fallen. Jim was proud down to the very marrow of his bones. You remember the guinea that the young lord had thrown him from the box of the coach? Two days later somebody picked it from the roadside mud. Jim only had seen where it had fallen, and he would not deign even to point it out to a beggar. Nor would he stoop to give a reason in such a case, but would answer all remonstrances with a curl of his lip and a flash of his dark eyes. Even at school he was the same, with such a sense of his own dignity, that other folk had to think of it too. He might say, as he did say, that a right angle was a proper sort of angle, or put Panama in Sicily, but old Joshua Allen would as soon have thought of raising his cane against him as he would of letting me off if I had said as much. And so it was that, although Jim was the son of nobody, and I of a King's officer, it always seemed to me to have been a condescension on his part that he should have chosen me as his friend.

It was this pride of Boy Jim's which led to an adventure which makes me shiver now when I think of it.

It happened in the August of '99, or it may have been in the early days of September; but I remember that we heard the cuckoo in Patcham Wood, and that Jim said that perhaps it was the last of him. I was still at school, but Jim had left, he being nigh sixteen and I thirteen. It was my Saturday half-holiday, and we spent it, as we often did, out upon the Downs. Our favourite place was beyond Wolstonbury, where we could stretch ourselves upon the soft, springy, chalk grass among the plump little Southdown sheep, chatting with the shepherds, as they leaned upon their queer old Pyecombe crooks, made in the days when Sussex turned out more iron than all the counties of England.

It was there that we lay upon that glorious afternoon. If we chose to roll upon our right sides, the whole weald lay in front of us, with the North Downs curving away in olive-green folds, with here and there the snow-white rift of a chalk-pit; if we turned upon our left, we overlooked the huge blue stretch of the Channel. A convoy, as I can well remember, was coming up it that day, the timid flock of merchantmen in front; the frigates, like well-trained dogs, upon the skirts; and two burly drover line-of-battle ships rolling along behind them. My fancy was soaring out to my father upon the waters, when a word from Jim brought it back on to the grass like a broken-winged gull.

"Roddy," said he, "have you heard that Cliffe Royal is haunted?"

Had I heard it? Of course I had heard it. Who was there in all the Down country who had not heard of the Walker of Cliffe Royal?

"Do you know the story of it, Roddy?"

"Why," said I, with some pride, "I ought to know it, seeing that my mother's brother, Sir Charles Tregellis, was the nearest friend of Lord Avon, and was at this card-party when the thing happened. I heard the vicar and my mother talking about it last week, and it was all so clear to me that I might have been there when the murder was done."

"It is a strange story," said Jim, thoughtfully; "but when I asked my aunt about it, she would give me no answer; and as to my uncle, he cut me short at the very mention of it."

"There is a good reason for that," said I, "for Lord Avon was, as I have heard, your uncle's best friend; and it is but natural that he would not wish to speak of his disgrace."

"Tell me the story, Roddy."

"It is an old one now—fourteen years old—and yet they have not got to the end of it. There were four of them who had come down from London to spend a few days in Lord Avon's old house. One was his own young brother, Captain Barrington; another was his cousin, Sir Lothian Hume; Sir Charles Tregellis, my uncle, was the third; and Lord Avon the fourth. They are fond of playing cards for money, these great people, and they played and played for two days and a night. Lord Avon lost, and Sir Lothian lost, and my uncle lost, and Captain

Barrington won until he could win no more. He won their money, but above all he won papers from his elder brother which meant a great deal to him. It was late on a Monday night that they stopped playing. On the Tuesday morning Captain Barrington was found dead beside his bed with his throat cut.

"And Lord Avon did it?"

"His papers were found burned in the grate, his wristband was clutched in the dead man's hand, and his knife lay beside the body."

"Did they hang him, then?"

"They were too slow in laying hands upon him. He waited until he saw that they had brought it home to him, and then he fled. He has never been seen since, but it is said that he reached America."

"And the ghost walks?"

"There are many who have seen it."

"Why is the house still empty?"

"Because it is in the keeping of the law. Lord Avon had no children, and Sir Lothian Hume—the same who was at the card-party—is his nephew and heir. But he can touch nothing until he can prove Lord Avon to be dead."

Jim lay silent for a bit, plucking at the short grass with his fingers.

"Roddy," said he at last, "will you come with me to-night and look for the ghost?"

It turned me cold, the very thought of it.

"My mother would not let me."

"Slip out when she's abed. I'll wait for you at the smithy."

"Cliffe Royal is locked."

"I'll open a window easy enough."

"I'm afraid, Jim."

"But you are not afraid if you are with me, Roddy. I'll promise you that no ghost shall hurt you."

So I gave him my word that I would come, and then all the rest of the day I went about the most sad-faced lad in Sussex. It was all very well for Boy Jim! It was that pride of his which was taking him there. He would go because there was no one else on the country side that would dare. But I had no pride of that sort. I was quite of the same way of thinking as the others, and would as soon have thought of passing my night at Jacob's gibbet on Ditchling Common as in the haunted house of Cliffe Royal. Still, I could not bring myself to desert Jim; and so, as I say, I slunk about the house with so pale and peaky a face that my dear mother would have it that I had been at the green apples, and sent me to bed early with a dish of camomile tea for my supper.

England went to rest betimes in those days, for there were few who could afford the price of candles. When I looked out of my window just after the clock had gone ten, there was not a light in the village save only at the inn. It was but a few feet from the ground, so I slipped out, and there was Jim waiting for me at the smithy corner. We crossed John's Common together, and so past Ridden's Farm, meeting only one or two riding officers upon the way. There was a brisk wind blowing, and the moon kept peeping through the rifts of the scud, so that our road was sometimes silver-clear, and sometimes so black that we found ourselves among the brambles and gorse-bushes which lined it. We came at last to the wooden gate with the high stone pillars by the roadside, and, looking through between the rails, we saw the long avenue of oaks, and at the end of this ill-boding tunnel, the pale face of the house glimmered in the moonshine.

That would have been enough for me, that one glimpse of it, and the sound of the night wind sighing and groaning among the branches. But Jim swung the gate open, and up we went, the gravel squeaking beneath our tread. It towered high, the old house, with many little windows in which the moon glinted, and with a strip of water running round three sides of it. The arched door stood right in the face of us, and on one side a lattice hung open upon its hinges.

"We're in luck, Roddy," whispered Jim. "Here's one of the windows open."

"Don't you think we've gone far enough, Jim?" said I, with my teeth chattering.

"I'll lift you in first."

"No, no, I'll not go first."

"Then I will." He gripped the sill, and had his knee on it in an instant. "Now, Roddy, give me your hands." With a pull he had me up beside him, and a moment later we were both in the haunted house.

How hollow it sounded when we jumped down on to the wooden floor! There was such a sudden boom and reverberation that we both stood silent for a moment. Then Jim burst out laughing.

"What an old drum of a place it is!" he cried; "we'll strike a light, Roddy, and see where we are."

He had brought a candle and a tinder-box in his pocket. When the flame burned up, we saw an arched stone roof above our heads, and broad deal shelves all round us covered with dusty dishes. It was the pantry.

"I'll show you round," said Jim, merrily; and, pushing the door open, he led the way into the hall. I remember the high, oak-panelled walls, with the heads of deer jutting out, and a single white bust, which sent my heart into my mouth, in the corner. Many rooms opened out of this, and we wandered from one to the other—the kitchens, the still-room, the morning-room, the dining-room, all filled with the same choking smell of dust and of mildew.

"This is where they played the cards, Jim," said I, in a hushed voice. "It was on that very table."

"Why, here are the cards themselves!" cried he; and he pulled a brown towel from something in the centre of the sideboard. Sure enough it was a pile of playing-cards—forty packs, I should think, at the least—which had lain there ever since that tragic game which was played before I was born.

"I wonder whence that stair leads?" said Jim.

"Don't go up there, Jim!" I cried, clutching at his arm. "That must lead to the room of the murder."

"How do you know that?"

"The vicar said that they saw on the ceiling—Oh, Jim, you can see it even now!"

He held up his candle, and there was a great, dark smudge upon the white plaster above us.

"I believe you're right," said he; "but anyhow I'm going to have a look at it."

"Don't, Jim, don't!" I cried.

"Tut, Roddy! you can stay here if you are afraid. I won't be more than a minute. There's no use going on a ghost hunt unless—Great Lord, there's something coming down the stairs!"

I heard it too—a shuffling footstep in the room above, and then a creak from the steps, and then another creak, and another. I saw Jim's face as if it had been carved out of ivory, with his parted lips and his staring eyes fixed upon the black square of the stair opening. He still held the light, but his fingers twitched, and with every twitch the shadows sprang from the walls to the ceiling. As to myself, my knees gave way under me, and I found myself on the floor crouching down behind Jim, with a scream frozen in my throat. And still the step came slowly from stair to stair.

Then, hardly daring to look and yet unable to turn away my eyes, I saw a figure dimly outlined in the corner upon which the stair opened. There was a silence in which I could hear my poor heart thumping, and then when I looked again the figure was gone, and the low creak, creak was heard once more upon the stairs. Jim sprang after it, and I was left half-fainting in the moonlight.

But it was not for long. He was down again in a minute, and, passing his hand under my arm, he half led and half carried me out of the house. It was not until we were in the fresh night air again that he opened his mouth.

"Can you stand, Roddy?"

"Yes, but I'm shaking."

"So am I," said he, passing his hand over his forehead. "I ask your pardon, Roddy. I was a fool to bring you on such an errand. But I never believed in such things. I know better now."

"Could it have been a man, Jim?" I asked, plucking up my courage now that I could hear the dogs barking on the farms.

"It was a spirit, Rodney."

"How do you know?"

"Because I followed it and saw it vanish into a wall, as easily as an eel into sand. Why, Roddy, what's amiss now?"

My fears were all back upon me, and every nerve creeping with horror.

"Take me away, Jim! Take me away!" I cried.

I was glaring down the avenue, and his eyes followed mine. Amid the gloom of the oak trees something was coming towards us.

"Quiet, Roddy!" whispered Jim. "By heavens, come what may, my arms are going round it this time."

We crouched as motionless as the trunks behind us. Heavy steps ploughed their way through the soft gravel, and a broad figure loomed upon us in the darkness.

Jim sprang upon it like a tiger.

"You're not a spirit, anyway!" he cried.

The man gave a shout of surprise, and then a growl of rage.

"What the deuce!" he roared, and then, "I'll break your neck if you don't let go."

The threat might not have loosened Jim's grip, but the voice did.

"Why, uncle!" he cried.

"Well, I'm blessed if it isn't Boy Jim! And what's this? Why, it's young Master Rodney Stone, as I'm a living sinner! What in the world are you two doing up at Cliffe Royal at this time of night?"

We had all moved out into the moonlight, and there was Champion Harrison with a big bundle on his arm,—and such a look of amazement upon his face as would have brought a smile back on to mine had my heart not still been cramped with fear.

"We're exploring," said Jim.

"Exploring, are you? Well, I don't think you were meant to be Captain Cooks, either of you, for I never saw such a pair of peeled-turnip faces. Why, Jim, what are you afraid of?"

"I'm not afraid, uncle. I never was afraid; but spirits are new to me, and—"

"Spirits?"

"I've been in Cliffe Royal, and we've seen the ghost."

The Champion gave a whistle.

"That's the game, is it?" said he. "Did you have speech with it?"

"It vanished first."

The Champion whistled once more.

"I've heard there is something of the sort up yonder," said he; "but it's not a thing as I would advise you to meddle with. There's enough trouble with the folk of this world, Boy Jim, without going out of your way to mix up with those of another. As to young Master Rodney Stone, if his good mother saw that white face of his, she'd never let him come to the smithy more. Walk slowly on, and I'll see you back to Friar's Oak."

We had gone half a mile, perhaps, when the Champion overtook us, and I could not but observe that the bundle was no longer under his arm. We were nearly at the smithy before Jim asked the question which was already in my mind.

"What took you up to Cliffe Royal, uncle?"

"Well, as a man gets on in years," said the Champion, "there's many a duty turns up that the likes of you have no idea of. When you're near forty yourself, you'll maybe know the truth of what I say."

So that was all we could draw from him; but, young as I was, I had heard of coast smuggling and of packages carried to lonely places at night, so that from that time on, if I had heard that the preventives had made a capture, I was never easy until I saw the jolly face of Champion Harrison looking out of his smithy door.

CHAPTER III—THE PLAY-ACTRESS OF ANSTEY CROSS

I have told you something about Friar's Oak, and about the life that we led there. Now that my memory goes back to the old place it would gladly linger, for every thread which I draw from the skein of the past brings out half a dozen others that were entangled with it. I was in two minds when I began whether I had enough in me to make a book of, and now I know that I could write one about Friar's Oak alone, and the folk whom I knew in my childhood. They were hard and uncouth, some of them, I doubt not; and yet, seen through the golden haze of time, they all seem sweet and lovable. There was our good vicar, Mr. Jefferson, who loved the whole world save only Mr. Slack, the Baptist minister of Clayton; and there was kindly Mr. Slack, who was all men's brother save only of Mr. Jefferson, the vicar of Friar's Oak. Then there was Monsieur Rudin, the French Royalist refugee who lived over on the Pangdean road, and who, when the news of a victory came in, was convulsed with joy because we had beaten Bonaparte, and shaken with rage because we had beaten the French, so that after the Nile he wept for a whole day out of delight and then for another one out of fury, alternately clapping his hands and stamping his feet. Well I remember his thin, upright figure and the way in which he jauntily twirled his little cane; for cold and hunger could not cast him down, though we knew that he had his share of both. Yet he was so proud and had such a grand manner of talking, that no one dared to offer him a cloak or a meal. I can see his face now, with a flush over each craggy cheek-bone when the butcher made him the present of some ribs of beef. He could not but take it, and yet whilst he was stalking off he threw a proud glance over his shoulder at the butcher, and he said, "Monsieur, I have a dog!" Yet it was Monsieur Rudin and not his dog who looked plumper for a week to come.

Then I remember Mr. Paterson, the farmer, who was what you would now call a Radical, though at that time some called him a Priestley-ite, and some a Fox-ite, and nearly everybody a traitor. It certainly seemed to me at the time to be very wicked that a man should look glum when he heard of a British victory; and when they burned his straw image at the gate of his farm, Boy Jim and I were among those who lent a hand. But we were bound to confess that he was game, though he might be a traitor, for down he came, striding into the midst of us with his brown coat and his buckled shoes, and the fire beating upon his grim, schoolmaster face. My word, how he rated us, and how glad we were at last to sneak quietly away.

"You livers of a lie!" said he. "You and those like you have been preaching peace for nigh two thousand years, and cutting throats the whole time. If the money that is lost in taking French lives were spent in saving English ones, you would have more right to burn candles in your windows. Who are you that dare to come here to insult a law-abiding man?"

"We are the people of England!" cried young Master Ovington, the son of the Tory Squire.

"You! you horse-racing, cock-fighting ne'er-do-weel! Do you presume to talk for the people of England? They are a deep, strong, silent stream, and you are the scum, the bubbles, the poor, silly froth that floats upon the surface."

We thought him very wicked then, but, looking back, I am not sure that we were not very wicked ourselves.

And then there were the smugglers! The Downs swarmed with them, for since there might be no lawful trade betwixt France and England, it had all to run in that channel. I have been up on St. John's Common upon a dark night, and, lying among the bracken, I have seen as many as seventy mules and a man at the head of each go flitting past me as silently as trout in a stream. Not one of them but bore its two ankers of the right French cognac, or its bale of silk of Lyons and lace of Valenciennes. I knew Dan Scales, the head of them, and I knew Tom Hislop, the riding officer, and I remember the night they met.

"Do you fight, Dan?" asked Tom.

"Yes, Tom; thou must fight for it."

On which Tom drew his pistol, and blew Dan's brains out.

"It was a sad thing to do," he said afterwards, "but I knew Dan was too good a man for me, for we tried it out before."

It was Tom who paid a poet from Brighton to write the lines for the tombstone, which we all thought were very true and good, beginning—

"Alas! Swift flew the fatal lead
Which piercéd through the young man's head.
He instantly fell, resigned his breath,
And closed his languid eyes in death."

There was more of it, and I dare say it is all still to be read in Patcham Churchyard.

One day, about the time of our Cliffe Royal adventure, I was seated in the cottage looking round at the curios which my father had fastened on to the walls, and wishing, like the lazy lad that I was, that Mr. Lilly had died before ever he wrote his Latin grammar, when my mother, who was sitting knitting in the window, gave a little cry of surprise.

"Good gracious!" she cried. "What a vulgar-looking woman!"

It was so rare to hear my mother say a hard word against any-body (unless it were General Bonaparte) that I was across the room and at the window in a jump. A pony-chaise was coming slowly down the village street, and in it was the queerest-looking person that I had ever seen. She was very stout, with a face that was of so dark a red that it shaded away into purple over the nose and cheeks. She wore a great hat with a white curling ostrich feather, and from under its brim her two bold, black eyes stared out with a look of anger and defiance as if to tell the folk that she thought less of them than they could do of her. She had some sort of scarlet pelisse with white swans-down about her neck, and she held the reins slack in her hands, while the pony wandered from side to side of the road as the fancy took him. Each time the chaise swayed, her head with the great hat swayed also, so that sometimes we saw the crown of it and sometimes the brim.

"What a dreadful sight!" cried my mother.

"What is amiss with her, mother?"

"Heaven forgive me if I misjudge her, Rodney, but I think that the unfortunate woman has been drinking."

"Why," I cried, "she has pulled the chaise up at the smithy. I'll find out all the news for you;" and, catching up my cap, away I scampered.

Champion Harrison had been shoeing a horse at the forge door, and when I got into the street I could see him with the creature's hoof still under his arm, and the rasp in his hand, kneeling down amid the white parings. The woman was beckoning him from the chaise, and he staring up at her with the queerest expression upon his face. Presently he threw down his rasp and went across to her, standing by the wheel and shaking his head as he talked to her. For my part, I slipped into the smithy, where Boy Jim was finishing the shoe, and I watched the neatness of his work and the deft way in which he turned up the caulkens. When he had done with it he carried it out, and there was the strange woman still talking with his uncle.

"Is that he?" I heard her ask.

Champion Harrison nodded.

She looked at Jim, and I never saw such eyes in a human head, so large, and black, and wonderful. Boy as I was, I knew that, in spite of that bloated face, this woman had once been very beautiful. She put out a hand, with all the fingers going as if she were playing on the harpsichord, and she touched Jim on the shoulder.

"I hope—I hope you're well," she stammered.

"Very well, ma'am," said Jim, staring from her to his uncle.

"And happy too?"

"Yes, ma'am, I thank you."

"Nothing that you crave for?"

"Why, no, ma'am, I have all that I lack."

"That will do, Jim," said his uncle, in a stern voice. "Blow up the forge again, for that shoe wants reheating."

But it seemed as if the woman had something else that she would say, for she was angry that he should be sent away. Her eyes gleamed, and her head tossed, while the smith with his two big hands outspread seemed to be soothing her as best he could. For a long time they whispered until at last she appeared to be satisfied.

"To-morrow, then?" she cried loud out.

"To-morrow," he answered.

"You keep your word and I'll keep mine," said she, and dropped the lash on the pony's back. The smith stood with the rasp in his hand, looking after her until she was just a little red spot on the white road. Then he turned, and I never saw his face so grave.

"Jim," said he, "that's Miss Hinton, who has come to live at The Maples, out Anstey Cross way. She's taken a kind of a fancy to you, Jim, and maybe she can help you on a bit. I promised her that you would go over and see her to-morrow."

"I don't want her help, uncle, and I don't want to see her."

"But I've promised, Jim, and you wouldn't make me out a liar. She does but want to talk with you, for it is a lonely life she leads."

"What would she want to talk with such as me about?"

"Why, I cannot say that, but she seemed very set upon it, and women have their fancies. There's young Master Stone here who wouldn't refuse to go and see a good lady, I'll warrant, if he thought he might better his fortune by doing so."

"Well, uncle, I'll go if Roddy Stone will go with me," said Jim.

"Of course he'll go. Won't you, Master Rodney?"

So it ended in my saying "yes," and back I went with all my news to my mother, who dearly loved a little bit of gossip. She shook her head when she heard where I was going, but she did not say nay, and so it was settled.

It was a good four miles of a walk, but when we reached it you would not wish to see a more cosy little house: all honeysuckle and creepers, with a wooden porch and lattice windows. A common-looking woman opened the door for us.

"Miss Hinton cannot see you," said she.

"But she asked us to come," said Jim.

"I can't help that," cried the woman, in a rude voice. "I tell you that she can't see you."

We stood irresolute for a minute.

"Maybe you would just tell her I am here," said Jim, at last.

"Tell her! How am I to tell her when she couldn't so much as hear a pistol in her ears? Try and tell her yourself, if you have a mind to."

She threw open a door as she spoke, and there, in a reclining chair at the further end of the room, we caught a glimpse of a figure all lumped together, huge and shapeless, with tails of black hair hanging down.

The sound of dreadful, swine-like breathing fell upon our ears. It was but a glance, and then we were off hot-foot for home. As for me, I was so young that I was not sure whether this was funny or terrible; but when I looked at Jim to see how he took it, he was looking quite white and ill.

"You'll not tell any one, Roddy," said he.

"Not unless it's my mother."

"I won't even tell my uncle. I'll say she was ill, the poor lady! It's enough that we should have seen her in her shame, without its being the gossip of the village. It makes me feel sick and heavy at heart."

"She was so yesterday, Jim."

"Was she? I never marked it. But I know that she has kind eyes and a kind heart, for I saw the one in the other when she looked at me. Maybe it's the want of a friend that has driven her to this."

It blighted his spirits for days, and when it had all gone from my mind it was brought back to me by his manner. But it was not to be our last memory of the lady with the scarlet pelisse, for before the week was out Jim came round to ask me if I would again go up with him.

"My uncle has had a letter," said he. "She would speak with me, and it would be easier if you came with me, Rod."

For me it was only a pleasure outing, but I could see, as we drew near the house, that Jim was troubling in his mind lest we should find that things were amiss.

His fears were soon set at rest, however, for we had scarce clicked the garden gate before the woman was out of the door of the cottage and running down the path to meet us. She was so strange a figure, with some sort of purple wrapper on, and her big, flushed face smiling out of it, that I might, if I had been alone, have taken to my heels at the sight of her. Even Jim stopped for a moment as if he were not very sure of himself, but her hearty ways soon set us at our ease.

"It is indeed good of you to come and see an old, lonely woman," said she, "and I owe you an apology that I should give you a fruitless journey on Tuesday, but in a sense you were yourselves the cause of it, since the thought of your coming had excited me, and any excitement throws me into a nervous fever. My poor nerves! You can see for yourselves how they serve me."

She held out her twitching hands as she spoke. Then she passed one of them through Jim's arm, and walked with him up the path.

"You must let me know you, and know you well," said she. "Your uncle and aunt are quite old acquaintances of mine, and though you cannot remember me, I have held you in my arms when you were an infant. Tell me, little man," she added, turning to me, "what do you call your friend?"

"Boy Jim, ma'am," said I.

"Then if you will not think me forward, I will call you Boy Jim also. We elderly people have our privileges, you know. And now you shall come in with me, and we will take a dish of tea together."

She led the way into a cosy room—the same which we had caught a glimpse of when last we came—and there, in the middle, was a table with white napery, and shining glass, and gleaming china, and red-cheeked apples piled upon a centre-dish, and a great plateful of smoking muffins which the cross-faced maid had just carried in. You can think that we did justice to all the good things, and Miss Hinton would ever keep pressing us to pass our cup and to fill our plate. Twice during our meal she rose from her chair and withdrew into a cupboard at the end of the room, and each time I saw Jim's face cloud, for we heard a gentle clink of glass against glass.

"Come now, little man," said she to me, when the table had been cleared. "Why are you looking round so much?"

"Because there are so many pretty things upon the walls."

"And which do you think the prettiest of them?"

"Why, that!" said I, pointing to a picture which hung opposite to me. It was of a tall and slender girl, with the rosiest cheeks and the tenderest eyes—so daintily dressed, too, that I had never seen anything more perfect. She had a posy of flowers in her hand and another one was lying upon the planks of wood upon which she was standing.

"Oh, that's the prettiest, is it?" said she, laughing. "Well, now, walk up to it, and let us hear what is writ beneath it."

I did as she asked, and read out: "Miss Polly Hinton, as 'Peggy,' in The Country Wife, played for her benefit at the Haymarket Theatre, September 14th, 1782."

"It's a play-actress," said I.

"Oh, you rude little boy, to say it in such a tone," said she; "as if a play-actress wasn't as good as any one else. Why, 'twas but the other day that the Duke of Clarence, who may come to call himself King of England, married Mrs. Jordan, who is herself only a play-actress. And whom think you that this one is?"

She stood under the picture with her arms folded across her great body, and her big black eyes looking from one to the other of us.

"Why, where are your eyes?" she cried at last. "I was Miss Polly Hinton of the Haymarket Theatre. And perhaps you never heard the name before?"

We were compelled to confess that we never had. And the very name of play-actress had filled us both with a kind of vague horror, like the country-bred folk that we were. To us they were a class apart, to be hinted at rather than named, with the wrath of the Almighty hanging over them like a thundercloud. Indeed, His judgments seemed to be in visible operation before us when we looked upon what this woman was, and what she had been.

"Well," said she, laughing like one who is hurt, "you have no cause to say anything, for I read on your face what you have been taught to think of me. So this is the upbringing that you have had, Jim—to think evil of that which you do not understand! I wish you had been in the theatre that very night with Prince Florizel and four Dukes in the boxes, and all the wits and macaronis of London rising at me in the pit. If Lord Avon had not given me a cast in his carriage, I had never got my flowers back to my lodgings in York Street, Westminster. And now two little country lads are sitting in judgment upon me!"

Jim's pride brought a flush on to his cheeks, for he did not like to be called a country lad, or to have it supposed that he was so far behind the grand folk in London.

"I have never been inside a play-house," said he; "I know nothing of them."

"Nor I either."

"Well," said she, "I am not in voice, and it is ill to play in a little room with but two to listen, but you must conceive me to be the Queen of the Peruvians, who is exhorting her countrymen to rise up against the Spaniards, who are oppressing them."

And straightway that coarse, swollen woman became a queen—the grandest, haughtiest queen that you could dream of—and she turned upon us with such words of fire, such lightning eyes and sweeping of her white hand, that she held us spellbound in our chairs. Her voice was soft and sweet, and persuasive at the first, but louder it rang and louder as it spoke of wrongs and freedom and the joys of death in a good cause, until it thrilled into my every nerve, and I asked nothing more than to run out of the cottage and to die then and there in the cause of my country. And then in an instant she changed. She was a poor woman now, who had lost her only child, and who was bewailing it. Her voice was full of tears, and what she said was so simple, so true, that we both seemed to see the dead babe stretched there on the carpet before us, and we could have joined in with words of pity and of grief. And then, before our cheeks were dry, she was back into her old self again.

"How like you that, then?" she cried. "That was my way in the days when Sally Siddons would turn green at the name of Polly Hinton. It's a fine play, is Pizarro."

"And who wrote it, ma'am?"

"Who wrote it? I never heard. What matter who did the writing of it! But there are some great lines for one who knows how they should be spoken."

"And you play no longer, ma'am?"

"No, Jim, I left the boards when—when I was weary of them. But my heart goes back to them sometimes. It seems to me there is no smell like that of the hot oil in the footlights and of the oranges in the pit. But you are sad, Jim."

"It was but the thought of that poor woman and her child."

"Tut, never think about her! I will soon wipe her from your mind. This is 'Miss Priscilla Tomboy,' from The Romp. You must conceive that the mother is speaking, and that the forward young minx is answering.

And she began a scene between the two of them, so exact in voice and manner that it seemed to us as if there were really two folk before us: the stern old mother with her hand up like an ear-trumpet, and her flouncing, bouncing daughter. Her great figure danced about with a wonderful lightness, and she tossed her head and pouted her lips as she answered back to the old, bent figure that addressed her. Jim and I had forgotten our tears, and were holding our ribs before she came to the end of it.

"That is better," said she, smiling at our laughter. "I would not have you go back to Friar's Oak with long faces, or maybe they would not let you come to me again."

She vanished into her cupboard, and came out with a bottle and glass, which she placed upon the table.

"You are too young for strong waters," she said, "but this talking gives one a dryness, and—"

Then it was that Boy Jim did a wonderful thing. He rose from his chair, and he laid his hand upon the bottle.

"Don't!" said he.

She looked him in the face, and I can still see those black eyes of hers softening before the gaze.

"Am I to have none?"

"Please, don't."

With a quick movement she wrested the bottle out of his hand and raised it up so that for a moment it entered my head that she was about to drink it off. Then she flung it through the open lattice, and we heard the crash of it on the path outside.

"There, Jim!" said she; "does that satisfy you? It's long since any one cared whether I drank or no."

"You are too good and kind for that," said he.

"Good!" she cried. "Well, I love that you should think me so. And it would make you happier if I kept from the brandy, Jim? Well, then, I'll make you a promise, if you'll make me one in return."

"What's that, miss?"

"No drop shall pass my lips, Jim, if you will swear, wet or shine, blow or snow, to come up here twice in every week, that I may see you and speak with you, for, indeed, there are times when I am very lonesome."

So the promise was made, and very faithfully did Jim keep it, for many a time when I have wanted him to go fishing or rabbit-snaring, he has remembered that it was his day for Miss Hinton, and has tramped off to Anstey Cross. At first I think that she found her share of the bargain hard to keep, and I have seen Jim come back with a black face on him, as if things were going amiss. But after a time the fight was won—as all fights are won if one does but fight long enough—and in the year before my father came back Miss Hinton had become another woman. And it was not her ways only, but herself as well, for from being the person that I have described, she became in one twelve-month as fine a looking lady as there was in the whole country-side. Jim was prouder of it by far than of anything he had had a hand in in his life, but it was only to me that he ever spoke about it, for he had that tenderness towards her that one has for those whom one has helped. And she helped him also, for by her talk of the world and of what she had seen, she took his mind away from the Sussex country-side and prepared it for a broader life beyond. So matters stood between them at the time when peace was made and my father came home from the sea.

CHAPTER IV—THE PEACE OF AMIENS

Many a woman's knee was on the ground, and many a woman's soul spent itself in joy and thankfulness when the news came with the fall of the leaf in 1801 that the preliminaries of peace had been settled. All England waved her gladness by day and twinkled it by night. Even in little Friar's Oak we had our flags flying bravely, and a candle in every window, with a big G.R. guttering in the wind over the door of the inn. Folk were weary of the war, for we had been at it for eight years, taking Holland, and Spain, and France each in turn and all together. All that we had learned during that time was that our little army was no match for the French on land, and that our large navy was more than a match for them upon the water. We had gained some credit, which we were sorely in need of after the American business; and a few Colonies, which were welcome also for the same reason; but our debt had gone on rising and our consols sinking, until even Pitt stood aghast. Still, if we had known that there never could be peace between Napoleon and ourselves, and that this was only the end of a round and not of the battle, we should have been better advised had we fought it out without a break. As it was, the French got back the twenty thousand good seamen whom we had captured, and a fine dance they led

us with their Boulogne flotillas and fleets of invasion before we were
able to catch them again.

My father, as I remember him best, was a tough, strong little man, of
no great breadth, but solid and well put together. His face was burned
of a reddish colour, as bright as a flower-pot, and in spite of his age (for
he was only forty at the time of which I speak) it was shot with lines,
which deepened if he were in any way perturbed, so that I have seen
him turn on the instant from a youngish man to an elderly. His eyes
especially were meshed round with wrinkles, as is natural for one who
had puckered them all his life in facing foul wind and bitter weather.
These eyes were, perhaps, his strangest feature, for they were of a very
clear and beautiful blue, which shone the brighter out of that ruddy
setting. By nature he must have been a fair-skinned man, for his upper
brow, where his cap came over it, was as white as mine, and his close-
cropped hair was tawny.

He had served, as he was proud to say, in the last of our ships which
had been chased out of the Mediterranean in '97, and in the first which
had re-entered it in '98. He was under Miller, as third lieutenant of the
Theseus, when our fleet, like a pack of eager fox hounds in a covert,
was dashing from Sicily to Syria and back again to Naples, trying to
pick up the lost scent. With the same good fighting man he served
at the Nile, where the men of his command sponged and rammed
and trained until, when the last tricolour had come down, they hove
up the sheet anchor and fell dead asleep upon the top of each other
under the capstan bars. Then, as a second lieutenant, he was in one of
those grim three-deckers with powder-blackened hulls and crimson
scupper-holes, their spare cables tied round their keels and over their
bulwarks to hold them together, which carried the news into the Bay
of Naples. From thence, as a reward for his services, he was transferred
as first lieutenant to the Aurora frigate, engaged in cutting off supplies
from Genoa, and in her he still remained until long after peace was
declared.

How well I can remember his home-coming! Though it is now
eight-and-forty years ago, it is clearer to me than the doings of last

week, for the memory of an old man is like one of those glasses which shows out what is at a distance and blurs all that is near.

My mother had been in a tremble ever since the first rumour of the preliminaries came to our ears, for she knew that he might come as soon as his message. She said little, but she saddened my life by insisting that I should be for ever clean and tidy. With every rumble of wheels, too, her eyes would glance towards the door, and her hands steal up to smooth her pretty black hair. She had embroidered a white "Welcome" upon a blue ground, with an anchor in red upon each side, and a border of laurel leaves; and this was to hang upon the two lilac bushes which flanked the cottage door. He could not have left the Mediterranean before we had this finished, and every morning she looked to see if it were in its place and ready to be hanged.

But it was a weary time before the peace was ratified, and it was April of next year before our great day came round to us. It had been raining all morning, I remember—a soft spring rain, which sent up a rich smell from the brown earth and pattered pleasantly upon the budding chestnuts behind our cottage. The sun had shone out in the evening, and I had come down with my fishing-rod (for I had promised Boy Jim to go with him to the mill-stream), when what should I see but a post-chaise with two smoking horses at the gate, and there in the open door of it were my mother's black skirt and her little feet jutting out, with two blue arms for a waist-belt, and all the rest of her buried in the chaise. Away I ran for the motto, and I pinned it up on the bushes as we had agreed, but when I had finished there were the skirts and the feet and the blue arms just the same as before.

"Here's Rod," said my mother at last, struggling down on to the ground again. "Roddy, darling, here's your father!"

I saw the red face and the kindly, light-blue eyes looking out at me.

"Why, Roddy, lad, you were but a child and we kissed good-bye when last we met; but I suppose we must put you on a different rating now. I'm right glad from my heart to see you, dear lad; and as to you, sweetheart—"

The blue arms flew out, and there were the skirt and the two feet fixed in the door again.

"Here are the folk coming, Anson," said my mother, blushing. "Won't you get out and come in with us?"

And then suddenly it came home to us both that for all his cheery face he had never moved more than his arms, and that his leg was resting on the opposite seat of the chaise.

"Oh, Anson, Anson!" she cried.

"Tut, 'tis but the bone of my leg," said he, taking his knee between his hands and lifting it round. "I got it broke in the Bay, but the surgeon has fished it and spliced it, though it's a bit crank yet. Why, bless her kindly heart, if I haven't turned her from pink to white. You can see for yourself that it's nothing."

He sprang out as he spoke, and with one leg and a staff he hopped swiftly up the path, and under the laurel-bordered motto, and so over his own threshold for the first time for five years. When the post-boy and I had carried up the sea-chest and the two canvas bags, there he was sitting in his armchair by the window in his old weather-stained blue coat. My mother was weeping over his poor leg, and he patting her hair with one brown hand. His other he threw round my waist, and drew me to the side of his chair.

"Now that we have peace, I can lie up and refit until King George needs me again," said he. "'Twas a carronade that came adrift in the Bay when it was blowing a top-gallant breeze with a beam sea. Ere we could make it fast it had me jammed against the mast. Well, well," he added, looking round at the walls of the room, "here are all my old curios, the same as ever: the narwhal's horn from the Arctic, and the blowfish from the Moluccas, and the paddles from Fiji, and the picture of the Ca Ira with Lord Hotham in chase. And here you are, Mary, and you also, Roddy, and good luck to the carronade which has sent me into so snug a harbour without fear of sailing orders."

My mother had his long pipe and his tobacco all ready for him, so that he was able now to light it and to sit looking from one of us to the other and then back again, as if he could never see enough of us. Young as I was, I could still understand that this was the moment which he had thought of during many a lonely watch, and that the expectation of it had cheered his heart in many a dark hour. Sometimes he would touch one of us with his hand, and sometimes the other, and so he sat, with his soul too satiated for words, whilst the shadows gathered in the little room and the lights of the inn windows glimmered through the gloom. And then, after my mother had lit our own lamp, she slipped suddenly down upon her knees, and he got one knee to the ground also, so that, hand-in-hand, they joined their thanks to Heaven for manifold mercies. When I look back at my parents as they were in those days, it is at that very moment that I can picture them most clearly: her sweet face with the wet shining upon her cheeks, and his blue eyes upturned to the smoke-blackened ceiling. I remember that he swayed his reeking pipe in the earnestness of his prayer, so that I was half tears and half smiles as I watched him.

"Roddy, lad," said he, after supper was over, "you're getting a man now, and I suppose you will go afloat like the rest of us. You're old enough to strap a dirk to your thigh."

"And leave me without a child as well as without a husband!" cried my mother.

"Well, there's time enough yet," said he, "for they are more inclined to empty berths than to fill them, now that peace has come. But I've never tried what all this schooling has done for you, Rodney. You have had a great deal more than ever I had, but I dare say I can make shift to test it. Have you learned history?"

"Yes, father," said I, with some confidence.

"Then how many sail of the line were at the Battle of Camperdown?"

He shook his head gravely when he found that I could not answer him.

"Why, there are men in the fleet who never had any schooling at all who could tell you that we had seven 74's, seven 64's, and two 50-gun ships in the action. There's a picture on the wall of the chase of the Ca Ira. Which were the ships that laid her aboard?"

Again I had to confess that he had beaten me.

"Well, your dad can teach you something in history yet," he cried, looking in triumph at my mother. "Have you learned geography?"

"Yes, father," said I, though with less confidence than before.

"Well, how far is it from Port Mahon to Algeciras?"

I could only shake my head.

"If Ushant lay three leagues upon your starboard quarter, what would be your nearest English port?"

Again I had to give it up.

"Well, I don't see that your geography is much better than your history," said he. "You'd never get your certificate at this rate. Can you do addition? Well, then, let us see if you can tot up my prize-money."

He shot a mischievous glance at my mother as he spoke, and she laid down her knitting on her lap and looked very earnestly at him.

"You never asked me about that, Mary," said he.

"The Mediterranean is not the station for it, Anson. I have heard you say that it is the Atlantic for prize-money, and the Mediterranean for honour."

"I had a share of both last cruise, which comes from changing a line-of-battleship for a frigate. Now, Rodney, there are two pounds in every hundred due to me when the prize-courts have done with them. When we were watching Massena, off Genoa, we got a matter of seventy schooners, brigs, and tartans, with wine, food, and powder. Lord Keith will want his finger in the pie, but that's for the Courts to settle. Put them at four pounds apiece to me, and what will the seventy bring?"

"Two hundred and eighty pounds," I answered.

"Why, Anson, it is a fortune!" cried my mother, clapping her hands.

"Try you again, Roddy!" said he, shaking his pipe at me. "There was the Xebec frigate out of Barcelona with twenty thousand Spanish dollars aboard, which make four thousand of our pounds. Her hull should be worth another thousand. What's my share of that?"

"A hundred pounds."

"Why, the purser couldn't work it out quicker," he cried in his delight. "Here's for you again! We passed the Straits and worked up to the

Azores, where we fell in with the La Sabina from the Mauritius with sugar and spices. Twelve hundred pounds she's worth to me, Mary, my darling, and never again shall you soil your pretty fingers or pinch upon my beggarly pay.

My dear mother had borne her long struggle without a sign all these years, but now that she was so suddenly eased of it she fell sobbing upon his neck. It was a long time before my father had a thought to spare upon my examination in arithmetic.

"It's all in your lap, Mary," said he, dashing his own hand across his eyes. "By George, lass, when this leg of mine is sound we'll bear down for a spell to Brighton, and if there is a smarter frock than yours upon the Steyne, may I never tread a poop again. But how is it that you are so quick at figures, Rodney, when you know nothing of history or geography?"

I tried to explain that addition was the same upon sea or land, but that history and geography were not.

"Well," he concluded, "you need figures to take a reckoning, and you need nothing else save what your mother wit will teach you. There never was one of our breed who did not take to salt water like a young gull. Lord Nelson has promised me a vacancy for you, and he'll be as good as his word."

So it was that my father came home to us, and a better or kinder no lad could wish for. Though my parents had been married so long, they had really seen very little of each other, and their affection was as warm and as fresh as if they were two newly-wedded lovers. I have learned since that sailors can be coarse and foul, but never did I know it from my father; for, although he had seen as much rough work as the wildest could wish for, he was always the same patient, good-humoured man, with a smile and a jolly word for all the village. He could suit himself to his company, too, for on the one hand he could take his wine with the vicar, or with Sir James Ovington, the squire of the parish; while on the other he would sit by the hour amongst my humble friends down in the smithy, with Champion Harrison, Boy Jim, and the rest of them, telling them such stories of Nelson and his men that

I have seen the Champion knot his great hands together, while Jim's eyes have smouldered like the forge embers as he listened.

My father had been placed on half-pay, like so many others of the old war officers, and so, for nearly two years, he was able to remain with us. During all this time I can only once remember that there was the slightest disagreement between him and my mother. It chanced that I was the cause of it, and as great events sprang out of it, I must tell you how it came about. It was indeed the first of a series of events which affected not only my fortunes, but those of very much more important people.

The spring of 1803 was an early one, and the middle of April saw the leaves thick upon the chestnut trees. One evening we were all seated together over a dish of tea when we heard the scrunch of steps outside our door, and there was the postman with a letter in his hand.

"I think it is for me," said my mother, and sure enough it was addressed in the most beautiful writing to Mrs. Mary Stone, of Friar's Oak, and there was a red seal the size of a half-crown upon the outside of it with a flying dragon in the middle.

"Whom think you that it is from, Anson?" she asked.

"I had hoped that it was from Lord Nelson," answered my father. "It is time the boy had his commission. But if it be for you, then it cannot be from any one of much importance."

"Can it not!" she cried, pretending to be offended. "You will ask my pardon for that speech, sir, for it is from no less a person than Sir Charles Tregellis, my own brother."

My mother seemed to speak with a hushed voice when she mentioned this wonderful brother of hers, and always had done as long as I can remember, so that I had learned also to have a subdued and reverent feeling when I heard his name. And indeed it was no wonder, for that name was never mentioned unless it were in connection with something brilliant and extraordinary. Once we heard that he was at Windsor with the King. Often he was at Brighton with the Prince. Sometimes it was as a sportsman that his reputation reached us, as when his Meteor beat the Duke of Queensberry's Egham, at

Newmarket, or when he brought Jim Belcher up from Bristol, and sprang him upon the London fancy. But usually it was as the friend of the great, the arbiter of fashions, the king of bucks, and the best-dressed man in town that his reputation reached us. My father, however, did not appear to be elated at my mother's triumphant rejoinder.

"Ay, and what does he want?" asked he, in no very amiable voice.

"I wrote to him, Anson, and told him that Rodney was growing a man now, thinking, since he had no wife or child of his own, he might be disposed to advance him."

"We can do very well without him," growled my father. "He sheered off from us when the weather was foul, and we have no need of him now that the sun is shining."

"Nay, you misjudge him, Anson," said my mother, warmly. "There is no one with a better heart than Charles; but his own life moves so smoothly that he cannot understand that others may have trouble. During all these years I have known that I had but to say the word to receive as much as I wished from him."

"Thank God that you never had to stoop to it, Mary. I want none of his help."

"But we must think of Rodney."

"Rodney has enough for his sea-chest and kit. He needs no more."

"But Charles has great power and influence in London. He could make Rodney known to all the great people. Surely you would not stand in the way of his advancement."

"Let us hear what he says, then," said my father; and this was the letter which she read to him—

14, Jermyn Street, St. James's,
"April 15th, 1803.
"MY DEAR SISTER MARY,

"In answer to your letter, I can assure you that you must not conceive me to be wanting in those finer feelings which are the chief adornment of humanity. It is true that for some years, absorbed as I have been in affairs of the highest importance, I have seldom taken a pen in hand, for which I can assure you that I have been reproached by many *des plus charmantes* of your charming sex. At the present moment I lie abed (having stayed late in order to pay a compliment to the Marchioness of Dover at her ball last night), and this is writ to my dictation by Ambrose, my clever rascal of a valet. I am interested to hear of my nephew Rodney (*Mon dieu, quel nom!*), and as I shall be on my way to visit the Prince at Brighton next week, I shall break my journey at Friar's Oak for the sake of seeing both you and him. Make my compliments to your husband.

"I am ever, my dear sister Mary,

"Your brother,

"CHARLES TREGELLIS."

"What do you think of that?" cried my mother in triumph when she had finished.

"I think it is the letter of a fop," said my father, bluntly.

"You are too hard on him, Anson. You will think better of him when you know him. But he says that he will be here next week, and this is Thursday, and the best curtains unhung, and no lavender in the sheets!"

Away she bustled, half distracted, while my father sat moody, with his chin upon his hands, and I remained lost in wonder at the thought of this grand new relative from London, and of all that his coming might mean to us.

CHAPTER V—BUCK TREGELLIS

Now that I was in my seventeenth year, and had already some need for a razor, I had begun to weary of the narrow life of the village, and to long to see something of the great world beyond. The craving was all the stronger because I durst not speak openly about it, for the least hint of it brought the tears into my mother's eyes. But now there was the less reason that I should stay at home, since my father was at her side, and so my mind was all filled by this prospect of my uncle's visit, and of the chance that he might set my feet moving at last upon the road of life.

As you may think, it was towards my father's profession that my thoughts and my hopes turned, for from my childhood I have never seen the heave of the sea or tasted the salt upon my lips without feeling the blood of five generations of seamen thrill within my veins. And think of the challenge which was ever waving in those days before the eyes of a coast-living lad! I had but to walk up to Wolstonbury in the war time to see the sails of the French chasse-marées and privateers. Again and again I have heard the roar of the guns coming from far out over the waters. Seamen would tell us how they had left London and been engaged ere nightfall, or sailed out of Portsmouth and been yard-arm to yard-arm before they had lost sight of St. Helen's light. It was this imminence of the danger which warmed our hearts to our sailors, and made us talk, round the winter fires, of our little Nelson, and Cuddie Collingwood, and Johnnie Jarvis, and the rest of them, not as being great High Admirals with titles and dignities, but as good friends whom we loved and honoured above all others. What boy was there through the length and breadth of Britain who did not long to be out with them under the red-cross flag?

But now that peace had come, and the fleets which had swept the Channel and the Mediterranean were lying dismantled in our harbours, there was less to draw one's fancy seawards. It was London now of which I thought by day and brooded by night: the huge city, the home of the wise and the great, from which came this constant stream of carriages, and those crowds of dusty people who were for ever flashing past our window-pane. It was this one side of life which first presented itself to me, and so, as a boy, I used to picture the City as a gigantic stable with a huge huddle of coaches, which were for ever streaming off down the country roads. But, then, Champion Harrison told me how the fighting-men lived there, and my father how the heads of the Navy lived there, and my mother how her brother and his grand friends were there, until at last I was consumed with impatience to see this marvellous heart of England. This coming of my uncle, then, was the breaking of light through the darkness, though I hardly dared to hope that he would take me with him into those high circles in which he lived. My mother, however, had such confidence either in his good nature or in her own powers of persuasion, that she already began to make furtive preparations for my departure.

But if the narrowness of the village life chafed my easy spirit, it was a torture to the keen and ardent mind of Boy Jim. It was but a few days after the coming of my uncle's letter that we walked over the Downs together, and I had a peep of the bitterness of his heart.

"What is there for me to do, Rodney?" he cried. "I forge a shoe, and I fuller it, and I clip it, and I caulken it, and I knock five holes in it, and there it is finished. Then I do it again and again, and blow up the bellows and feed the forge, and rasp a hoof or two, and there is a day's work done, and every day the same as the other. Was it for this only, do you think, that I was born into the world?"

I looked at him, his proud, eagle face, and his tall, sinewy figure, and I wondered whether in the whole land there was a finer, handsomer man.

"The Army or the Navy is the place for you, Jim," said I.

"That is very well," he cried. "If you go into the Navy, as you are likely to do, you go as an officer, and it is you who do the ordering. If I go in, it is as one who was born to receive orders."

"An officer gets his orders from those above him."

"But an officer does not have the lash hung over his head. I saw a poor fellow at the inn here—it was some years ago—who showed us his back in the tap-room, all cut into red diamonds with the boat-swain's whip. 'Who ordered that?' I asked. 'The captain,' said he. 'And what would you have had if you had struck him dead?' said I. 'The yard-arm,' he answered. 'Then if I had been you that's where I should have been,' said I, and I spoke the truth. I can't help it, Rod! There's something here in my heart, something that is as much a part of myself as this hand is, which holds me to it."

"I know that you are as proud as Lucifer," said I.

"It was born with me, Roddy, and I can't help it. Life would be easier if I could. I was made to be my own master, and there's only one place where I can hope to be so."

"Where is that, Jim?"

"In London. Miss Hinton has told me of it, until I feel as if I could find my way through it from end to end. She loves to talk of it as well as I do to listen. I have it all laid out in my mind, and I can see where the playhouses are, and how the river runs, and where the King's house is, and the Prince's, and the place where the fighting-men live. I could make my name known in London."

"How?"

"Never mind how, Rod. I could do it, and I will do it, too. 'Wait!' says my uncle—'wait, and it will all come right for you.' That is what he always says, and my aunt the same. Why should I wait? What am I to wait for? No, Roddy, I'll stay no longer eating my heart out in this little village, but I'll leave my apron behind me and I'll seek my fortune in London, and when I come back to Friar's Oak, it will be in such style as that gentleman yonder."

He pointed as he spoke, and there was a high crimson curricle coming down the London road, with two bay mares harnessed tandem fashion before it. The reins and fittings were of a light fawn colour, and the gentleman had a driving-coat to match, with a servant in dark livery behind. They flashed past us in a rolling cloud of dust, and I had just a glimpse of the pale, handsome face of the master, and of the dark, shrivelled features of the man. I should never have given them another thought had it not chanced that when the village came into view there was the curricle again, standing at the door of the inn, and the grooms busy taking out the horses.

"Jim," I cried, "I believe it is my uncle!" and taking to my heels I ran for home at the top of my speed. At the door was standing the dark-faced servant. He carried a cushion, upon which lay a small and fluffy lapdog.

"You will excuse me, young sir," said he, in the suavest, most soothing of voices, "but am I right in supposing that this is the house of Lieutenant Stone? In that case you will, perhaps, do me the favour to hand to Mrs. Stone this note which her brother, Sir Charles Tregellis, has just committed to my care."

I was quite abashed by the man's flowery way of talking—so unlike anything which I had ever heard. He had a wizened face, and sharp little dark eyes, which took in me and the house and my mother's startled face at the window all in the instant. My parents were together, the two of them, in the sitting-room, and my mother read the note to us.

"My dear Mary," it ran, "I have stopped at the inn, because I am somewhat *ravagé* by the dust of your Sussex roads. A lavender-water bath may restore me to a condition in which I may fitly pay my compliments to a lady. Meantime, I send you Fidelio as a hostage. Pray give him a half-pint of warmish milk with six drops of pure brandy in it. A better or more faithful creature never lived. *Toujours à toi.*—Charles."

"Have him in! Have him in!" cried my father, heartily, running to the door. "Come in, Mr. Fidelio. Every man to his own taste, and six drops to the half-pint seems a sinful watering of grog—but if you like it so, you shall have it."

A smile flickered over the dark face of the servant, but his features reset themselves instantly into their usual mask of respectful observance.

"You are labouring under a slight error, sir, if you will permit me to say so. My name is Ambrose, and I have the honour to be the valet of Sir Charles Tregellis. This is Fidelio upon the cushion."

"Tut, the dog!" cried my father, in disgust. "Heave him down by the fireside. Why should he have brandy, when many a Christian has to go without?"

"Hush, Anson!" said my mother, taking the cushion. "You will tell Sir Charles that his wishes shall be carried out, and that we shall expect him at his own convenience."

The man went off noiselessly and swiftly, but was back in a few minutes with a flat brown basket.

"It is the refection, madam," said he. "Will you permit me to lay the table? Sir Charles is accustomed to partake of certain dishes and to drink certain wines, so that we usually bring them with us when we visit." He opened the basket, and in a minute he had the table all shining with silver and glass, and studded with dainty dishes. So quick and neat and silent was he in all he did, that my father was as taken with him as I was.

"You'd have made a right good foretopman if your heart is as stout as your fingers are quick," said he. "Did you never wish to have the honour of serving your country?"

"It is my honour, sir, to serve Sir Charles Tregellis, and I desire no other master," he answered. "But I will convey his dressing-case from the inn, and then all will be ready."

He came back with a great silver-mounted box under his arm, and close at his heels was the gentleman whose coming had made such a disturbance.

My first impression of my uncle as he entered the room was that one of his eyes was swollen to the size of an apple. It caught the breath from my lips—that monstrous, glistening eye. But the next instant I perceived that he held a round glass in the front of it, which magnified it in this fashion. He looked at us each in turn, and then he bowed very gracefully to my mother and kissed her upon either cheek.

"You will permit me to compliment you, my dear Mary," said he, in a voice which was the most mellow and beautiful that I have ever heard. "I can assure you that the country air has used you wondrous well, and that I should be proud to see my pretty sister in the Mall. I am your servant, sir," he continued, holding out his hand to my father. "It was but last week that I had the honour of dining with my friend, Lord St. Vincent, and I took occasion to mention you to him. I may tell you that your name is not forgotten at the Admiralty, sir, and I hope that I may see you soon walking the poop of a 74-gun ship of your own. So this is my nephew, is it?" He put a hand upon each of my shoulders in a very friendly way and looked me up and down.

"How old are you, nephew?" he asked.

"Seventeen, sir."

"You look older. You look eighteen, at the least. I find him very passable, Mary—very passable, indeed. He has not the bel air, the tournure—in our uncouth English we have no word for it. But he is as healthy as a May-hedge in bloom."

So within a minute of his entering our door he had got himself upon terms with all of us, and with so easy and graceful a manner that it seemed as if he had known us all for years. I had a good look at him now as he stood upon the hearthrug with my mother upon one side and my father on the other. He was a very large man, with noble shoulders, small waist, broad hips, well-turned legs, and the smallest of hands and feet. His face was pale and handsome, with a prominent chin, a jutting nose, and large blue staring eyes, in which a sort of dancing, mischievous light was for ever playing. He wore a deep brown coat with a collar as high as his ears and tails as low as his knees. His black breeches and silk stockings ended in very small pointed shoes, so highly polished that they twinkled with every movement. His vest was of black velvet, open at the top to show an embroidered shirt-front, with a high, smooth, white cravat above it, which kept his neck for ever on the stretch. He stood easily, with one thumb in the arm-pit, and two fingers of the other hand in his vest pocket. It made me proud as I watched him to think that so magnificent a man, with such easy, masterful ways, should be my own blood relation, and I could see from my mother's eyes as they turned towards him that the same thought was in her mind.

All this time Ambrose had been standing like a dark-clothed, bronze-faced image by the door, with the big silver-bound box under his arm. He stepped forward now into the room.

"Shall I convey it to your bedchamber, Sir Charles?" he asked.

"Ah, pardon me, sister Mary," cried my uncle, "I am old-fashioned enough to have principles—an anachronism, I know, in this lax age. One of them is never to allow my *batterie de toilette* out of my sight when I am travelling. I cannot readily forget the agonies which I endured some years ago through neglecting this precaution. I will do Ambrose the justice to say that it was before he took charge of my affairs. I was compelled to wear the same ruffles upon two consecutive days. On the third morning my fellow was so affected by the sight of my condition, that he burst into tears and laid out a pair which he had stolen from me."

As he spoke his face was very grave, but the light in his eyes danced and gleamed. He handed his open snuff-box to my father, as Ambrose followed my mother out of the room.

"You number yourself in an illustrious company by upping your finger and thumb into it," said he.

"Indeed, sir!" said my father, shortly.

"You are free of my box, as being a relative by marriage. You are free also, nephew, and I pray you to take a pinch. It is the most intimate sign of my goodwill. Outside ourselves there are four, I think, who have had access to it—the Prince, of course; Mr Pitt; Monsieur Otto, the French Ambassador; and Lord Hawkesbury. I have sometimes thought that I was premature with Lord Hawkesbury."

"I am vastly honoured, sir," said my father, looking suspiciously at his guest from under his shaggy eyebrows, for with that grave face and those twinkling eyes it was hard to know how to take him.

"A woman, sir, has her love to bestow," said my uncle. "A man has his snuff-box. Neither is to be lightly offered. It is a lapse of taste; nay, more, it is a breach of morals. Only the other day, as I was seated in Watier's, my box of prime macouba open upon the table beside me, an Irish bishop thrust in his intrusive fingers. 'Waiter,' I cried, 'my box has been soiled! Remove it!' The man meant no insult, you understand, but that class of people must be kept in their proper sphere.'

"A bishop!" cried my father. "You draw your line very high, sir."

"Yes, sir," said my uncle; "I wish no better epitaph upon my tombstone."

My mother had in the meanwhile descended, and we all drew up to the table.

"You will excuse my apparent grossness, Mary, in venturing to bring my own larder with me. Abernethy has me under his orders, and I must eschew your rich country dainties. A little white wine and a cold bird—it is as much as the niggardly Scotchman will allow me."

"We should have you on blockading service when the levanters are blowing," said my father. "Salt junk and weevilly biscuits, with a rib of a tough Barbary ox when the tenders come in. You would have your spare diet there, sir."

Straightway my uncle began to question him about the sea service, and for the whole meal my father was telling him of the Nile and of the Toulon blockade, and the siege of Genoa, and all that he had seen and done. But whenever he faltered for a word, my uncle always had it ready for him, and it was hard to say which knew most about the business.

"No, I read little or nothing," said he, when my father marvelled where he got his knowledge. "The fact is that I can hardly pick up a print without seeing some allusion to myself: 'Sir C. T. does this,' or 'Sir C. T. says the other,' so I take them no longer. But if a man is in my position all knowledge comes to him. The Duke of York tells me of the Army in the morning, and Lord Spencer chats with me of the Navy in the afternoon, and Dundas whispers me what is going forward in the Cabinet, so that I have little need of the Times or the Morning Chronicle."

This set him talking of the great world of London, telling my father about the men who were his masters at the Admiralty, and my mother about the beauties of the town, and the great ladies at Almack's, but all in the same light, fanciful way, so that one never knew whether to laugh or to take him gravely. I think it flattered him to see the way in which we all three hung upon his words. Of some he thought highly and of some lowly, but he made no secret that the highest of all, and the one against whom all others should be measured, was Sir Charles Tregellis himself.

"As to the King," said he, "of course, I am l'ami de famille there; and even with you I can scarce speak freely, as my relations are confidential."

"God bless him and keep him from ill!" cried my father.

"It is pleasant to hear you say so," said my uncle. "One has to come into the country to hear honest loyalty, for a sneer and a gibe are more the fashions in town. The King is grateful to me for the interest which I have ever shown in his son. He likes to think that the Prince has a man of taste in his circle."

"And the Prince?" asked my mother. "Is he well-favoured?"

"He is a fine figure of a man. At a distance he has been mistaken for me. And he has some taste in dress, though he gets slovenly if I am too long away from him. I warrant you that I find a crease in his coat to-morrow."

We were all seated round the fire by this time, for the evening had turned chilly. The lamp was lighted and so also was my father's pipe.

"I suppose," said he, "that this is your first visit to Friar's Oak?"

My uncle's face turned suddenly very grave and stern.

"It is my first visit for many years," said he. "I was but one-and-twenty years of age when last I came here. I am not likely to forget it."

I knew that he spoke of his visit to Cliffe Royal at the time of the murder, and I saw by her face that my mother knew it also. My father, however, had either never heard of it, or had forgotten the circumstance.

"Was it at the inn you stayed?" he asked.

"I stayed with the unfortunate Lord Avon. It was the occasion when he was accused of slaying his younger brother and fled from the country."

We all fell silent, and my uncle leaned his chin upon his hand, looking thoughtfully into the fire. If I do but close my eyes now, I can see the light upon his proud, handsome face, and see also my dear father, concerned at having touched upon so terrible a memory, shooting little slanting glances at him betwixt the puffs of his pipe.

"I dare say that it has happened with you, sir," said my uncle at last, "that you have lost some dear messmate, in battle or wreck, and that you have put him out of your mind in the routine of your daily life, until suddenly some word or some scene brings him back to your memory, and you find your sorrow as raw as upon the first day of your loss."

My father nodded.

"So it is with me to-night. I never formed a close friendship with a man—I say nothing of women—save only the once. That was with Lord Avon. We were of an age, he a few years perhaps my senior, but our tastes, our judgments, and our characters were alike, save only that he had in him a touch of pride such as I have never known in any other man. Putting aside the little foibles of a rich young man of fashion, *les indescrétions d'une jeunesse dorée*, I could have sworn that he was as good a man as I have ever known."

"How came he, then, to such a crime?" asked my father.

My uncle shook his head.

"Many a time have I asked myself that question, and it comes home to me more to-night than ever."

All the jauntiness had gone out of his manner, and he had turned suddenly into a sad and serious man.

"Was it certain that he did it, Charles?" asked my mother.

My uncle shrugged his shoulders.

"I wish I could think it were not so. I have thought sometimes that it was this very pride, turning suddenly to madness, which drove him to it. You have heard how he returned the money which we had lost?"

"Nay, I have heard nothing of it," my father answered.

"It is a very old story now, though we have not yet found an end to it. We had played for two days, the four of us: Lord Avon, his brother Captain Barrington, Sir Lothian Hume, and myself. Of the Captain I knew little, save that he was not of the best repute, and was deep in the hands of the Jews. Sir Lothian has made an evil name for himself since—'tis the same Sir Lothian who shot Lord Carton in the affair at Chalk Farm—but in those days there was nothing against him. The oldest of us was but twenty-four, and we gamed on, as I say, until the Captain had cleared the board. We were all hit, but our host far the hardest.

"That night—I tell you now what it would be a bitter thing for me to tell in a court of law—I was restless and sleepless, as often happens when a man has kept awake over long. My mind would dwell upon the fall of the cards, and I was tossing and turning in my bed, when suddenly a cry fell upon my ears, and then a second louder one, coming from the direction of Captain Barrington's room. Five minutes later I heard steps passing down the passage, and, without striking a light, I opened my door and peeped out, thinking that some one was taken unwell. There was Lord Avon walking towards me. In one hand he held a guttering candle and in the other a brown bag, which chinked as he moved. His face was all drawn and distorted—so much so that my question was frozen upon my lips. Before I could utter it he turned into his chamber and softly closed the door.

"Next morning I was awakened by finding him at my bedside.

"'Charles,' said he, 'I cannot abide to think that you should have lost this money in my house. You will find it here upon your table.'

"It was in vain that I laughed at his squeamishness, telling him that I should most certainly have claimed my money had I won, so that it would be strange indeed if I were not permitted to pay it when I lost.

"'Neither I nor my brother will touch it,' said he. 'There it lies, and you may do what you like about it.'

"He would listen to no argument, but dashed out of the room like a madman. But perhaps these details are familiar to you, and God knows they are painful to me to tell."

My father was sitting with staring eyes, and his forgotten pipe reeking in his hand.

"Pray let us hear the end of it, sir," he cried.

"Well, then, I had finished my toilet in an hour or so—for I was less exigeant in those days than now—and I met Sir Lothian Hume at breakfast. His experience had been the same as my own, and he was eager to see Captain Barrington; and to ascertain why he had directed his brother to return the money to us. We were talking the matter over when suddenly I raised my eyes to the corner of the ceiling, and I saw—I saw—"

My uncle had turned quite pale with the vividness of the memory, and he passed his hand over his eyes.

"It was crimson," said he, with a shudder—"crimson with black cracks, and from every crack—but I will give you dreams, sister Mary. Suffice it that we rushed up the stair which led direct to the Captain's room, and there we found him lying with the bone gleaming white through his throat. A hunting-knife lay in the room—and the knife was Lord Avon's. A lace ruffle was found in the dead man's grasp—and the ruffle was Lord Avon's. Some papers were found charred in the grate—and the papers were Lord Avon's. Oh, my poor friend, in what moment of madness did you come to do such a deed?"

The light had gone out of my uncle's eyes and the extravagance from his manner. His speech was clear and plain, with none of those strange London ways which had so amazed me. Here was a second uncle, a man of heart and a man of brains, and I liked him better than the first.

"And what said Lord Avon?" cried my father.

"He said nothing. He went about like one who walks in his sleep, with horror-stricken eyes. None dared arrest him until there should be due inquiry, but when the coroner's court brought wilful murder against him, the constables came for him in full cry. But they found him fled. There was a rumour that he had been seen in Westminster in the next week, and then that he had escaped for America, but nothing more is known. It will be a bright day for Sir Lothian Hume when they can prove him dead, for he is next of kin, and till then he can touch neither title nor estate."

The telling of this grim story had cast a chill upon all of us. My uncle held out his hands towards the blaze, and I noticed that they were as white as the ruffles which fringed them.

"I know not how things are at Cliffe Royal now," said he, thoughtfully. "It was not a cheery house, even before this shadow fell upon it. A fitter stage was never set forth for such a tragedy. But seventeen years have passed, and perhaps even that horrible ceiling—"

"It still bears the stain," said I.

I know not which of the three was the more astonished, for my mother had not heard of my adventures of the night. They never took their wondering eyes off me as I told my story, and my heart swelled with pride when my uncle said that we had carried ourselves well, and that he did not think that many of our age would have stood it as stoutly.

"But as to this ghost, it must have been the creature of your own minds," said he. "Imagination plays us strange tricks, and though I have as steady a nerve as a man might wish, I cannot answer for what I might see if I were to stand under that blood-stained ceiling at midnight."

"Uncle," said I, "I saw a figure as plainly as I see that fire, and I heard the steps as clearly as I hear the crackle of the fagots. Besides, we could not both be deceived."

"There is truth in that," said be, thoughtfully. "You saw no features, you say?"

"It was too dark."

"But only a figure?"

"The dark outline of one."

"And it retreated up the stairs?"

"Yes."

"And vanished into the wall?"

"Yes."

"What part of the wall?" cried a voice from behind us.

My mother screamed, and down came my father's pipe on to the hearthrug. I had sprung round with a catch of my breath, and there was the valet, Ambrose, his body in the shadow of the doorway, his dark face protruded into the light, and two burning eyes fixed upon mine.

"What the deuce is the meaning of this, sir?" cried my uncle.

It was strange to see the gleam and passion fade out of the man's face, and the demure mask of the valet replace it. His eyes still smouldered, but his features regained their prim composure in an instant.

"I beg your pardon, Sir Charles," said he. "I had come in to ask you if you had any orders for me, and I did not like to interrupt the young gentleman's story. I am afraid that I have been somewhat carried away by it."

"I never knew you forget yourself before," said my uncle.

"You will, I am sure, forgive me, Sir Charles, if you will call to mind the relation in which I stood to Lord Avon." He spoke with some dignity of manner, and with a bow he left the room.

"We must make some little allowance," said my uncle, with a sudden return to his jaunty manner. "When a man can brew a dish of chocolate, or tie a cravat, as Ambrose does, he may claim consideration. The fact is that the poor fellow was valet to Lord Avon, that he was at Cliffe Royal upon the fatal night of which I have spoken, and that he is most devoted to his old master. But my talk has been somewhat triste, sister Mary, and now we shall return, if you please, to the dresses of the Countess Lieven, and the gossip of St. James."

CHAPTER VI—ON THE THRESHOLD

My father sent me to bed early that night, though I was very eager to stay up, for every word which this man said held my attention. His face, his manner, the large waves and sweeps of his white hands, his easy air of superiority, his fantastic fashion of talk, all filled me with interest and wonder. But, as I afterwards learned, their conversation was to be about myself and my own prospects, so I was despatched to my room, whence far into the night I could hear the deep growl of my father and the rich tones of my uncle, with an occasional gentle murmur from my mother, as they talked in the room beneath.

I had dropped asleep at last, when I was awakened suddenly by something wet being pressed against my face, and by two warm arms which were cast round me. My mother's cheek was against my own, and I could hear the click of her sobs, and feel her quiver and shake in the darkness. A faint light stole through the latticed window, and I could dimly see that she was in white, with her black hair loose upon her shoulders.

"You won't forget us, Roddy? You won't forget us?"

"Why, mother, what is it?"

"Your uncle, Roddy—he is going to take you away from us."

"When, mother?"

"To-morrow."

God forgive me, how my heart bounded for joy, when hers, which was within touch of it, was breaking with sorrow!

"Oh, mother!" I cried. "To London?"

"First to Brighton, that he may present you to the Prince. Next day to London, where you will meet the great people, Roddy, and learn to look down upon—to look down upon your poor, simple, old-fashioned father and mother."

I put my arms about her to console her, but she wept so that, for all my seventeen years and pride of manhood, it set me weeping also, and with such a hiccoughing noise, since I had not a woman's knack of quiet tears, that it finally turned her own grief to laughter.

"Charles would be flattered if he could see the gracious way in which we receive his kindness," said she. "Be still, Roddy dear, or you will certainly wake him."

"I'll not go if it is to grieve you," I cried.

"Nay, dear, you must go, for it may be the one great chance of your life. And think how proud it will make us all when we hear of you in the company of Charles's grand friends. But you will promise me not to gamble, Roddy? You heard to-night of the dreadful things which come from it."

"I promise you, mother."

"And you will be careful of wine, Roddy? You are young and unused to it."

"Yes, mother."

"And play-actresses also, Roddy. And you will not cast your under-clothing until June is in. Young Master Overton came by his death through it. Think well of your dress, Roddy, so as to do your uncle credit, for it is the thing for which he is himself most famed. You have but to do what he will direct. But if there is a time when you are not meeting grand people, you can wear out your country things, for your brown coat is as good as new, and the blue one, if it were ironed and relined, would take you through the summer. I have put out your Sunday clothes with the nankeen vest, since you are to see the Prince to-morrow, and you will wear your brown silk stockings and buckle shoes. Be guarded in crossing the London streets, for I am told that the hackney coaches are past all imagining. Fold your clothes when you go to bed, Roddy, and do not forget your evening prayers, for, oh, my dear boy, the days of temptation are at hand, when I will no longer be with you to help you."

So with advice and guidance both for this world and the next did my mother, with her soft, warm arms around me, prepare me for the great step which lay before me.

My uncle did not appear at breakfast in the morning, but Ambrose brewed him a dish of chocolate and took it to his room. When at last, about midday, he did descend, he was so fine with his curled hair, his shining teeth, his quizzing glass, his snow-white ruffles, and his laughing eyes, that I could not take my gaze from him.

"Well, nephew," he cried, "what do you think of the prospect of coming to town with me?"

"I thank you, sir, for the kind interest which you take in me," said I.

"But you must be a credit to me. My nephew must be of the best if he is to be in keeping with the rest of me."

"You'll find him a chip of good wood, sir," said my father.

"We must make him a polished chip before we have done with him. Your aim, my dear nephew, must always be to be in bon ton. It is not a case of wealth, you understand. Mere riches cannot do it. Golden Price has forty thousand a year, but his clothes are disastrous. I assure you that I saw him come down St. James's Street the other day, and I was so shocked at his appearance that I had to step into Vernet's for a glass of orange brandy. No, it is a question of natural taste, and of following the advice and example of those who are more experienced than yourself."

"I fear, Charles, that Roddy's wardrobe is country-made," said my mother.

"We shall soon set that right when we get to town. We shall see what Stultz or Weston can do for him," my uncle answered. "We must keep him quiet until he has some clothes to wear."

This slight upon my best Sunday suit brought a flush to my mother's cheeks, which my uncle instantly observed, for he was quick in noticing trifles.

"The clothes are very well for Friar's Oak, sister Mary," said he. "And yet you can understand that they might seem rococo in the Mall. If you leave him in my hands I shall see to the matter."

"On how much, sir," asked my father, "can a young man dress in town?"

"With prudence and reasonable care, a young man of fashion can dress upon eight hundred a year," my uncle answered.

I saw my poor father's face grow longer.

"I fear, sir, that Roddy must keep his country clothes," said he. "Even with my prize-money—"

"Tut, sir!" cried my uncle. "I already owe Weston something over a thousand, so how can a few odd hundreds affect it? If my nephew comes with me, my nephew is my care. The point is settled, and I must refuse to argue upon it." He waved his white hands as if to brush aside all opposition.

My parents tried to thank him, but he cut them short.

"By the way, now that I am in Friar's Oak, there is another small piece of business which I have to perform," said he. "I believe that there is a fighting-man named Harrison here, who at one time might have held the championship. In those days poor Avon and I were his principal backers. I should like to have a word with him."

You may think how proud I was to walk down the village street with my magnificent relative, and to note out of the corner of my eye how the folk came to the doors and windows to see us pass. Champion Harrison was standing outside the smithy, and he pulled his cap off when he saw my uncle.

"God bless me, sir! Who'd ha' thought of seem' you at Friar's Oak? Why, Sir Charles, it brings old memories back to look at your face again."

"Glad to see you looking so fit, Harrison," said my uncle, running his eyes over him. "Why, with a week's training you would be as good a man as ever. I don't suppose you scale more than thirteen and a half?"

"Thirteen ten, Sir Charles. I'm in my fortieth year, but I am sound in wind and limb, and if my old woman would have let me off my promise, I'd ha' had a try with some of these young ones before now. I hear that they've got some amazin' good stuff up from Bristol of late."

"Yes, the Bristol yellowman has been the winning colour of late. How d'ye do, Mrs. Harrison? I don't suppose you remember me?"

She had come out from the house, and I noticed that her worn face—on which some past terror seemed to have left its shadow—hardened into stern lines as she looked at my uncle.

"I remember you too well, Sir Charles Tregellis," said she. "I trust that you have not come here to-day to try to draw my husband back into the ways that he has forsaken."

"That's the way with her, Sir Charles," said Harrison, resting his great hand upon the woman's shoulder. "She's got my promise, and she holds me to it! There was never a better or more hard-working wife, but she ain't what you'd call a patron of sport, and that's a fact."

"Sport!" cried the woman, bitterly. "A fine sport for you, Sir Charles, with your pleasant twenty-mile drive into the country and your luncheon-basket and your wines, and so merrily back to London in the cool of the evening, with a well-fought battle to talk over. Think of the sport that it was to me to sit through the long hours, listening for the wheels of the chaise which would bring my man back to me. Sometimes he could walk in, and sometimes he was led in, and sometimes he was carried in, and it was only by his clothes that I could know him—"

"Come, wifie," said Harrison, patting her on the shoulder. "I've been cut up in my time, but never as bad as that."

"And then to live for weeks afterwards with the fear that every knock at the door may be to tell us that the other is dead, and that my man may have to stand in the dock and take his trial for murder."

"No, she hasn't got a sportin' drop in her veins," said Harrison. "She'd never make a patron, never! It's Black Baruk's business that did it, when we thought he'd napped it once too often. Well, she has my promise, and I'll never sling my hat over the ropes unless she gives me leave."

"You'll keep your hat on your head like an honest, God-fearing man, John," said his wife, turning back into the house.

"I wouldn't for the world say anything to make you change your resolutions," said my uncle. "At the same time, if you had wished to take a turn at the old sport, I had a good thing to put in your way." .

"Well, it's no use, sir," said Harrison, "but I'd be glad to hear about it all the same."

"They have a very good bit of stuff at thirteen stone down Gloucester way. Wilson is his name, and they call him Crab on account of his style."

Harrison shook his head. "Never heard of him, sir."

"Very likely not, for he has never shown in the P.R. But they think great things of him in the West, and he can hold his own with either of the Belchers with the mufflers."

"Sparrin' ain't fightin'," said the smith

"I am told that he had the best of it in a by-battle with Noah James, of Cheshire."

"There's no gamer man on the list, sir, than Noah James, the guardsman," said Harrison. "I saw him myself fight fifty rounds after his jaw had been cracked in three places. If Wilson could beat him, Wilson will go far."

"So they think in the West, and they mean to spring him on the London talent. Sir Lothian Hume is his patron, and to make a long story short, he lays me odds that I won't find a young one of his weight to meet him. I told him that I had not heard of any good young ones, but that I had an old one who had not put his foot into a ring for many years, who would make his man wish he had never come to London.

"'Young or old, under twenty or over thirty-five, you may bring whom you will at the weight, and I shall lay two to one on Wilson,' said he. I took him in thousands, and here I am."

"It won't do, Sir Charles," said the smith, shaking his head. "There's nothing would please me better, but you heard for yourself."

"Well, if you won't fight, Harrison, I must try to get some promising colt. I'd be glad of your advice in the matter. By the way, I take the chair at a supper of the Fancy at the Waggon and Horses in St. Martin's Lane next Friday. I should be very glad if you will make one of my guests. Halloa, who's this?" Up flew his glass to his eye.

Boy Jim had come out from the forge with his hammer in his hand. He had, I remember, a grey flannel shirt, which was open at the neck and turned up at the sleeves. My uncle ran his eyes over the fine lines of his magnificent figure with the glance of a connoisseur.

"That's my nephew, Sir Charles."

"Is he living with you?"

"His parents are dead."

"Has he ever been in London?"

"No, Sir Charles. He's been with me here since he was as high as that hammer."

My uncle turned to Boy Jim.

"I hear that you have never been in London," said he. "Your uncle is coming up to a supper which I am giving to the Fancy next Friday. Would you care to make one of us?"

Boy Jim's dark eyes sparkled with pleasure.

"I should be glad to come, sir."

"No, no, Jim," cried the smith, abruptly. "I'm sorry to gainsay you, lad, but there are reasons why I had rather you stayed down here with your aunt."

"Tut, Harrison, let the lad come!" cried my uncle.

"No, no, Sir Charles. It's dangerous company for a lad of his mettle. There's plenty for him to do when I'm away."

Poor Jim turned away with a clouded brow and strode into the smithy again. For my part, I slipped after him to try to console him, and to tell him all the wonderful changes which had come so suddenly into my life. But I had not got half through my story, and Jim, like the good fellow that he was, had just begun to forget his own troubles in his delight at my good fortune, when my uncle called to me from without. The curricle with its tandem mares was waiting for us outside the cottage, and Ambrose had placed the refection-basket, the lap-dog, and the precious toilet-box inside of it. He had himself climbed up behind, and I, after a hearty handshake from my father, and a last sobbing embrace from my mother, took my place beside my uncle in the front.

"Let go her head!" cried he to the ostler, and with a snap, a crack, and a jingle, away we went upon our journey.

Across all the years how clearly I can see that spring day, with the green English fields, the windy English sky, and the yellow, beetle-browed cottage in which I had grown from a child to a man. I see, too, the figures at the garden gate: my mother, with her face turned away and her handkerchief waving; my father, with his blue coat and his white shorts, leaning upon his stick with his hand shading his eyes as he peered after us. All the village was out to see young Roddy Stone go off with his grand relative from London to call upon the Prince in his own palace. The Harrisons were waving to me from the smithy, and John Cummings from the steps of the inn, and I saw Joshua Allen, my old schoolmaster, pointing me out to the people, as if he were showing what came from his teaching. To make it complete, who should drive past just as we cleared the village but Miss Hinton, the play-actress, the pony and phaeton the same as when first I saw her, but she herself another woman; and I thought to myself that if Boy Jim had done nothing but that one thing, he need not think that his youth had been wasted in the country. She was driving to see him, I have no doubt, for they were closer than ever, and she never looked up nor saw the hand that I waved to her. So as we took the curve of the road the little village vanished, and there in the dip of the Downs, past the spires of Patcham and of Preston, lay the broad blue sea and the grey houses of Brighton, with the strange Eastern domes and minarets of the Prince's Pavilion shooting out from the centre of it.

To every traveller it was a sight of beauty, but to me it was the world—the great wide free world—and my heart thrilled and fluttered as the young bird's may when it first hears the whirr of its own flight, and skims along with the blue heaven above it and the green fields beneath. The day may come when it may look back regretfully to the snug nest in the thornbush, but what does it reck of that when spring is in the air and youth in its blood, and the old hawk of trouble has not yet darkened the sunshine with the ill-boding shadow of its wings?

CHAPTER VII—THE HOPE
OF ENGLAND

My uncle drove for some time in silence, but I was conscious that his eye was always coming round to me, and I had an uneasy conviction that he was already beginning to ask himself whether he could make anything of me, or whether he had been betrayed into an indiscretion when he had allowed his sister to persuade him to show her son something of the grand world in which he lived.

"You sing, don't you, nephew?" he asked, suddenly.

"Yes, sir, a little."

"A baritone, I should fancy?"

"Yes, sir."

"And your mother tells me that you play the fiddle. These things will be of service to you with the Prince. Music runs in his family. Your education has been what you could get at a village school. Well, you are not examined in Greek roots in polite society, which is lucky for some of us. It is as well just to have a tag or two of Horace or Virgil: *sub tegmine fagi*, or *habet fœnum in cornu*, which gives a flavour to one's conversation like the touch of garlic in a salad. It is not *bon ton* to be learned, but it is a graceful thing to indicate that you have forgotten a good deal. Can you write verse?"

"I fear not, sir."

"A small book of rhymes may be had for half a crown. *Vers de Société* are a great assistance to a young man. If you have the ladies on your side, it does not matter whom you have against you. You must learn to open a door, to enter a room, to present a snuff-box, raising the lid with the forefinger of the hand in which you hold it. You must acquire the bow for a man, with its necessary touch of dignity, and that for a lady, which cannot be too humble, and should still contain the least suspicion of abandon. You must cultivate a manner with women which shall be deprecating and yet audacious. Have you any eccentricity?"

It made me laugh, the easy way in which he asked the question, as if it were a most natural thing to possess.

"You have a pleasant, catching laugh, at all events," said he. "But an eccentricity is very bon ton at present, and if you feel any leaning towards one, I should certainly advise you to let it run its course. Petersham would have remained a mere peer all his life had it not come out that he had a snuff-box for every day in the year, and that he had caught cold through a mistake of his valet, who sent him out on a bitter winter day with a thin *Sèvres* china box instead of a thick tortoiseshell. That brought him out of the ruck, you see, and people remember him. Even some small characteristic, such as having an apricot tart on your sideboard all the year round, or putting your candle out at night by stuffing it under your pillow, serves to separate you from your neighbour. In my own case, it is my precise judgment upon matter of dress and decorum which has placed me where I am. I do not profess to follow a law. I set one. For example, I am taking you to-day to see the Prince in a nankeen vest. What do you think will be the consequence of that?"

My fears told me that it might be my own very great discomfiture, but I did not say so.

"Why, the night coach will carry the news to London. It will be in Brookes's and White's to-morrow morning. Within, a week St. James's Street and the Mall will be full of nankeen waistcoats. A most painful incident happened to me once. My cravat came undone in the street, and I actually walked from Carlton House to Watier's in Bruton Street with the two ends hanging loose. Do you suppose it shook my position? The same evening there were dozens of young bloods walking the streets of London with their cravats loose. If I had not rearranged mine there would not be one tied in the whole kingdom now, and a great art would have been prematurely lost. You have not yet began to practise it?"

I confessed that I had not.

"You should begin now in your youth. I will myself teach you the *coup d'archet*. By using a few hours in each day, which would otherwise be wasted, you may hope to have excellent cravats in middle life. The whole knack lies in pointing your chin to the sky, and then arranging your folds by the gradual descent of your lower jaw."

When my uncle spoke like this there was always that dancing, mischievous light in his dark blue eyes, which showed me that this humour of his was a conscious eccentricity, depending, as I believe, upon a natural fastidiousness of taste, but wilfully driven to grotesque lengths for the very reason which made him recommend me also to develop some peculiarity of my own. When I thought of the way in which he had spoken of his unhappy friend, Lord Avon, upon the evening before, and of the emotion which he showed as he told the horrible story, I was glad to think that there was the heart of a man there, however much it might please him to conceal it.

And, as it happened, I was very soon to have another peep at it, for a most unexpected event befell us as we drew up in front of the Crown hotel. A swarm of ostlers and grooms had rushed out to us, and my uncle, throwing down the reins, gathered Fidelio on his cushion from under the seat.

"Ambrose," he cried, "you may take Fidelio."

But there came no answer. The seat behind was unoccupied. Ambrose was gone.

We could hardly believe our eyes when we alighted and found that it was really so. He had most certainly taken his seat there at Friar's Oak, and from there on we had come without a break as fast as the mares could travel. Whither, then, could he have vanished to?

"He's fallen off in a fit!" cried my uncle. "I'd drive back, but the Prince is expecting us. Where's the landlord? Here, Coppinger, send your best man back to Friar's Oak as fast as his horse can go, to find news of my valet, Ambrose. See that no pains be spared. Now, nephew, we shall lunch, and then go up to the Pavilion."

My uncle was much disturbed by the strange loss of his valet, the more so as it was his custom to go through a whole series of washings and changings after even the shortest journey. For my own part, mindful of my mother's advice, I carefully brushed the dust from my clothes and made myself as neat as possible. My heart was down in the soles of my little silver-buckled shoes now that I had the immediate prospect of meeting so great and terrible a person as the Prince of Wales. I had seen his flaring yellow barouche flying through Friar's Oak many a time, and had halloaed and waved my hat with the others as it passed, but never in my wildest dreams had it entered my head that I should ever be called upon to look him in the face and answer his questions. My mother had taught me to regard him with reverence, as one of those whom God had placed to rule over us; but my uncle smiled when I told him of her teaching.

"You are old enough to see things as they are, nephew," said he, "and your knowledge of them is the badge that you are in that inner circle where I mean to place you. There is no one who knows the Prince better than I do, and there is no one who trusts him less. A stranger contradiction of qualities was never gathered under one hat. He is a man who is always in a hurry, and yet has never anything to do. He fusses about things with which he has no concern, and he neglects every obvious duty. He is generous to those who have no claim upon him, but he has ruined his tradesmen by refusing to pay his just debts. He is affectionate to casual acquaintances, but he dislikes his father, loathes his mother, and is not on speaking terms with his wife. He claims to be the first gentleman of England, but the gentlemen of England have responded by blackballing his friends at their clubs, and by warning him off from Newmarket under suspicion of having tampered with a horse. He spends his days in uttering noble sentiments, and contradicting them by ignoble actions. He tells stories of his own doings which are so grotesque that they can only be explained by the madness which runs in his blood. And yet, with all this, he can be courteous, dignified, and kindly upon occasion, and I have seen an impulsive good-heartedness in the man which has made me overlook faults which come mainly from his being placed in a position which no one upon this earth was ever less fitted to fill. But this is between ourselves, nephew; and now you will come with me and you will form an opinion for yourself."

It was but a short walk, and yet it took us some time, for my uncle stalked along with great dignity, his lace-bordered handkerchief in one hand, and his cane with the clouded amber head dangling from the other. Every one that we met seemed to know him, and their hats flew from their heads as we passed. He took little notice of these greetings, save to give a nod to one, or to slightly raise his forefinger to another. It chanced, however, that as we turned into the Pavilion Grounds, we met a magnificent team of four coal-black horses, driven by a rough-looking, middle-aged fellow in an old weather-stained cape. There was nothing that I could see to distinguish him from any professional driver, save that he was chatting very freely with a dainty little woman who was perched on the box beside him.

"Halloa, Charlie! Good drive down?" he cried.

My uncle bowed and smiled to the lady.

"Broke it at Friar's Oak," said he. "I've my light curricle and two new mares—half thorough-bred, half Cleveland bay."

"What d'you think of my team of blacks?" asked the other.

"Yes, Sir Charles, what d'you think of them? Ain't they damnation smart?" cried the little woman.

"Plenty of power. Good horses for the Sussex clay. Too thick about the fetlocks for me. I like to travel."

"Travel!" cried the woman, with extraordinary vehemence. "Why, what the—" and she broke into such language as I had never heard from a man's lips before. "We'd start with our swingle-bars touching, and we'd have your dinner ordered, cooked, laid, and eaten before you were there to claim it."

"By George, yes, Letty is right!" cried the man. "D'you start to-morrow?"

"Yes, Jack."

"Well, I'll make you an offer. Look ye here, Charlie! I'll spring my cattle from the Castle Square at quarter before nine. You can follow as the clock strikes. I've double the horses and double the weight. If you so much as see me before we cross Westminster Bridge, I'll pay you a cool hundred. If not, it's my money—play or pay. Is it a match?"

"Very good," said my uncle, and, raising his hat, he led the way into the grounds. As I followed, I saw the woman take the reins, while the man looked after us, and squirted a jet of tobacco-juice from between his teeth in coachman fashion.

"That's Sir John Lade," said my uncle, "one of the richest men and best whips in England. There isn't a professional on the road that can handle either his tongue or his ribbons better; but his wife, Lady Letty, is his match with the one or the other."

"It was dreadful to hear her," said I.

"Oh, it's her eccentricity. We all have them; and she amuses the Prince. Now, nephew, keep close at my elbow, and have your eyes open and your mouth shut."

Two lines of magnificent red and gold footmen who guarded the door bowed deeply as my uncle and I passed between them, he with his head in the air and a manner as if he entered into his own, whilst I tried to look assured, though my heart was beating thin and fast. Within there was a high and large hall, ornamented with Eastern decorations, which harmonized with the domes and minarets of the exterior. A number of people were moving quietly about, forming into groups and whispering to each other. One of these, a short, burly, red-faced man, full of fuss and self-importance, came hurrying up to my uncle.

"I have de goot news, Sir Charles," said he, sinking his voice as one who speaks of weighty measures. "*Es ist vollendet*—dat is, I have it at last thoroughly done."

"Well, serve it hot," said my uncle, coldly, "and see that the sauces are a little better than when last I dined at Carlton House."

"Ah, *mein Gott*, you tink I talk of de cuisine. It is de affair of de Prince dat I speak of. Dat is one little vol-au-vent dat is worth one hundred tousand pound. Ten per cent., and double to be repaid when de Royal pappa die. *Alles ist fertig.* Goldshmidt of de Hague have took it up, and de Dutch public has subscribe de money."

"God help the Dutch public!" muttered my uncle, as the fat little man bustled off with his news to some new-comer. "That's the Prince's famous cook, nephew. He has not his equal in England for a *filet sauté aux champignons.* He manages his master's money affairs."

"The cook!" I exclaimed, in bewilderment.

"You look surprised, nephew."

"I should have thought that some respectable banking firm—"

My uncle inclined his lips to my ear.

"No respectable house would touch them," he whispered. "Ah, Mellish, is the Prince within?"

"In the private saloon, Sir Charles," said the gentleman addressed.

"Any one with him?"

"Sheridan and Francis. He said he expected you."

"Then we shall go through."

I followed him through the strangest succession of rooms, full of curious barbaric splendour which impressed me as being very rich and wonderful, though perhaps I should think differently now. Gold and scarlet in arabesque designs gleamed upon the walls, with gilt dragons and monsters writhing along cornices and out of corners. Look where I would, on panel or ceiling, a score of mirrors flashed back the picture of the tall, proud, white-faced man, and the youth who walked so demurely at his elbow. Finally, a footman opened a door, and we found ourselves in the Prince's own private apartment.

Two gentlemen were lounging in a very easy fashion upon luxurious fauteuils at the further end of the room and a third stood between them, his thick, well-formed legs somewhat apart and his hands clasped behind him. The sun was shining in upon them through a side-window, and I can see the three faces now—one in the dusk, one in the light, and one cut across by the shadow. Of those at the sides,

I recall the reddish nose and dark, flashing eyes of the one, and the hard, austere face of the other, with the high coat-collars and many-wreathed cravats. These I took in at a glance, but it was upon the man in the centre that my gaze was fixed, for this I knew must be the Prince of Wales.

George was then in his forty-first year, and with the help of his tailor and his hairdresser, he might have passed as somewhat less. The sight of him put me at my ease, for he was a merry-looking man, handsome too in a portly, full-blooded way, with laughing eyes and pouting, sensitive lips. His nose was turned upwards, which increased the good-humoured effect of his countenance at the expense of its dignity. His cheeks were pale and sodden, like those of a man who lived too well and took too little exercise. He was dressed in a single-breasted black coat buttoned up, a pair of leather pantaloons stretched tightly across his broad thighs, polished Hessian boots, and a huge white neckcloth.

"Halloa, Tregellis!" he cried, in the cheeriest fashion, as my uncle crossed the threshold, and then suddenly the smile faded from his face, and his eyes gleamed with resentment. "What the deuce is this?" he shouted, angrily.

A thrill of fear passed through me as I thought that it was my appearance which had produced this outburst. But his eyes were gazing past us, and glancing round we saw that a man in a brown coat and scratch wig had followed so closely at our heels, that the footmen had let him pass under the impression that he was of our party. His face was very red, and the folded blue paper which he carried in his hand shook and crackled in his excitement.

"Why, it's Vuillamy, the furniture man," cried the Prince. "What, am I to be dunned in my own private room? Where's Mellish? Where's Townshend? What the deuce is Tom Tring doing?"

"I wouldn't have intruded, your Royal Highness, but I must have the money—or even a thousand on account would do."

"Must have it, must you, Vuillamy? That's a fine word to use. I pay my debts in my own time, and I'm not to be bullied. Turn him out, footman! Take him away!"

"If I don't get it by Monday, I shall be in your papa's Bench," wailed the little man, and as the footman led him out we could hear him, amidst shouts of laughter, still protesting that he would wind up in "papa's Bench."

"That's the very place for a furniture man," said the man with the red nose.

"It should be the longest bench in the world, Sherry," answered the Prince, "for a good many of his subjects will want seats on it. Very glad to see you back, Tregellis, but you must really be more careful what you bring in upon your skirts. It was only yesterday that we had an infernal Dutchman here howling about some arrears of interest and the deuce knows what. 'My good fellow,' said I, 'as long as the Commons starve me, I have to starve you,' and so the matter ended."

"I think, sir, that the Commons would respond now if the matter were fairly put before them by Charlie Fox or myself," said Sheridan.

The Prince burst out against the Commons with an energy of hatred that one would scarce expect from that chubby, good-humoured face.

"Why, curse them!" he cried. "After all their preaching and throwing my father's model life, as they called it, in my teeth, they had to pay his debts to the tune of nearly a million, whilst I can't get a hundred thousand out of them. And look at all they've done for my brothers! York is Commander-in-Chief. Clarence is Admiral. What am I? Colonel of a damned dragoon regiment under the orders of my own younger brother. It's my mother that's at the bottom of it all. She always tried to hold me back. But what's this you've brought, Tregellis, eh?"

My uncle put his hand on my sleeve and led me forward.

"This is my sister's son, sir; Rodney Stone by name," said he. "He is coming with me to London, and I thought it right to begin by presenting him to your Royal Highness."

"Quite right! Quite right!" said the Prince, with a good-natured smile, patting me in a friendly way upon the shoulder. "Is your mother living?"

"Yes, sir," said I.

"If you are a good son to her you will never go wrong. And, mark my words, Mr. Rodney Stone, you should honour the King, love your country, and uphold the glorious British Constitution."

When I thought of the energy with which he had just been cursing the House of Commons, I could scarce keep from smiling, and I saw Sheridan put his hand up to his lips.

"You have only to do this, to show a regard for your word, and to keep out of debt in order to insure a happy and respected life. What is your father, Mr. Stone? Royal Navy! Well, it is a glorious service. I have had a touch of it myself. Did I ever tell you how we laid aboard the French sloop of war Minerve—hey, Tregellis?"

"No, sir," said my uncle. Sheridan and Francis exchanged glances behind the Prince's back.

"She was flying her tricolour out there within sight of my pavilion windows. Never saw such monstrous impudence in my life! It would take a man of less mettle than me to stand it. Out I went in my little cock-boat—you know my sixty-ton yawl, Charlie?—with two four-pounders on each side, and a six-pounder in the bows."

"Well, sir! Well, sir! And what then, sir?" cried Francis, who appeared to be an irascible, rough-tongued man.

"You will permit me to tell the story in my own way, Sir Philip," said the Prince, with dignity. "I was about to say that our metal was so light that I give you my word, gentlemen, that I carried my port broadside in one coat pocket, and my starboard in the other. Up we came to the big Frenchman, took her fire, and scraped the paint off her before we let drive. But it was no use. By George, gentlemen, our balls just stuck in her timbers like stones in a mud wall. She had her nettings up, but we scrambled aboard, and at it we went hammer and anvil. It was a sharp twenty minutes, but we beat her people down below, made the hatches fast on them, and towed her into Seaham. Surely you were with us, Sherry?"

"I was in London at the time," said Sheridan, gravely.

"You can vouch for it, Francis!"

"I can vouch to having heard your Highness tell the story."

"It was a rough little bit of cutlass and pistol work. But, for my own part, I like the rapier. It's a gentleman's weapon. You heard of my bout with the Chevalier d'Eon? I had him at my sword-point for forty minutes at Angelo's. He was one of the best blades in Europe, but I was a little too supple in the wrist for him. 'I thank God there was a button on your Highness's foil,' said he, when we had finished our breather. By the way, you're a bit of a duellist yourself, Tregellis. How often have you been out?"

"I used to go when I needed exercise," said my uncle, carelessly. "But I have taken to tennis now instead. A painful incident happened the last time that I was out, and it sickened me of it."

"You killed your man—?"

"No, no, sir, it was worse than that. I had a coat that Weston has never equalled. To say that it fitted me is not to express it. It was me—like the hide on a horse. I've had sixty from him since, but he could never approach it. The sit of the collar brought tears into my eyes, sir, when first I saw it; and as to the waist—"

"But the duel, Tregellis!" cried the Prince.

"Well, sir, I wore it at the duel, like the thoughtless fool that I was. It was Major Hunter, of the Guards, with whom I had had a little *tracasserie*, because I hinted that he should not come into Brookes's smelling of the stables. I fired first, and missed. He fired, and I shrieked in despair. 'He's hit! A surgeon! A surgeon!' they cried. 'A tailor! A tailor!' said I, for there was a double hole through the tails of my masterpiece. No, it was past all repair. You may laugh, sir, but I'll never see the like of it again."

I had seated myself on a settee in the corner, upon the Prince's invitation, and very glad I was to remain quiet and unnoticed, listening to the talk of these men. It was all in the same extravagant vein, garnished with many senseless oaths; but I observed this difference, that, whereas my uncle and Sheridan had something of humour in their exaggeration, Francis tended always to ill-nature, and the Prince to self-glorification. Finally, the conversation turned to music—I am not sure that my uncle did not artfully bring it there, and the Prince, hearing from him of my tastes, would have it that I should then and there sit down at the wonderful little piano, all inlaid with mother-of-pearl, which stood in the corner, and play him the accompaniment to his song. It was called, as I remember, "The Briton Conquers but to Save," and he rolled it out in a very fair bass voice, the others joining in the chorus, and clapping vigorously when he finished.

"Bravo, Mr. Stone!" said he. "You have an excellent touch; and I know what I am talking about when I speak of music. Cramer, of the Opera, said only the other day that he had rather hand his baton to me than to any amateur in England. Halloa, it's Charlie Fox, by all that's wonderful!"

He had run forward with much warmth, and was shaking the hand of a singular-looking person who had just entered the room. The new-comer was a stout, square-built man, plainly and almost carelessly dressed, with an uncouth manner and a rolling gait. His age might have been something over fifty, and his swarthy, harshly-featured face was already deeply lined either by his years or by his excesses. I have never seen a countenance in which the angel and the devil were more obviously wedded. Above, was the high, broad fore-head of the philosopher, with keen, humorous eyes looking out from under thick, strong brows. Below, was the heavy jowl of the sensualist curving in a broad crease over his cravat. That brow was the brow of the public Charles Fox, the thinker, the philanthropist, the man who rallied and led the Liberal party during the twenty most hazardous years of its existence. That jaw was the jaw of the private Charles Fox, the gambler, the libertine, the drunkard. Yet to his sins he never added the crowning one of hypocrisy. His vices were as open as his virtues. In some quaint freak of Nature, two spirits seemed to have been joined in one body, and the same frame to contain the best and the worst man of his age.

"I've run down from Chertsey, sir, just to shake you by the hand, and to make sure that the Tories have not carried you off."

"Hang it, Charlie, you know that I sink or swim with my friends! A Whig I started, and a Whig I shall remain."

I thought that I could read upon Fox's dark face that he was by no means so confident about the Prince's principles.

"Pitt has been at you, sir, I understand?"

"Yes, confound him! I hate the sight of that sharp-pointed snout of his, which he wants to be ever poking into my affairs. He and Addington have been boggling about the debts again. Why, look ye, Charlie, if Pitt held me in contempt he could not behave different."

I gathered from the smile which flitted over Sheridan's expressive face that this was exactly what Pitt did do. But straightway they all plunged into politics, varied by the drinking of sweet maraschino, which a footman brought round upon a salver. The King, the Queen, the Lords, and the Commons were each in succession cursed by the Prince, in spite of the excellent advice which he had given me about the British Constitution.

"Why, they allow me so little that I can't look after my own people. There are a dozen annuities to old servants and the like, and it's all I can do to scrape the money together to pay them. However, my"—he pulled himself up and coughed in a consequential way—"my financial agent has arranged for a loan, repayable upon the King's death. This liqueur isn't good for either of us, Charlie. We're both getting monstrous stout."

"I can't get any exercise for the gout," said Fox.

"I am blooded fifty ounces a month, but the more I take the more I make. You wouldn't think, to look at us, Tregellis, that we could do what we have done. We've had some days and nights together, Charlie!"

Fox smiled and shook his head.

"You remember how we posted to Newmarket before the races. We took a public coach, Tregellis, clapped the postillions into the rumble, and jumped on to their places. Charlie rode the leader and I the wheeler. One fellow wouldn't let us through his turnpike, and Charlie hopped off and had his coat off in a minute. The fellow thought he had to do with a fighting man, and soon cleared the way for us."

"By the way, sir, speaking of fighting men, I give a supper to the Fancy at the Waggon and Horses on Friday next," said my uncle. "If you should chance to be in town, they would think it a great honour if you should condescend to look in upon us."

"I've not seen a fight since I saw Tom Tyne, the tailor, kill Earl fourteen years ago. I swore off then, and you know me as a man of my word, Tregellis. Of course, I've been at the ringside incog many a time, but never as the Prince of Wales."

"We should be vastly honoured if you would come incog to our supper, sir."

"Well, well, Sherry, make a note of it. We'll be at Carlton House on Friday. The Prince can't come, you know, Tregellis, but you might reserve a chair for the Earl of Chester."

"Sir, we shall be proud to see the Earl of Chester there," said my uncle.

"By the way, Tregellis," said Fox, "there's some rumour about your having a sporting bet with Sir Lothian Hume. What's the truth of it?"

"Only a small matter of a couple of thous to a thou, he giving the odds. He has a fancy to this new Gloucester man, Crab Wilson, and I'm to find a man to beat him. Anything under twenty or over thirty-five, at or about thirteen stone."

"You take Charlie Fox's advice, then," cried the Prince. "When it comes to handicapping a horse, playing a hand, matching a cock, or picking a man, he has the best judgment in England. Now, Charlie, whom have we upon the list who can beat Crab Wilson, of Gloucester?"

I was amazed at the interest and knowledge which all these great people showed about the ring, for they not only had the deeds of the principal men of the time—Belcher, Mendoza, Jackson, or Dutch Sam—at their fingers' ends, but there was no fighting man so obscure that they did not know the details of his deeds and prospects. The old ones and then the young were discussed—their weight, their gameness, their hitting power, and their constitution. Who, as he saw Sheridan and Fox eagerly arguing as to whether Caleb Baldwin, the Westminster costermonger, could hold his own with Isaac Bittoon, the Jew, would have guessed that the one was the deepest political philosopher in

Europe, and that the other would be remembered as the author of the wittiest comedy and of the finest speech of his generation?

The name of Champion Harrison came very early into the discussion, and Fox, who had a high idea of Crab Wilson's powers, was of opinion that my uncle's only chance lay in the veteran taking the field again. "He may be slow on his pins, but he fights with his head, and he hits like the kick of a horse. When he finished Black Baruk the man flew across the outer ring as well as the inner, and fell among the spectators. If he isn't absolutely stale, Tregellis, he is your best chance."

My uncle shrugged his shoulders.

"If poor Avon were here we might do something with him, for he was Harrison's first patron, and the man was devoted to him. But his wife is too strong for me. And now, sir, I must leave you, for I have had the misfortune to-day to lose the best valet in England, and I must make inquiry for him. I thank your Royal Highness for your kindness in receiving my nephew in so gracious a fashion."

"Till Friday, then," said the Prince, holding out his hand. "I have to go up to town in any case, for there is a poor devil of an East India Company's officer who has written to me in his distress. If I can raise a few hundreds, I shall see him and set things right for him. Now, Mr. Stone, you have your life before you, and I hope it will be one which your uncle may be proud of. You will honour the King, and show respect for the Constitution, Mr. Stone. And, hark ye, you will avoid debt, and bear in mind that your honour is a sacred thing."

So I carried away a last impression of his sensual, good-humoured face, his high cravat, and his broad leather thighs. Again we passed the strange rooms, the gilded monsters, and the gorgeous footmen, and it was with relief that I found myself out in the open air once more, with the broad blue sea in front of us, and the fresh evening breeze upon our faces.

CHAPTER VIII—THE BRIGHTON ROAD

My uncle and I were up betimes next morning, but he was much out of temper, for no news had been heard of his valet Ambrose. He had indeed become like one of those ants of which I have read, who are so accustomed to be fed by smaller ants that when they are left to themselves they die of hunger. It was only by the aid of a man whom the landlord procured, and of Fox's valet, who had been sent expressly across, that his toilet was at last performed.

"I must win this race, nephew," said he, when he had finished breakfast; "I can't afford to be beat. Look out of the window and see if the Lades are there."

"I see a red four-in-hand in the square, and there is a crowd round it. Yes, I see the lady upon the box seat."

"Is our tandem out?"

"It is at the door."

"Come, then, and you shall have such a drive as you never had before."

He stood at the door pulling on his long brown driving-gauntlets and giving his orders to the ostlers.

"Every ounce will tell," said he. "We'll leave that dinner-basket behind. And you can keep my dog for me, Coppinger. You know him and understand him. Let him have his warm milk and curaçoa the same as usual. Whoa, my darlings, you'll have your fill of it before you reach Westminster Bridge."

"Shall I put in the toilet-case?" asked the landlord. I saw the struggle upon my uncle's face, but he was true to his principles.

"Put it under the seat—the front seat," said he. "Nephew, you must keep your weight as far forward as possible. Can you do anything on a yard of tin? Well, if you can't, we'll leave the trumpet. Buckle that girth up, Thomas. Have you greased the hubs, as I told you? Well, jump up, nephew, and we'll see them off."

Quite a crowd had gathered in the Old Square: men and women, dark-coated tradesmen, bucks from the Prince's Court, and officers from Hove, all in a buzz of excitement; for Sir John Lade and my uncle were two of the most famous whips of the time, and a match between them was a thing to talk of for many a long day.

"The Prince will be sorry to have missed the start," said my uncle. "He doesn't show before midday. Ah, Jack, good morning! Your servant, madam! It's a fine day for a little bit of waggoning."

As our tandem came alongside of the four-in-hand, with the two bonny bay mares gleaming like shot-silk in the sunshine, a murmur of admiration rose from the crowd. My uncle, in his fawn-coloured driving-coat, with all his harness of the same tint, looked the ideal of a Corinthian whip; while Sir John Lade, with his many-caped coat, his white hat, and his rough, weather-beaten face, might have taken his seat with a line of professionals upon any ale-house bench without any one being able to pick him out as one of the wealthiest landowners in England. It was an age of eccentricity, but he had carried his peculiarities to a length which surprised even the out-and-outers by marrying the sweetheart of a famous highwayman when the gallows had come between her and her lover. She was perched by his side, looking very smart in a flowered bonnet and grey travelling-dress, while in front of them the four splendid coal-black horses, with a flickering touch of gold upon their powerful, well-curved quarters, were pawing the dust in their eagerness to be off.

"It's a hundred that you don't see us before Westminster with a quarter of an hour's start," said Sir John.

"I'll take you another hundred that we pass you," answered my uncle.

"Very good. Time's up. Good-bye!" He gave a *tchk* of the tongue, shook his reins, saluted with his whip; in true coachman's style, and away he went, taking the curve out of the square in a workmanlike fashion that fetched a cheer from the crowd. We heard the dwindling roar of the wheels upon the cobblestones until they died away in the distance.

It seemed one of the longest quarters of an hour that I had ever known before the first stroke of nine boomed from the parish clock. For my part, I was fidgeting in my seat in my impatience, but my uncle's calm, pale face and large blue eyes were as tranquil and demure as those of the most unconcerned spectator. He was keenly on the alert, however, and it seemed to me that the stroke of the clock and the thong of his whip fell together—not in a blow, but in a sharp snap over the leader, which sent us flying with a jingle and a rattle upon our fifty miles' journey. I heard a roar from behind us, saw the gliding lines of windows with staring faces and waving handkerchiefs, and then we were off the stones and on to the good white road which curved away in front of us, with the sweep of the green downs upon either side.

I had been provided with shillings that the turnpike-gate might not stop us, but my uncle reined in the mares and took them at a very easy trot up all the heavy stretch which ends in Clayton Hill. He let them go then, and we flashed through Friar's Oak and across St. John's Common without more than catching a glimpse of the yellow cottage which contained all that I loved best. Never have I travelled at such a pace, and never have I felt such a sense of exhilaration from the rush of keen upland air upon our faces, and from the sight of those two glorious creatures stretched to their utmost, with the roar of their hoofs and the rattle of our wheels as the light curricle bounded and swayed behind them.

"It's a long four miles uphill from here to Hand Cross," said my uncle, as we flew through Cuckfield. "I must ease them a bit, for I cannot afford to break the hearts of my cattle. They have the right blood in them, and they would gallop until they dropped if I were brute enough to let them. Stand up on the seat, nephew, and see if you can get a glimpse of them."

I stood up, steadying myself upon my uncle's shoulder, but though I could see for a mile, or perhaps a quarter more, there was not a sign of the four-in-hand.

"If he has sprung his cattle up all these hills they'll be spent ere they see Croydon," said he.

"They have four to two," said I.

"*J'en suis bien sûr.* Sir John's black strain makes a good, honest creature, but not fliers like these. There lies Cuckfield Place, where the towers are, yonder. Get your weight right forward on the splashboard now that we are going uphill, nephew. Look at the action of that leader: did ever you see anything more easy and more beautiful?"

We were taking the hill at a quiet trot, but even so, we made the carrier, walking in the shadow of his huge, broad-wheeled, canvas-covered waggon, stare at us in amazement. Close to Hand Cross we passed the Royal Brighton stage, which had left at half-past seven, dragging heavily up the slope, and its passengers, toiling along through the dust behind, gave us a cheer as we whirled by. At Hand Cross we caught a glimpse of the old landlord, hurrying out with his gin and his gingerbread; but the dip of the ground was downwards now, and away we flew as fast as eight gallant hoofs could take us.

"Do you drive, nephew?"

"Very little, sir."

"There is no driving on the Brighton Road."

"How is that, sir?"

"Too good a road, nephew. I have only to give them their heads, and they will race me into Westminster. It wasn't always so. When I was a very young man one might learn to handle his twenty yards of tape here as well as elsewhere. There's not much really good waggoning now south of Leicestershire. Show me a man who can hit 'em and hold 'em on a Yorkshire dale-side, and that's the man who comes from the right school."

We had raced over Crawley Down and into the broad main street of Crawley village, flying between two country waggons in a way which showed me that even now a driver might do something on the road. With every turn I peered ahead, looking for our opponents, but my uncle seemed to concern himself very little about them, and occupied himself in giving me advice, mixed up with so many phrases of the craft, that it was all that I could do to follow him.

"Keep a finger for each, or you will have your reins clubbed," said he. "As to the whip, the less fanning the better if you have willing cattle; but when you want to put a little life into a coach, see that you get your thong on to the one that needs it, and don't let it fly round after you've hit. I've seen a driver warm up the off-side passenger on the roof behind him every time he tried to cut his off-side wheeler. I believe that is their dust over yonder."

A long stretch of road lay before us, barred with the shadows of wayside trees. Through the green fields a lazy blue river was drawing itself slowly along, passing under a bridge in front of us. Beyond was a young fir plantation, and over its olive line there rose a white whirl which drifted swiftly, like a cloud-scud on a breezy day.

"Yes, yes, it's they!" cried my uncle. "No one else would travel as fast. Come, nephew, we're half-way when we cross the mole at Kimberham Bridge, and we've done it in two hours and fourteen minutes. The Prince drove to Carlton House with a three tandem in four hours and a half. The first half is the worst half, and we might cut his time if all goes well. We should make up between this and Reigate."

And we flew. The bay mares seemed to know what that white puff in front of us signified, and they stretched themselves like greyhounds. We passed a phaeton and pair London-bound, and we left it behind as if it had been standing still. Trees, gates, cottages went dancing by. We heard the folks shouting from the fields, under the impression that we were a runaway. Faster and faster yet they raced, the hoofs rattling like castanets, the yellow manes flying, the wheels buzzing, and every joint and rivet creaking and groaning, while the curricle swung and swayed until I found myself clutching to the side-rail. My uncle eased them and glanced at his watch as we saw the grey tiles and dingy red houses of Reigate in the hollow beneath us.

"We did the last six well under twenty minutes," said he. "We've time in hand now, and a little water at the Red Lion will do them no harm. Red four-in-hand passed, ostler?"

"Just gone, sir."

"Going hard?"

"Galloping full split, sir! Took the wheel off a butcher's cart at the corner of the High Street, and was out o' sight before the butcher's boy could see what had hurt him."

Z-z-z-z-ack! went the long thong, and away we flew once more. It was market day at Redhill, and the road was crowded with carts of produce, droves of bullocks, and farmers' gigs. It was a sight to see how my uncle threaded his way amongst them all. Through the market-place we dashed amidst the shouting of men, the screaming of women, and the scuttling of poultry, and then we were out in the country again, with the long, steep incline of the Redhill Road before us. My uncle waved his whip in the air with a shrill view-halloa.

There was the dust-cloud rolling up the hill in front of us, and through it we had a shadowy peep of the backs of our opponents, with a flash of brass-work and a gleam of scarlet.

"There's half the game won, nephew. Now we must pass them. Hark forward, my beauties! By George, if Kitty isn't foundered!"

The leader had suddenly gone dead lame. In an instant we were both out of the curricle and on our knees beside her. It was but a stone, wedged between frog and shoe in the off fore-foot, but it was a minute or two before we could wrench it out. When we had regained our places the Lades were round the curve of the hill and out of sight.

"Bad luck!" growled my uncle. "But they can't get away from us!" For the first time he touched the mares up, for he had but cracked the whip over their heads before. "If we catch them in the next few miles we can spare them for the rest of the way."

They were beginning to show signs of exhaustion. Their breath came quick and hoarse, and their beautiful coats were matted with moisture. At the top of the hill, however, they settled down into their swing once more.

"Where on earth have they got to?" cried my uncle. "Can you make them out on the road, nephew?"

We could see a long white ribbon of it, all dotted with carts and waggons coming from Croydon to Redhill, but there was no sign of the big red four-in-hand.

"There they are! Stole away! Stole away!" he cried, wheeling the mares round into a side road which struck to the right out of that which we had travelled. "There they are, nephew! On the brow of the hill!"

Sure enough, on the rise of a curve upon our right the four-in-hand had appeared, the horses stretched to the utmost. Our mares laid themselves out gallantly, and the distance between us began slowly to decrease. I found that I could see the black band upon Sir John's white hat, then that I could count the folds of his cape; finally, that I could see the pretty features of his wife as she looked back at us.

"We're on the side road to Godstone and Warlingham," said my uncle. "I suppose he thought that he could make better time by getting out of the way of the market carts. But we've got the deuce of a hill to come down. You'll see some fun, nephew, or I am mistaken."

As he spoke I suddenly saw the wheels of the four-in-hand disappear, then the body of it, and then the two figures upon the box, as suddenly and abruptly as if it had bumped down the first three steps of some gigantic stairs. An instant later we had reached the same spot, and there was the road beneath us, steep and narrow, winding in long curves into the valley. The four-in-hand was swishing down it as hard as the horses could gallop.

"Thought so!" cried my uncle. "If he doesn't brake, why should I? Now, my darlings, one good spurt, and we'll show them the colour of our tailboard."

We shot over the brow and flew madly down the hill with the great red coach roaring and thundering before us. Already we were in her dust, so that we could see nothing but the dim scarlet blur in the heart of it, rocking and rolling, with its outline hardening at every stride. We could hear the crack of the whip in front of us, and the shrill voice of Lady Lade as she screamed to the horses. My uncle was very quiet, but when I glanced up at him I saw that his lips were set and his eyes shining, with just a little flush upon each pale cheek. There was no need to urge on the mares, for they were already flying at a pace which could neither be stopped nor controlled. Our leader's head came abreast of the off hind wheel, then of the off front one—then for a hundred yards we did not gain an inch, and then with a spurt the bay leader was neck to neck with the black wheeler, and our fore wheel within an inch of their hind one.

"Dusty work!" said my uncle, quietly.

"Fan 'em, Jack! Fan 'em!" shrieked the lady.

He sprang up and lashed at his horses.

"Look out, Tregellis!" he shouted. "There's a damnation spill coming for somebody."

We had got fairly abreast of them now, the rumps of the horses exactly a-line and the fore wheels whizzing together. There was not six inches to spare in the breadth of the road, and every instant I expected to feel the jar of a locking wheel. But now, as we came out from the dust, we could see what was ahead, and my uncle whistled between his teeth at the sight.

Two hundred yards or so in front of us there was a bridge, with wooden posts and rails upon either side. The road narrowed down at the point, so that it was obvious that the two carriages abreast could not possibly get over. One must give way to the other. Already our wheels were abreast of their wheelers.

"I lead!" shouted my uncle. "You must pull them, Lade!"

"Not I!" he roared.

"No, by George!" shrieked her ladyship. "Fan 'em, Jack; keep on fanning 'em!"

It seemed to me that we were all going to eternity together. But my uncle did the only thing that could have saved us. By a desperate effort we might just clear the coach before reaching the mouth of the bridge. He sprang up, and lashed right and left at the mares, who, maddened by the unaccustomed pain, hurled themselves on in a frenzy. Down we thundered together, all shouting, I believe, at the top of our voices in the madness of the moment; but still we were drawing steadily away, and we were almost clear of the leaders when we flew on to the bridge. I glanced back at the coach, and I saw Lady Lade, with her savage little white teeth clenched together, throw herself forward and tug with both hands at the off-side reins.

"Jam them, Jack!" she cried. "Jam the—before they can pass."

Had she done it an instant sooner we should have crashed against the wood-work, carried it away, and been hurled into the deep gully below. As it was, it was not the powerful haunch of the black leader which caught our wheel, but the forequarter, which had not weight enough to turn us from our course. I saw a red wet seam gape suddenly through the black hair, and next instant we were flying alone down the road, whilst the four-in-hand had halted, and Sir John and his lady were down in the road together tending to the wounded horse.

"Easy now, my beauties!" cried my uncle, settling down into his seat again, and looking back over his shoulder. "I could not have believed that Sir John Lade would have been guilty of such a trick as pulling that leader across. I do not permit a *mauvaise plaisanterie* of that sort. He shall hear from me to-night."

"It was the lady," said I.

My uncle's brow cleared, and he began to laugh.

"It was little Letty, was it?" said he. "I might have known it. There's a touch of the late lamented Sixteen-string Jack about the trick. Well, it is only messages of another kind that I send to a lady, so we'll just drive on our way, nephew, and thank our stars that we bring whole bones over the Thames."

We stopped at the Greyhound, at Croydon, where the two good little mares were sponged and petted and fed, after which, at an easier pace, we made our way through Norbury and Streatham. At last the fields grew fewer and the walls longer. The outlying villas closed up thicker and thicker, until their shoulders met, and we were driving between a double line of houses with garish shops at the corners, and such a stream of traffic as I had never seen, roaring down the centre. Then suddenly we were on a broad bridge with a dark coffee-brown river flowing sulkily beneath it, and bluff-bowed barges drifting down upon its bosom. To right and left stretched a broken, irregular line of many-coloured houses winding along either bank as far as I could see.

"That's the House of Parliament, nephew," said my uncle, pointing with his whip, "and the black towers are Westminster Abbey. How do, your Grace? How do? That's the Duke of Norfolk—the stout man in blue upon the swish-tailed mare. Now we are in Whitehall. There's the Treasury on the left, and the Horse Guards, and the Admiralty, where the stone dolphins are carved above the gate."

I had the idea, which a country-bred lad brings up with him, that London was merely a wilderness of houses, but I was astonished now to see the green slopes and the lovely spring trees showing between.

"Yes, those are the Privy Gardens," said my uncle, "and there is the window out of which Charles took his last step on to the scaffold. You wouldn't think the mares had come fifty miles, would you? See how les petites cheries step out for the credit of their master. Look at the barouche, with the sharp-featured man peeping out of the window. That's Pitt, going down to the House. We are coming into Pall Mall now, and this great building on the left is Carlton House, the Prince's Palace. There's St. James's, the big, dingy place with the clock, and the two red-coated sentries before it. And here's the famous street of the same name, nephew, which is the very centre of the world, and here's Jermyn Street opening out of it, and finally, here's my own little box, and we are well under the five hours from Brighton Old Square."

CHAPTER IX—WATIER'S

My uncle's house in Jermyn Street was quite a small one—five rooms and an attic. "A man-cook and a cottage," he said, "are all that a wise man requires." On the other hand, it was furnished with the neatness and taste which belonged to his character, so that his most luxurious friends found something in the tiny rooms which made them discontented with their own sumptuous mansions. Even the attic, which had been converted into my bedroom, was the most perfect little bijou attic that could possibly be imagined. Beautiful and valuable knick-knacks filled every corner of every apartment, and the house had become a perfect miniature museum which would have delighted a virtuoso. My uncle explained the presence of all these pretty things with a shrug of his shoulders and a wave of his hands. "They are *des petites cadeaux*," said he, "but it would be an indiscretion for me to say more."

We found a note from Ambrose waiting for us which increased rather than explained the mystery of his disappearance.

"My dear Sir Charles Tregellis," it ran, "it will ever be a subject of regret to me that the force of circumstances should have compelled me to leave your service in so abrupt a fashion, but something occurred during our journey from Friar's Oak to Brighton which left me without any possible alternative. I trust, however, that my absence may prove to be but a temporary one. The isinglass recipe for the shirt-fronts is in the strong-box at Drummond's Bank.—Yours obediently, AMBROSE."

"Well, I suppose I must fill his place as best I can," said my uncle, moodily. "But how on earth could something have occurred to make him leave me at a time when we were going full-trot down hill in my curricle? I shall never find his match again either for chocolate or cravats. *Je suis desolé*! But now, nephew, we must send to Weston and have you fitted up. It is not for a gentleman to go to a shop, but for the shop to come to the gentleman. Until you have your clothes you must remain *en retraite*."

The measuring was a most solemn and serious function, though it was nothing to the trying-on two days later, when my uncle stood by in an agony of apprehension as each garment was adjusted, he and Weston arguing over every seam and lapel and skirt until I was dizzy with turning round in front of them. Then, just as I had hoped that all was settled, in came young Mr. Brummell, who promised to be an even greater exquisite than my uncle, and the whole matter had to be thrashed out between them. He was a good-sized man, this Brummell, with a long, fair face, light brown hair, and slight sandy side-whiskers. His manner was languid, his voice drawling, and while he eclipsed my uncle in the extravagance of his speech, he had not the air of manliness and decision which underlay all my kinsman's affectations.

"Why, George," cried my uncle, "I thought you were with your regiment."

"I've sent in my papers," drawled the other.

"I thought it would come to that."

"Yes. The Tenth was ordered to Manchester, and they could hardly expect me to go to a place like that. Besides, I found the major monstrous rude."

"How was that?"

"He expected me to know about his absurd drill, Tregellis, and I had other things to think of, as you may suppose. I had no difficulty in taking my right place on parade, for there was a trooper with a red nose on a flea-bitten grey, and I had observed that my post was always immediately in front of him. This saved a great deal of trouble. The other day, however, when I came on parade, I galloped up one line and down the other, but the deuce a glimpse could I get of that long nose of his! Then, just as I was at my wits' end, I caught sight of him, alone at one side; so I formed up in front. It seems he had been put there to keep the ground, and the major so far forgot himself as to say that I knew nothing of my duties."

My uncle laughed, and Brummell looked me up and down with his large, intolerant eyes.

"These will do very passably," said he. "Buff and blue are always very gentlemanlike. But a sprigged waistcoat would have been better."

"I think not," said my uncle, warmly.

"My dear Tregellis, you are infallible upon a cravat, but you must allow me the right of my own judgment upon vests. I like it vastly as it stands, but a touch of red sprig would give it the finish that it needs."

They argued with many examples and analogies for a good ten minutes, revolving round me at the same time with their heads on one side and their glasses to their eyes. It was a relief to me when they at last agreed upon a compromise.

"You must not let anything I have said shake your faith in Sir Charles's judgment, Mr. Stone," said Brummell, very earnestly.

I assured him that I should not.

"If you were my nephew, I should expect you to follow my taste. But you will cut a very good figure as it is. I had a young cousin who came up to town last year with a recommendation to my care. But he would take no advice. At the end of the second week I met him coming down St. James's Street in a snuff-coloured coat cut by a country tailor. He bowed to me. Of course I knew what was due to myself. I looked all round him, and there was an end to his career in town. You are from the country, Mr. Stone?"

"From Sussex, sir."

"Sussex! Why, that is where I send my washing to. There is an excellent clear-starcher living near Hayward's Heath. I send my shirts two at a time, for if you send more it excites the woman and diverts her attention. I cannot abide anything but country washing. But I should be vastly sorry to have to live there. What can a man find to do?"

"You don't hunt, George?"

"When I do, it's a woman. But surely you don't go to hounds, Charles?"

"I was out with the Belvoir last winter."

"The Belvoir! Did you hear how I smoked Rutland? The story has been in the clubs this month past. I bet him that my bag would weigh more than his. He got three and a half brace, but I shot his liver-coloured pointer, so he had to pay. But as to hunting, what amusement can there be in flying about among a crowd of greasy, galloping farmers? Every man to his own taste, but Brookes's window by day and a snug corner of the macao table at Watier's by night, give me all I want for mind and body. You heard how I plucked Montague the brewer!"

"I have been out of town."

"I had eight thousand from him at a sitting. 'I shall drink your beer in future, Mr. Brewer,' said I. 'Every blackguard in London does,' said he. It was monstrous impolite of him, but some people cannot lose with grace. Well, I am going down to Clarges Street to pay Jew King a little of my interest. Are you bound that way? Well, good-bye, then! I'll see you and your young friend at the club or in the Mall, no doubt," and he sauntered off upon his way.

"That young man is destined to take my place," said my uncle, gravely, when Brummell had departed. "He is quite young and of no descent, but he has made his way by his cool effrontery, his natural taste, and his extravagance of speech. There is no man who can be impolite in so polished a fashion. He has a half-smile, and a way of raising his eyebrows, for which he will be shot one of these mornings. Already his opinion is quoted in the clubs as a rival to my own. Well, every man has his day, and when I am convinced that mine is past, St. James's Street shall know me no more, for it is not in my nature to be second to any man. But now, nephew, in that buff and blue suit you may pass anywhere; so, if you please, we will step into my vis-à-vis, and I will show you something of the town."

How can I describe all that we saw and all that we did upon that lovely spring day? To me it was as if I had been wafted to a fairy world, and my uncle might have been some benevolent enchanter in a high-collared, long-tailed coat, who was guiding me about in it. He showed me the West-end streets, with the bright carriages and the gaily dressed ladies and sombre-clad men, all crossing and hurrying and recrossing like an ants' nest when you turn it over with a stick. Never had I formed a conception of such endless banks of houses, and such a ceaseless stream of life flowing between. Then we passed down the Strand, where the crowd was thicker than ever, and even penetrated beyond Temple Bar and into the City, though my uncle begged me not to mention it, for he would not wish it to be generally known. There I saw the Exchange and the Bank and Lloyd's Coffee House, with the brown-coated, sharp-faced merchants and the hurrying clerks, the huge horses and the busy draymen. It was a very different world this from that which we had left in the West—a world of energy and of strength, where there was no place for the listless and the idle. Young as I was, I knew that it was here, in the forest of merchant shipping, in the bales which swung up to the warehouse windows, in the loaded waggons which roared over the cobblestones, that the power of Britain lay. Here, in the City of London, was the taproot from which Empire and wealth and so many other fine leaves had sprouted. Fashion and speech and manners may change, but the spirit of enterprise within that square mile or two of land must not change, for when it withers all that has grown from it must wither also.

We lunched at Stephen's, the fashionable inn in Bond Street, where I saw a line of tilburys and saddle-horses, which stretched from the door to the further end of the street. And thence we went to the Mail in St. James's Park, and thence to Brookes's, the great Whig club, and thence again to Watier's, where the men of fashion used to gamble. Everywhere I met the same sort of men, with their stiff figures and small waists, all showing the utmost deference to my uncle, and for his sake an easy tolerance of me. The talk was always such as I had already heard at the Pavilion: talk of politics, talk of the King's health, talk of the Prince's extravagance, of the expected renewal of war, of horse-racing, and of the ring. I saw, too, that eccentricity was, as my uncle had told me, the fashion; and if the folk upon the Continent look upon us even to this day as being a nation of lunatics, it is no doubt a tradition handed down from the time when the only travellers whom they were likely to see were drawn from the class which I was now meeting.

It was an age of heroism and of folly. On the one hand soldiers, sailors, and statesmen of the quality of Pitt, Nelson, and afterwards Wellington, had been forced to the front by the imminent menace of Buonaparte. We were great in arms, and were soon also to be great in literature, for Scott and Byron were in their day the strongest forces in Europe. On the other hand, a touch of madness, real or assumed, was a passport through doors which were closed to wisdom and to virtue. The man who could enter a drawing-room walking upon his hands, the man who had filed his teeth that he might whistle like a coach-man, the man who always spoke his thoughts aloud and so kept his guests in a quiver of apprehension, these were the people who found it easy to come to the front in London society. Nor could the heroism and the folly be kept apart, for there were few who could quite escape the contagion of the times. In an age when the Premier was a heavy drinker, the Leader of the Opposition a libertine, and the Prince of Wales a combination of the two, it was hard to know where to look for a man whose private and public characters were equally lofty. At the same time, with all its faults it was a strong age, and you will be fortunate if in your time the country produces five such names as Pitt, Fox, Scott, Nelson, and Wellington.

It was in Watier's that night, seated by my uncle on one of the red velvet settees at the side of the room, that I had pointed out to me some of those singular characters whose fame and eccentricities are even now not wholly forgotten in the world. The long, many-pillared room, with its mirrors and chandeliers, was crowded with full-blooded, loud-voiced men-about-town, all in the same dark evening dress with white silk stockings, cambric shirt-fronts, and little, flat chapeau-bras under their arms.

"The acid-faced old gentleman with the thin legs is the Marquis of Queensberry," said my uncle. "His chaise was driven nineteen miles in an hour in a match against the Count Taafe, and he sent a message fifty miles in thirty minutes by throwing it from hand to hand in a cricket-ball. The man he is talking to is Sir Charles Bunbury, of the Jockey Club, who had the Prince warned off the Heath at Newmarket on account of the in-and-out riding of Sam Chifney, his jockey. There's Captain Barclay going up to them now. He knows more about training than any man alive, and he has walked ninety miles in twenty-one hours. You have only to look at his calves to see that Nature built him for it. There's another walker there, the man with a flowered vest standing near the fireplace. That is Buck Whalley, who walked to Jerusalem in a long blue coat, top-boots, and buckskins."

"Why did he do that, sir?" I asked, in astonishment.

My uncle shrugged his shoulders.

"It was his humour," said he. "He walked into society through it, and that was better worth reaching than Jerusalem. There's Lord Petersham, the man with the beaky nose. He always rises at six in the evening, and he has laid down the finest cellar of snuff in Europe. It was he who ordered his valet to put half a dozen of sherry by his bed and call him the day after to-morrow. He's talking to Lord Panmure, who can take his six bottles of claret and argue with a bishop after it. The lean man with the weak knees is General Scott who lives upon toast and water and has won £200,000 at whist. He is talking to young Lord Blandford who gave £1800 for a Boccaccio the other day. Evening, Dudley!"

"Evening, Tregellis!" An elderly, vacant-looking man had stopped before us and was looking me up and down.

"Some young cub Charlie Tregellis has caught in the country," he murmured. "He doesn't look as if he would be much credit to him. Been out of town, Tregellis?"

"For a few days."

"Hem!" said the man, transferring his sleepy gaze to my uncle. "He's looking pretty bad. He'll be going into the country feet foremost some of these days if he doesn't pull up!" He nodded, and passed on.

"You mustn't look so mortified, nephew," said my uncle, smiling. "That's old Lord Dudley, and he has a trick of thinking aloud. People used to be offended, but they take no notice of him now. It was only last week, when he was dining at Lord Elgin's, that he apologized to the company for the shocking bad cooking. He thought he was at his own table, you see. It gives him a place of his own in society. That's Lord Harewood he has fastened on to now. Harewood's peculiarity is to mimic the Prince in everything. One day the Prince hid his queue behind the collar of his coat, so Harewood cut his off, thinking that they were going out of fashion. Here's Lumley, the ugly man. 'L'homme laid' they called him in Paris. The other one is Lord Foley—they call him No. 11, on account of his thin legs."

"There is Mr. Brummell, sir," said I.

"Yes, he'll come to us presently. That young man has certainly a future before him. Do you observe the way in which he looks round the room from under his drooping eyelids, as though it were a condescension that he should have entered it? Small conceits are intolerable, but when they are pushed to the uttermost they become respectable. How do, George?"

"Have you heard about Vereker Merton?" asked Brummell, strolling up with one or two other exquisites at his heels. "He has run away with his father's woman-cook, and actually married her."

"What did Lord Merton do?"

"He congratulated him warmly, and confessed that he had always underrated his intelligence. He is to live with the young couple, and make a handsome allowance on condition that the bride sticks to her old duties. By the way, there was a rumour that you were about to marry, Tregellis."

"I think not," answered my uncle. "It would be a mistake to overwhelm one by attentions which are a pleasure to many."

"My view, exactly, and very neatly expressed," cried Brummell. "Is it fair to break a dozen hearts in order to intoxicate one with rapture? I'm off to the Continent next week."

"Bailiffs?" asked one of his companions.

"Too bad, Pierrepoint. No, no; it is pleasure and instruction combined. Besides, it is necessary to go to Paris for your little things, and if there is a chance of the war breaking out again, it would be well to lay in a supply."

"Quite right," said my uncle, who seemed to have made up his mind to outdo Brummell in extravagance. "I used to get my sulphur-coloured gloves from the Palais Royal. When the war broke out in '93 I was cut off from them for nine years. Had it not been for a lugger which I specially hired to smuggle them, I might have been reduced to English tan."

"The English are excellent at a flat-iron or a kitchen poker, but anything more delicate is beyond them."

"Our tailors are good," cried my uncle, "but our stuffs lack taste and variety. The war has made us more rococo than ever. It has cut us off from travel, and there is nothing to match travel for expanding the mind. Last year, for example, I came upon some new waist-coating in the Square of San Marco, at Venice. It was yellow, with the prettiest little twill of pink running through it. How could I have seen it had I not travelled? I brought it back with me, and for a time it was all the rage."

"The Prince took it up."

"Yes, he usually follows my lead. We dressed so alike last year that we were frequently mistaken for each other. It tells against me, but so it was. He often complains that things do not look as well upon him as upon me, but how can I make the obvious reply? By the way, George, I did not see you at the Marchioness of Dover's ball."

"Yes, I was there, and lingered for a quarter of an hour or so. I am surprised that you did not see me. I did not go past the doorway, however, for undue preference gives rise to jealousy."

"I went early," said my uncle, "for I had heard that there were to be some tolerable débutantes. It always pleases me vastly when I am able to pass a compliment to any of them. It has happened, but not often, for I keep to my own standard."

So they talked, these singular men, and I, looking from one to the other, could not imagine how they could help bursting out a-laughing in each other's faces. But, on the contrary, their conversation was very grave, and filled out with many little bows, and opening and shutting of snuff-boxes, and flickings of laced handkerchiefs. Quite a crowd had gathered silently around, and I could see that the talk had been regarded as a contest between two men who were looked upon as rival arbiters of fashion. It was finished by the Marquis of Queensberry passing his arm through Brummell's and leading him off, while my uncle threw out his laced cambric shirt-front and shot his ruffles as if he were well satisfied with his share in the encounter. It is seven-and-forty years since I looked upon that circle of dandies, and where, now, are their dainty little hats, their wonderful waistcoats, and their boots, in which one could arrange one's cravat? They lived strange lives, these men, and they died strange deaths—some by their own hands, some as beggars, some in a debtor's gaol, some, like the most brilliant of them all, in a madhouse in a foreign land.

"There is the card-room, Rodney," said my uncle, as we passed an open door on our way out. Glancing in, I saw a line of little green baize tables with small groups of men sitting round, while at one side was a longer one, from which there came a continuous murmur of voices. "You may lose what you like in there, save only your nerve or your temper," my uncle continued. "Ah, Sir Lothian, I trust that the luck was with you?"

A tall, thin man, with a hard, austere face, had stepped out of the open doorway. His heavily thatched eyebrows covered quick, furtive grey eyes, and his gaunt features were hollowed at the cheek and temple like water-grooved flint. He was dressed entirely in black, and I noticed that his shoulders swayed a little as if he had been drinking.

"Lost like the deuce," he snapped.

"Dice?"

"No, whist."

"You couldn't get very hard hit over that."

"Couldn't you?" he snarled. "Play a hundred a trick and a thousand on the rub, losing steadily for five hours, and see what you think of it."

My uncle was evidently struck by the haggard look upon the other's face.

"I hope it's not very bad," he said.

"Bad enough. It won't bear talking about. By the way, Tregellis, have you got your man for this fight yet?"

"No."

"You seem to be hanging in the wind a long time. It's play or pay, you know. I shall claim forfeit if you don't come to scratch."

"If you will name your day I shall produce my man, Sir Lothian," said my uncle, coldly.

"This day four weeks, if you like."

"Very good. The 18th of May."

"I hope to have changed my name by then!"

"How is that?" asked my uncle, in surprise.

"It is just possible that I may be Lord Avon."

"What, you have had some news?" cried my uncle, and I noticed a tremor in his voice.

"I've had my agent over at Monte Video, and he believes he has proof that Avon died there. Anyhow, it is absurd to suppose that because a murderer chooses to fly from justice—"

"I won't have you use that word, Sir Lothian," cried my uncle, sharply.

"You were there as I was. You know that he was a murderer."

"I tell you that you shall not say so."

Sir Lothian's fierce little grey eyes had to lower themselves before the imperious anger which shone in my uncle's.

"Well, to let that point pass, it is monstrous to suppose that the title and the estates can remain hung up in this way for ever. I'm the heir, Tregellis, and I'm going to have my rights."

"I am, as you are aware, Lord Avon's dearest friend," said my uncle, sternly. "His disappearance has not affected my love for him, and until his fate is finally ascertained, I shall exert myself to see that his rights also are respected."

"His rights would be a long drop and a cracked spine," Sir Lothian answered, and then, changing his manner suddenly, he laid his hand upon my uncle's sleeve.

"Come, come, Tregellis, I was his friend as well as you," said he. "But we cannot alter the facts, and it is rather late in the day for us to fall out over them. Your invitation holds good for Friday night?"

"Certainly."

"I shall bring Crab Wilson with me, and finally arrange the conditions of our little wager."

"Very good, Sir Lothian: I shall hope to see you." They bowed, and my uncle stood a little time looking after him as he made his way amidst the crowd.

"A good sportsman, nephew," said he. "A bold rider, the best pistol-shot in England, but . . . a dangerous man!"

CHAPTER X—THE MEN OF THE RING

It was at the end of my first week in London that my uncle gave a supper to the fancy, as was usual for gentlemen of that time if they wished to figure before the public as Corinthians and patrons of sport. He had invited not only the chief fighting-men of the day, but also those men of fashion who were most interested in the ring: Mr. Fletcher Reid, Lord Say and Sele, Sir Lothian Hume, Sir John Lade, Colonel Montgomery, Sir Thomas Apreece, the Hon. Berkeley Craven, and many more. The rumour that the Prince was to be present had already spread through the clubs, and invitations were eagerly sought after.

The Waggon and Horses was a well-known sporting house, with an old prize-fighter for landlord. And the arrangements were as primitive as the most Bohemian could wish. It was one of the many curious fashions which have now died out, that men who were blasé from luxury and high living seemed to find a fresh piquancy in life by descending to the lowest resorts, so that the night-houses and gambling-dens in Covent Garden or the Haymarket often gathered illustrious company under their smoke-blackened ceilings. It was a change for them to turn their backs upon the cooking of Weltjie and of Ude, or the chambertin of old Q., and to dine upon a porter-house steak washed down by a pint of ale from a pewter pot.

A rough crowd had assembled in the street to see the fighting-men go in, and my uncle warned me to look to my pockets as we pushed our way through it. Within was a large room with faded red curtains, a sanded floor, and walls which were covered with prints of pugilists and race-horses. Brown liquor-stained tables were dotted about in it, and round one of these half a dozen formidable-looking men were seated, while one, the roughest of all, was perched upon the table itself, swinging his legs to and fro. A tray of small glasses and pewter mugs stood beside them.

"The boys were thirsty, sir, so I brought up some ale and some lip-trap," whispered the landlord; "I thought you would have no objection, sir."

"Quite right, Bob! How are you all? How are you, Maddox? How are you, Baldwin? Ah, Belcher, I am very glad to see you."

The fighting-men rose and took their hats off, except the fellow on the table, who continued to swing his legs and to look my uncle very coolly in the face.

"How are you, Berks?"

"Pretty tidy. 'Ow are you?"

"Say 'sir' when you speak to a genelman," said Belcher, and with a sudden tilt of the table he sent Berks flying almost into my uncle's arms.

"See now, Jem, none o' that!" said Berks, sulkily.

"I'll learn you manners, Joe, which is more than ever your father did. You're not drinkin' black-jack in a boozin' ken, but you are meetin' noble, slap-up Corinthians, and it's for you to behave as such."

"I've always been reckoned a genelman-like sort of man," said Berks, thickly, "but if so be as I've said or done what I 'adn't ought to—"

"There, there, Berks, that's all right!" cried my uncle, only too anxious to smooth things over and to prevent a quarrel at the outset of the evening. "Here are some more of our friends. How are you, Apreece? How are you, Colonel? Well, Jackson, you are looking vastly better. Good evening, Lade. I trust Lady Lade was none the worse for our pleasant drive. Ah, Mendoza, you look fit enough to throw your hat over the ropes this instant. Sir Lothian, I am glad to see you. You will find some old friends here."

Amid the stream of Corinthians and fighting-men who were thronging into the room I had caught a glimpse of the sturdy figure and broad, good-humoured face of Champion Harrison. The sight of him was like a whiff of South Down air coming into that low-roofed, oil-smelling room, and I ran forward to shake him by the hand.

"Why, Master Rodney—or I should say Mr. Stone, I suppose— you've changed out of all knowledge. I can't hardly believe that it was really you that used to come down to blow the bellows when Boy Jim and I were at the anvil. Well, you are fine, to be sure!"

"What's the news of Friar's Oak?" I asked eagerly.

"Your father was down to chat with me, Master Rodney, and he tells me that the war is going to break out again, and that he hopes to see you here in London before many days are past; for he is coming up to see Lord Nelson and to make inquiry about a ship. Your mother is well, and I saw her in church on Sunday."

"And Boy Jim?"

Champion Harrison's good-humoured face clouded over.

"He'd set his heart very much on comin' here to-night, but there were reasons why I didn't wish him to, and so there's a shadow betwixt us. It's the first that ever was, and I feel it, Master Rodney. Between ourselves, I have very good reason to wish him to stay with me, and I am sure that, with his high spirit and his ideas, he would never settle down again after once he had a taste o' London. I left him behind me with enough work to keep him busy until I get back to him."

A tall and beautifully proportioned man, very elegantly dressed, was strolling towards us. He stared in surprise and held out his hand to my companion.

"Why, Jack Harrison!" he cried. "This is a resurrection. Where in the world did you come from?"

"Glad to see you, Jackson," said my companion. "You look as well and as young as ever."

"Thank you, yes. I resigned the belt when I could get no one to fight me for it, and I took to teaching."

"I'm doing smith's work down Sussex way."

"I've often wondered why you never had a shy at my belt. I tell you honestly, between man and man, I'm very glad you didn't."

"Well, it's real good of you to say that, Jackson. I might ha' done it, perhaps, but the old woman was against it. She's been a good wife to me and I can't go against her. But I feel a bit lonesome here, for these boys are since my time."

"You could do some of them over now," said Jackson, feeling my friend's upper arm. "No better bit of stuff was ever seen in a twenty-four foot ring. It would be a rare treat to see you take some of these young ones on. Won't you let me spring you on them?"

Harrison's eyes glistened at the idea, but he shook his head.

"It won't do, Jackson. My old woman holds my promise. That's Belcher, ain't it—the good lookin' young chap with the flash coat?"

"Yes, that's Jem. You've not seen him! He's a jewel."

"So I've heard. Who's the youngster beside him? He looks a tidy chap."

"That's a new man from the West. Crab Wilson's his name."

Harrison looked at him with interest. "I've heard of him," said he. "They are getting a match on for him, ain't they?"

"Yes. Sir Lothian Hume, the thin-faced gentleman over yonder, has backed him against Sir Charles Tregellis's man. We're to hear about the match to-night, I understand. Jem Belcher thinks great things of Crab Wilson. There's Belcher's young brother, Tom. He's looking out for a match, too. They say he's quicker than Jem with the mufflers, but he can't hit as hard. I was speaking of your brother, Jem."

"The young 'un will make his way," said Belcher, who had come across to us. "He's more a sparrer than a fighter just at present, but when his gristle sets he'll take on anything on the list. Bristol's as full o' young fightin'-men now as a bin is of bottles. We've got two more comin' up—Gully and Pearce—who'll make you London mill-ing coves wish they was back in the west country again."

"Here's the Prince," said Jackson, as a hum and bustle rose from the door.

I saw George come bustling in, with a good-humoured smile upon his comely face. My uncle welcomed him, and led some of the Corinthians up to be presented.

"We'll have trouble, gov'nor," said Belcher to Jackson. "Here's Joe Berks drinkin' gin out of a mug, and you know what a swine he is when he's drunk."

"You must put a stopper on 'im gov'nor," said several of the other prize-fighters. "'E ain't what you'd call a charmer when 'e's sober, but there's no standing 'im when 'e's fresh."

Jackson, on account of his prowess and of the tact which he possessed, had been chosen as general regulator of the whole prize-fighting body, by whom he was usually alluded to as the Commander-in-Chief. He and Belcher went across now to the table upon which Berks was still perched. The ruffian's face was already flushed, and his eyes heavy and bloodshot.

"You must keep yourself in hand to-night, Berks," said Jackson. "The Prince is here, and—"

"I never set eyes on 'im yet," cried Berks, lurching off the table. "Where is 'e, gov'nor? Tell 'im Joe Berks would like to do 'isself proud by shakin' 'im by the 'and."

"No, you don't, Joe," said Jackson, laying his hand upon Berks's chest, as he tried to push his way through the crowd. "You've got to keep your place, Joe, or we'll put you where you can make all the noise you like."

"Where's that, gov'nor?"

"Into the street, through the window. We're going to have a peaceful evening, as Jem Belcher and I will show you if you get up to any of your Whitechapel games."

"No 'arm, gov'nor," grumbled Berks. "I'm sure I've always 'ad the name of bein' a very genelman-like man."

"So I've always said, Joe Berks, and mind you prove yourself such. But the supper is ready for us, and there's the Prince and Lord Sole

going in. Two and two, lads, and don't forget whose company you
are in."

The supper was laid in a large room, with Union Jacks and mottoes
hung thickly upon the walls. The tables were arranged in three sides
of a square, my uncle occupying the centre of the principal one, with
the Prince upon his right and Lord Sele upon his left. By his wise precaution the seats had been allotted beforehand, so that the gentlemen
might be scattered among the professionals and no risk run of two
enemies finding themselves together, or a man who had been recently
beaten falling into the company of his conqueror. For my own part, I
had Champion Harrison upon one side of me and a stout, florid-faced
man upon the other, who whispered to me that he was "Bill Warr,
landlord of the One Tun public-house, of Jermyn Street, and one of
the gamest men upon the list."

"It's my flesh that's beat me, sir," said he. "It creeps over me amazin'
fast. I should fight at thirteen-eight, and 'ere I am nearly seventeen. It's
the business that does it, what with loflin' about behind the bar all day,
and bein' afraid to refuse a wet for fear of offendin' a customer. It's been
the ruin of many a good fightin'-man before me."

"You should take to my job," said Harrison. "I'm a smith by trade,
and I've not put on half a stone in fifteen years."

"Some take to one thing and some to another, but the most of us try
to 'ave a bar-parlour of our own. There's Will Wood, that I beat in forty
rounds in the thick of a snowstorm down Navestock way, 'e drives a
'ackney. Young Firby, the ruffian, 'e's a waiter now. Dick 'Umphries sells
coals—'e was always of a genelmanly disposition. George Ingleston
is a brewer's drayman. We all find our own cribs. But there's one
thing you are saved by livin' in the country, and that is 'avin' the young
Corinthians and bloods about town smackin' you eternally in the face."

This was the last inconvenience which I should have expected a
famous prize-fighter to be subjected to, but several bull-faced fellows
at the other side of the table nodded their concurrence.

"You're right, Bill," said one of them. "There's no one has had more
trouble with them than I have. In they come of an evenin' into my bar,

with the wine in their heads. 'Are you Tom Owen the bruiser?' says one o' them. 'At your service, sir,' says I. 'Take that, then,' says he, and it's a clip on the nose, or a backhanded slap across the chops as likely as not. Then they can brag all their lives that they had hit Tom Owen."

"D'you draw their cork in return?" asked Harrison.

"I argey it out with them. I say to them, 'Now, gents, fightin' is my profession, and I don't fight for love any more than a doctor doctors for love, or a butcher gives away a loin chop. Put up a small purse, master, and I'll do you over and proud. But don't expect that you're goin' to come here and get glutted by a middle-weight champion for nothing."

"That's my way too, Tom," said my burly neighbour. "If they put down a guinea on the counter—which they do if they 'ave been drinkin' very 'eavy—I give them what I think is about a guinea's worth and take the money."

"But if they don't?"

"Why, then, it's a common assault, d'ye see, against the body of 'is Majesty's liege, William Warr, and I 'as 'em before the beak next mornin', and it's a week or twenty shillin's."

Meanwhile the supper was in full swing—one of those solid and uncompromising meals which prevailed in the days of your grandfathers, and which may explain to some of you why you never set eyes upon that relative.

Great rounds of beef, saddles of mutton, smoking tongues, veal and ham pies, turkeys and chickens, and geese, with every variety of vegetables, and a succession of fiery cherries and heavy ales were the main staple of the feast. It was the same meal and the same cooking as their Norse or German ancestors might have sat down to fourteen centuries before, and, indeed, as I looked through the steam of the dishes at the lines of fierce and rugged faces, and the mighty shoulders which rounded themselves over the board, I could have imagined myself at one of those old-world carousals of which I had read, where the savage company gnawed the joints to the bone, and then, with murderous horseplay, hurled the remains at their prisoners. Here and there the pale, aquiline features of a sporting Corinthian recalled rather the

Norman type, but in the main these stolid, heavy-jowled faces, belonging to men whose whole life was a battle, were the nearest suggestion which we have had in modern times of those fierce pirates and rovers from whose loins we have sprung.

And yet, as I looked carefully from man to man in the line which faced me, I could see that the English, although they were ten to one, had not the game entirely to themselves, but that other races had shown that they could produce fighting-men worthy to rank with the best.

There were, it is true, no finer or braver men in the room than Jackson and Jem Belcher, the one with his magnificent figure, his small waist and Herculean shoulders; the other as graceful as an old Grecian statue, with a head whose beauty many a sculptor had wished to copy, and with those long, delicate lines in shoulder and loins and limbs, which gave him the litheness and activity of a panther. Already, as I looked at him, it seemed to me that there was a shadow of tragedy upon his face, a forecast of the day then but a few months distant when a blow from a racquet ball darkened the sight of one eye for ever. Had he stopped there, with his unbeaten career behind him, then indeed the evening of his life might have been as glorious as its dawn. But his proud heart could not permit his title to be torn from him without a struggle. If even now you can read how the gallant fellow, unable with his one eye to judge his distances, fought for thirty-five minutes against his young and formidable opponent, and how, in the bitterness of defeat, he was heard only to express his sorrow for a friend who had backed him with all he possessed, and if you are not touched by the story there must be something wanting in you which should go to the making of a man.

But if there were no men at the tables who could have held their own against Jackson or Jem Belcher, there were others of a different race and type who had qualities which made them dangerous bruisers. A little way down the room I saw the black face and woolly head of Bill Richmond, in a purple-and-gold footman's livery—destined to be the predecessor of Molineaux, Sutton, and all that line of black boxers who have shown that the muscular power and insensibility to pain which distinguish the African give him a peculiar advantage in the sports of the ring. He could boast also of the higher honour of having been the first born American to win laurels in the British ring. There also I saw the keen features of Dada Mendoza, the Jew, just retired from active work, and leaving behind him a reputation for elegance and perfect science which has, to this day, never been exceeded. The worst fault that the critics could find with him was that there was a want of power in his blows—a remark which certainly could not have been made about his neighbour, whose long face, curved nose, and dark, flashing eyes proclaimed him as a member of the same ancient race. This was the formidable Dutch Sam, who fought at nine stone six, and yet possessed such hitting powers, that his admirers, in after years, were willing to back him against the fourteen-stone Tom Cribb, if each were strapped a-straddle to a bench. Half a dozen other sallow Hebrew faces showed how energetically the Jews of Houndsditch and Whitechapel had taken to the sport of the land of their adoption, and that in this, as in more serious fields of human effort, they could hold their own with the best.

It was my neighbour Warr who very good-humouredly pointed out to me all these celebrities, the echoes of whose fame had been wafted down even to our little Sussex village.

"There's Andrew Gamble, the Irish champion," said he. "It was 'e that beat Noah James, the Guardsman, and was afterwards nearly killed by Jem Belcher, in the 'ollow of Wimbledon Common by Abbershaw's gibbet. The two that are next 'im are Irish also, Jack O'Donnell and Bill Ryan. When you get a good Irishman you can't better 'em, but they're dreadful 'asty. That little cove with the leery face is Caleb Baldwin the Coster, 'im that they call the Pride of Westminster. 'E's but five foot seven, and nine stone five, but 'e's got the 'eart of a giant. 'E's never been beat, and there ain't a man within a stone of 'im that could beat 'im, except only Dutch Sam. There's George Maddox, too, another o' the same breed, and as good a man as ever pulled his coat off. The genelmanly man that eats with a fork, 'im what looks like a Corinthian, only that the bridge of 'is nose ain't quite as it ought to be, that's Dick 'Umphries, the same that was cock of the middle-weights until Mendoza cut his comb for 'im. You see the other with the grey 'ead and the scars on his face?"

"Why, it's old Tom Faulkner the cricketer!" cried Harrison, following the line of Bill Warr's stubby forefinger. "He's the fastest bowler in the Midlands, and at his best there weren't many boxers in England that could stand up against him."

"You're right there, Jack 'Arrison. 'E was one of the three who came up to fight when the best men of Birmingham challenged the best men of London. 'E's an evergreen, is Tom. Why, he was turned five-and-fifty when he challenged and beat, after fifty minutes of it, Jack Thornhill, who was tough enough to take it out of many a youngster. It's better to give odds in weight than in years."

"Youth will be served," said a crooning voice from the other side of the table. "Ay, masters, youth will be served."

The man who had spoken was the most extraordinary of all the many curious figures in the room. He was very, very old, so old that he was past all comparison, and no one by looking at his mummy skin and fish-like eyes could give a guess at his years. A few scanty grey hairs still hung about his yellow scalp. As to his features, they were scarcely human in their disfigurement, for the deep wrinkles and pouchings of extreme age had been added to a face which had always been grotesquely ugly, and had been crushed and smashed in addition by many a blow. I had noticed this creature at the beginning of the meal, leaning his chest against the edge of the table as if its support was a welcome one, and feebly picking at the food which was placed before him. Gradually, however, as his neighbours plied him with drink, his shoulders grew squarer, his back stiffened, his eyes brightened, and he looked about him, with an air of surprise at first, as if he had no clear recollection of how he came there, and afterwards with an expression of deepening interest, as he listened, with his ear scooped up in his hand, to the conversation around him.

"That's old Buckhorse," whispered Champion Harrison. "He was just the same as that when I joined the ring twenty years ago. Time was when he was the terror of London."

"'E was so," said Bill Warr. "'E would fight like a stag, and 'e was that 'ard that 'e would let any swell knock 'im down for 'alf-a-crown. 'E 'ad no face to spoil, d'ye see, for 'e was always the ugliest man in England. But 'e's been on the shelf now for near sixty years, and it cost 'im many a beatin' before 'e could understand that 'is strength was slippin' away from 'im."

"Youth will be served, masters," droned the old man, shaking his head miserably.

"Fill up 'is glass," said Warr. "'Ere, Tom, give old Buckhorse a sup o' liptrap. Warm his 'eart for 'im."

The old man poured a glass of neat gin down his shrivelled throat, and the effect upon him was extraordinary. A light glimmered in each of his dull eyes, a tinge of colour came into his wax-like cheeks, and, opening his toothless mouth, he suddenly emitted a peculiar, bell-like, and most musical cry. A hoarse roar of laughter from all the company answered it, and flushed faces craned over each other to catch a glimpse of the veteran.

"There's Buckhorse!" they cried. "Buckhorse is comin' round again."

"You can laugh if you vill, masters," he cried, in his Lewkner Lane dialect, holding up his two thin, vein-covered hands. "It von't be long that you'll be able to see my crooks vich 'ave been on Figg's conk, and on Jack Broughton's, and on 'Arry Gray's, and many another good fightin' man that was millin' for a livin' before your fathers could eat pap."

The company laughed again, and encouraged the old man by half-derisive and half-affectionate cries.

"Let 'em 'ave it, Buckhorse! Give it 'em straight! Tell us how the millin' coves did it in your time."

The old gladiator looked round him in great contempt.

"Vy, from vot I see," he cried, in his high, broken treble, "there's some on you that ain't fit to flick a fly from a joint o' meat. You'd make werry good ladies' maids, the most of you, but you took the wrong turnin' ven you came into the ring."

"Give 'im a wipe over the mouth," said a hoarse voice.

"Joe Berks," said Jackson, "I'd save the hangman the job of breaking your neck if His Royal Highness wasn't in the room."

"That's as it may be, guv'nor," said the half-drunken ruffian, staggering to his feet. "If I've said anything wot isn't genelmanlike—"

"Sit down, Berks!" cried my uncle, with such a tone of command that the fellow collapsed into his chair.

"Vy, vitch of you would look Tom Slack in the face?" piped the old fellow; "or Jack Broughton?—him vot told the old Dook of Cumberland that all he vanted vas to fight the King o' Proosia's guard, day by day, year in, year out, until 'e 'ad worked out the whole regiment of 'em—and the smallest of 'em six foot long. There's not more'n a few of you could 'it a dint in a pat o' butter, and if you gets a smack or two it's all over vith you. Vich among you could get up again after such a vipe as the Eytalian Gondoleery cove gave to Bob Vittaker?"

"What was that, Buckhorse?" cried several voices.

"'E came over 'ere from voreign parts, and 'e was so broad 'e 'ad to come edgewise through the doors. 'E 'ad so, upon my davy! 'E was that strong that wherever 'e 'it the bone had got to go; and when 'e'd cracked a jaw or two it looked as though nothing in the country could stan' against him. So the King 'e sent one of his genelmen down to Figg and he said to him: "Ere's a cove vot cracks a bone every time 'e lets vly, and it'll be little credit to the Lunnon boys if they lets 'im get avay vithout a vacking.' So Figg he ups, and he says, 'I do not know, master, but he may break one of 'is countrymen's jawbones vid 'is vist, but I'll bring 'im a Cockney lad and 'e shall not be able to break 'is jawbone with a sledge 'ammer.' I was with Figg in Slaughter's coffee-'ouse, as then vas, ven 'e says this to the King's genelman, and I goes so, I does!" Again he emitted the curious bell-like cry, and again the Corinthians and the fighting-men laughed and applauded him.

"His Royal Highness—that is, the Earl of Chester—would be glad to hear the end of your story, Buckhorse," said my uncle, to whom the Prince had been whispering.

"Vell, your R'yal 'Ighness, it vas like this. Ven the day came round, all the volk came to Figg's Amphitheatre, the same that vos in Tottenham

Court, an' Bob Vittaker 'e vos there, and the Eytalian Gondoleery cove 'e vas there, and all the purlitest, genteelest crowd that ever vos, twenty thousand of 'em, all sittin' with their 'eads like purtaties on a barrer, banked right up round the stage, and me there to pick up Bob, d'ye see, and Jack Figg 'imself just for fair play to do vot was right by the cove from voreign parts. They vas packed all round, the folks was, but down through the middle of 'em was a passage just so as the gentry could come through to their seats, and the stage it vas of wood, as the custom then vas, and a man's 'eight above the 'eads of the people. Vell, then, ven Bob was put up opposite this great Eytalian man I says 'Slap 'im in the vind, Bob,''cos I could see vid 'alf an eye that he vas as puffy as a cheesecake; so Bob he goes in, and as he comes the vorriner let 'im 'ave it amazin' on the conk. I 'eard the thump of it, and I kind o' velt somethin' vistle past me, but ven I looked there vas the Eytalian a feelin' of 'is muscles in the middle o' the stage, and as to Bob, there vern't no sign' of 'im at all no more'n if 'e'd never been."

His audience was riveted by the old prize-fighter's story. "Well," cried a dozen voices, "what then, Buckhorse: 'ad 'e swallowed 'im, or what?"

"Yell, boys, that vas vat I wondered, when sudden I seed two legs a-stickin' up out o' the crowd a long vay off, just like these two vingers, d'ye see, and I knewed they vas Bob's legs, seein' that 'e 'ad kind o' yellow small clothes vid blue ribbons—vich blue vas 'is colour—at the knee. So they up-ended 'im, they did, an' they made a lane for 'im an' cheered 'im to give 'im 'eart, though 'e never lacked for that. At virst 'e vas that dazed that 'e didn't know if 'e vas in church or in 'Orsemonger Gaol; but ven I'd bit 'is two ears 'e shook 'isself together. 'Ve'll try it again, Buck,' says 'e. 'The mark!' says I. And 'e vinked all that vas left o' one eye. So the Eytalian 'e lets swing again, but Bob 'e jumps inside an' 'e lets 'im 'ave it plumb square on the meat safe as 'ard as ever the Lord would let 'im put it in."

"Well? Well?"

"Vell, the Eytalian 'e got a touch of the gurgles, an' 'e shut 'imself right up like a two-foot rule. Then 'e pulled 'imself straight, an' 'e gave the most awful Glory Allelujah screech as ever you 'eard. Off 'e jumps from the stage an' down the passage as 'ard as 'is 'oofs would carry 'im. Up jumps the 'ole crowd, and after 'im as 'ard as they could move for laughin'. They vas lyin' in the kennel three deep all down Tottenham Court road wid their 'ands to their sides just vit to break themselves in two. Vell, ve chased 'im down 'Olburn, an' down Fleet Street, an' down Cheapside, an' past the 'Change, and on all the vay to Voppin' an' we only catched 'im in the shippin' office, vere 'e vas askin' 'ow soon 'e could get a passage to voreign parts."

There was much laughter and clapping of glasses upon the table at the conclusion of old Buckhorse's story, and I saw the Prince of Wales hand something to the waiter, who brought it round and slipped it into the skinny hand of the veteran, who spat upon it before thrusting it into his pocket. The table had in the meanwhile been cleared, and was now studded with bottles and glasses, while long clay pipes and tobacco-boxes were handed round. My uncle never smoked, thinking that the habit might darken his teeth, but many of the Corinthians, and the Prince amongst the first of them, set the example of lighting up. All restraint had been done away with, and the prize-fighters, flushed with wine, roared across the tables to each other, or shouted their greetings to friends at the other end of the room. The amateurs, falling into the humour of their company, were hardly less noisy, and loudly debated the merits of the different men, criticizing their styles of fighting before their faces, and making bets upon the results of future matches.

In the midst of the uproar there was an imperative rap upon the table, and my uncle rose to speak. As he stood with his pale, calm face and fine figure, I had never seen him to greater advantage, for he seemed, with all his elegance, to have a quiet air of domination amongst these fierce fellows, like a huntsman walking carelessly through a springing and yapping pack. He expressed his pleasure at seeing so many good sportsmen under one roof, and acknowledged the honour which had been done both to his guests and himself by the presence there that night of the illustrious personage whom he should refer to as the Earl of Chester. He was sorry that the season prevented him from placing game upon the table, but there was so much sitting round it that it would perhaps be hardly missed (cheers and laughter). The sports of the ring had, in his opinion, tended to that contempt of pain and of danger which had contributed so much in the past to the safety of the country, and which might, if what he heard was true, be very quickly needed once more. If an enemy landed upon our shores it was then that, with our small army, we should be forced to fall back upon native valour trained into hardihood by the practice and contemplation of manly sports. In time of peace also the rules of the ring had been of service in enforcing the principles of fair play, and in turning public opinion against that use of the knife or of the boot which was so common in foreign countries. He begged, therefore, to drink "Success to the Fancy," coupled with the name of John Jackson, who might stand as a type of all that was most admirable in British boxing.

Jackson having replied with a readiness which many a public man might have envied, my uncle rose once more.

"We are here to-night," said he, "not only to celebrate the past glories of the prize ring, but also to arrange some sport for the future. It should be easy, now that backers and fighting men are gathered together under one roof, to come to terms with each other. I have myself set an example by making a match with Sir Lothian Hume, the terms of which will be communicated to you by that gentleman."

Sir Lothian rose with a paper in his hand.

"The terms, your Royal Highness and gentlemen, are briefly these," said he. "My man, Crab Wilson, of Gloucester, having never yet fought a prize battle, is prepared to meet, upon May the 18th of this year, any man of any weight who may be selected by Sir Charles Tregellis. Sir Charles Tregellis's selection is limited to men below twenty or above thirty-five years of age, so as to exclude Belcher and the other candidates for championship honours. The stakes are two thousand pounds against a thousand, two hundred to be paid by the winner to his man; play or pay."

It was curious to see the intense gravity of them all, fighters and backers, as they bent their brows and weighed the conditions of the match.

"I am informed," said Sir John Lade, "that Crab Wilson's age is twenty-three, and that, although he has never fought a regular P.R. battle, he has none the less fought within ropes for a stake on many occasions."

"I've seen him half a dozen times at the least," said Belcher.

"It is precisely for that reason, Sir John, that I am laying odds of two to one in his favour."

"May I ask," said the Prince, "what the exact height and weight of Wilson may be?"

"Five foot eleven and thirteen-ten, your Royal Highness."

"Long enough and heavy enough for anything on two legs," said Jackson, and the professionals all murmured their assent.

"Read the rules of the fight, Sir Lothian."

"The battle to take place on Tuesday, May the 18th, at the hour of ten in the morning, at a spot to be afterwards named. The ring to be twenty foot square. Neither to fall without a knock-down blow, subject to the decision of the umpires. Three umpires to be chosen upon the ground, namely, two in ordinary and one in reference. Does that meet your wishes, Sir Charles?"

My uncle bowed.

"Have you anything to say, Wilson?"

The young pugilist, who had a curious, lanky figure, and a craggy, bony face, passed his fingers through his close-cropped hair.

"If you please, zir," said he, with a slight west-country burr, "a twenty-voot ring is too small for a thirteen-stone man."

There was another murmur of professional agreement.

"What would you have it, Wilson?"

"Vour-an'-twenty, Sir Lothian."

"Have you any objection, Sir Charles?"

"Not the slightest."

"Anything else, Wilson?"

"If you please, zir, I'd like to know whom I'm vighting with."

"I understand that you have not publicly nominated your man, Sir Charles?"

"I do not intend to do so until the very morning of the fight. I believe I have that right within the terms of our wager."

"Certainly, if you choose to exercise it."

"I do so intend. And I should be vastly pleased if Mr. Berkeley Craven will consent to be stake-holder."

That gentleman having willingly given his consent, the final formalities which led up to these humble tournaments were concluded.

And then, as these full-blooded, powerful men became heated with their wine, angry eyes began to glare across the table, and amid the grey swirls of tobacco-smoke the lamp-light gleamed upon the fierce, hawk-like Jews, and the flushed, savage Saxons. The old quarrel as to whether Jackson had or had not committed a foul by seizing Mendoza by the hair on the occasion of their battle at Hornchurch, eight years before, came to the front once more. Dutch Sam hurled a shilling down upon the table, and offered to fight the Pride of Westminster for it if he ventured to say that Mendoza had been fairly beaten. Joe Berks, who had grown noisier and more quarrelsome as the evening went on, tried to clamber across the table, with horrible blasphemies, to come to blows with an old Jew named Fighting Yussef, who had plunged into the discussion. It needed very little more to finish the supper by a general and ferocious battle, and it was only the exertions of Jackson, Belcher, Harrison, and others of the cooler and steadier men, which saved us from a riot.

And then, when at last this question was set aside, that of the rival claims to championships at different weights came on in its stead, and again angry words flew about and challenges were in the air. There was no exact limit between the light, middle, and heavyweights, and yet it would make a very great difference to the standing of a boxer whether he should be regarded as the heaviest of the light-weights, or the lightest of the heavy-weights. One claimed to be ten-stone champion, another was ready to take on anything at eleven, but would not run to twelve, which would have brought the invincible Jem Belcher down upon him. Faulkner claimed to be champion of the seniors, and even old Buckhorse's curious call rang out above the tumult as he turned the whole company to laughter and good humour again by challenging anything over eighty and under seven stone.

But in spite of gleams of sunshine, there was thunder in the air, and Champion Harrison had just whispered in my ear that he was quite sure that we should never get through the night without trouble, and was advising me, if it got very bad, to take refuge under the table, when the landlord entered the room hurriedly and handed a note to my uncle.

He read it, and then passed it to the Prince, who returned it with raised eyebrows and a gesture of surprise. Then my uncle rose with the scrap of paper in his hand and a smile upon his lips.

"Gentlemen," said he, "there is a stranger waiting below who desires a fight to a finish with the best men in the room."

CHAPTER XI—THE FIGHT IN THE COACH-HOUSE

The curt announcement was followed by a moment of silent surprise, and then by a general shout of laughter. There might be argument as to who was champion at each weight; but there could be no question that all the champions of all the weights were seated round the tables. An audacious challenge which embraced them one and all, without regard to size or age, could hardly be regarded otherwise than as a joke—but it was a joke which might be a dear one for the joker.

"Is this genuine?" asked my uncle.

"Yes, Sir Charles," answered the landlord; "the man is waiting below."

"It's a kid!" cried several of the fighting-men. "Some cove is a gammonin' us."

"Don't you believe it," answered the landlord. "He's a real slap-up Corinthian, by his dress; and he means what he says, or else I ain't no judge of a man."

My uncle whispered for a few moments with the Prince of Wales. "Well, gentlemen," said he, at last, "the night is still young, and if any of you should wish to show the company a little of your skill, you could not ask a better opportunity."

"What weight is he, Bill?" asked Jem Belcher.

"He's close on six foot, and I should put him well into the thirteen stones when he's buffed."

"Heavy metal!" cried Jackson. "Who takes him on?"

They all wanted to, from nine-stone Dutch Sam upwards. The air was filled with their hoarse shouts and their arguments why each should be the chosen one. To fight when they were flushed with wine and ripe for mischief—above all, to fight before so select a company with the Prince at the ringside, was a chance which did not often come in their way. Only Jackson, Belcher, Mendoza, and one or two others of the senior and more famous men remained silent, thinking it beneath their dignity that they should condescend to so irregular a bye-battle.

"Well, you can't all fight him," remarked Jackson, when the babel had died away. "It's for the chairman to choose."

"Perhaps your Royal Highness has a preference," said my uncle.

"By Jove, I'd take him on myself if my position was different," said the Prince, whose face was growing redder and his eyes more glazed. "You've seen me with the mufflers, Jackson! You know my form!"

"I've seen your Royal Highness, and I have felt your Royal Highness," said the courtly Jackson.

"Perhaps Jem Belcher would give us an exhibition," said my uncle.

Belcher smiled and shook his handsome head.

"There's my brother Tom here who has never been blooded in London yet, sir. He might make a fairer match of it."

"Give him over to me!" roared Joe Berks. "I've been waitin' for a turn all evenin', an' I'll fight any man that tries to take my place. 'E's my meat, my masters. Leave 'im to me if you want to see 'ow a calf's 'ead should be dressed. If you put Tom Belcher before me I'll fight Tom Belcher, an' for that matter I'll fight Jem Belcher, or Bill Belcher, or any other Belcher that ever came out of Bristol."

It was clear that Berks had got to the stage when he must fight some one. His heavy face was gorged and the veins stood out on his low forehead, while his fierce grey eyes looked viciously from man to man in quest of a quarrel. His great red hands were bunched into huge, gnarled fists, and he shook one of them menacingly as his drunken gaze swept round the tables.

"I think you'll agree with me, gentlemen, that Joe Berks would be all the better for some fresh air and exercise," said my uncle. "With the concurrence of His Royal Highness and of the company, I shall select him as our champion on this occasion."

"You do me proud," cried the fellow, staggering to his feet and pulling at his coat. "If I don't glut him within the five minutes, may I never see Shropshire again."

"Wait a bit, Berks," cried several of the amateurs. "Where's it going to be held?"

"Where you like, masters. I'll fight him in a sawpit, or on the outside of a coach if it please you. Put us toe to toe, and leave the rest with me."

"They can't fight here with all this litter," said my uncle. "Where shall it be?"

"'Pon my soul, Tregellis," cried the Prince, "I think our unknown friend might have a word to say upon that matter. He'll be vastly ill-used if you don't let him have his own choice of conditions."

"You are right, sir. We must have him up."

"That's easy enough," said the landlord, "for here he comes through the doorway."

I glanced round and had a side view of a tall and well-dressed young man in a long, brown travelling coat and a black felt hat. The next instant he had turned and I had clutched with both my hands on to Champion Harrison's arm.

"Harrison!" I gasped. "It's Boy Jim!"

And yet somehow the possibility and even the probability of it had occurred to me from the beginning, and I believe that it had to Harrison also, for I had noticed that his face grew grave and troubled from the very moment that there was talk of the stranger below. Now, the instant that the buzz of surprise and admiration caused by Jim's face and figure had died away, Harrison was on his feet, gesticulating in his excitement.

"It's my nephew Jim, gentlemen," he cried. "He's not twenty yet, and it's no doing of mine that he should be here."

"Let him alone, Harrison," cried Jackson. "He's big enough to take care of himself."

"This matter has gone rather far," said my uncle. "I think, Harrison, that you are too good a sportsman to prevent your nephew from showing whether he takes after his uncle."

"It's very different from me," cried Harrison, in great distress. "But I'll tell you what I'll do, gentlemen. I never thought to stand up in a ring again, but I'll take on Joe Berks with pleasure, just to give a bit o' sport to this company."

Boy Jim stepped across and laid his hand upon the prize-fighter's shoulder.

"It must be so, uncle," I heard him whisper. "I am sorry to go against your wishes, but I have made up my mind, and I must carry it through."

Harrison shrugged his huge shoulders.

"Jim, Jim, you don't know what you are doing! But I've heard you speak like that before, boy, and I know that it ends in your getting your way."

"I trust, Harrison, that your opposition is withdrawn?" said my uncle.

"Can I not take his place?"

"You would not have it said that I gave a challenge and let another carry it out?" whispered Jim. "This is my one chance. For Heaven's sake don't stand in my way."

The smith's broad and usually stolid face was all working with his conflicting emotions. At last he banged his fist down upon the table.

"It's no fault of mine!" he cried. "It was to be and it is. Jim, boy, for the Lord's sake remember your distances, and stick to out-fightin' with a man that could give you a stone."

"I was sure that Harrison would not stand in the way of sport," said my uncle. "We are glad that you have stepped up, that we might consult you as to the arrangements for giving effect to your very sporting challenge."

"Whom am I to fight?" asked Jim, looking round at the company, who were now all upon their feet.

"Young man, you'll know enough of who you 'ave to fight before you are through with it," cried Berks, lurching heavily through the crowd. "You'll need a friend to swear to you before I've finished, d'ye see?"

Jim looked at him with disgust in every line of his face.

"Surely you are not going to set me to fight a drunken man!" said he. "Where is Jem Belcher?"

"My name, young man."

"I should be glad to try you, if I may."

"You must work up to me, my lad. You don't take a ladder at one jump, but you do it rung by rung. Show yourself to be a match for me, and I'll give you a turn."

"I'm much obliged to you."

"And I like the look of you, and wish you well," said Belcher, holding out his hand. They were not unlike each other, either in face or figure, though the Bristol man was a few years the older, and a murmur of critical admiration was heard as the two tall, lithe figures, and keen, clean-cut faces were contrasted.

"Have you any choice where the fight takes place?" asked my uncle.

"I am in your hands, sir," said Jim.

"Why not go round to the Five's Court?" suggested Sir John Lade.

"Yes, let us go to the Five's Court."

But this did not at all suit the views of the landlord, who saw in this lucky incident a chance of reaping a fresh harvest from his spendthrift company.

"If it please you," he cried, "there is no need to go so far. My coach-house at the back of the yard is empty, and a better place for a mill you'll never find."

There was a general shout in favour of the coach-house, and those who were nearest the door began to slip through, in the hope of scouring the best places. My stout neighbour, Bill Warr, pulled Harrison to one side.

"I'd stop it if I were you," he whispered.

"I would if I could. It's no wish of mine that he should fight. But there's no turning him when once his mind is made up." All his own fights put together had never reduced the pugilist to such a state of agitation.

"Wait on 'im yourself, then, and chuck up the sponge when things begin to go wrong. You know Joe Berks's record?"

"He's since my time."

"Well, 'e's a terror, that's all. It's only Belcher that can master 'im. You see the man for yourself, six foot, fourteen stone, and full of the devil. Belcher's beat 'im twice, but the second time 'e 'ad all 'is work to do it."

"Well, well, we've got to go through with it. You've not seen Boy Jim put his mawleys up, or maybe you'd think better of his chances. When he was short of sixteen he licked the Cock of the South Downs, and he's come on a long way since then."

The company was swarming through the door and clattering down the stair, so we followed in the stream. A fine rain was falling, and the yellow lights from the windows glistened upon the wet cobblestones of the yard. How welcome was that breath of sweet, damp air after the fetid atmosphere of the supper-room. At the other end of the yard was an open door sharply outlined by the gleam of lanterns within, and through this they poured, amateurs and fighting-men jostling each other in their eagerness to get to the front. For my own part, being a smallish man, I should have seen nothing had I not found an upturned bucket in a corner, upon which I perched myself with the wall at my back.

It was a large room with a wooden floor and an open square in the ceiling, which was fringed with the heads of the ostlers and stable boys who were looking down from the harness-room above. A carriage-lamp was slung in each corner, and a very large stable-lantern hung from a rafter in the centre. A coil of rope had been brought in, and under the direction of Jackson four men had been stationed to hold it.

"What space do you give them?" asked my uncle.

"Twenty-four, as they are both big ones, sir."

"Very good, and half-minutes between rounds, I suppose? I'll umpire if Sir Lothian Hume will do the same, and you can hold the watch and referee, Jackson."

With great speed and exactness every preparation was rapidly made by these experienced men. Mendoza and Dutch Sam were commissioned to attend to Berks, while Belcher and Jack Harrison did the same for Boy Jim. Sponges, towels, and some brandy in a bladder were passed over the heads of the crowd for the use of the seconds.

"Here's our man," cried Belcher. "Come along, Berks, or we'll go to fetch you."

Jim appeared in the ring stripped to the waist, with a coloured handkerchief tied round his middle. A shout of admiration came from the spectators as they looked upon the fine lines of his figure, and I found myself roaring with the rest. His shoulders were sloping rather than bulky, and his chest was deep rather than broad, but the muscle was all in the right place, rippling down in long, low curves from neck to shoulder, and from shoulder to elbow. His work at the anvil had developed his arms to their utmost, and his healthy country living gave a sleek gloss to his ivory skin, which shone in the lamplight. His expression was full of spirit and confidence, and he wore a grim sort of half-smile which I had seen many a time in our boyhood, and which meant, I knew, that his pride had set iron hard, and that his senses would fail him long before his courage.

Joe Berks in the meanwhile had swaggered in and stood with folded arms between his seconds in the opposite corner. His face had none of the eager alertness of his opponent, and his skin, of a dead white, with heavy folds about the chest and ribs, showed, even to my inexperienced eyes, that he was not a man who should fight without training. A life of toping and ease had left him flabby and gross. On the other hand, he was famous for his mettle and for his hitting power, so that, even in the face of the advantages of youth and condition, the betting was three to one in his favour. His heavy-jowled, clean-shaven face expressed ferocity as well as courage, and he stood with his small, blood-shot eyes fixed viciously upon Jim, and his lumpy shoulders stooping a little forwards, like a fierce hound training on a leash.

The hubbub of the betting had risen until it drowned all other sounds, men shouting their opinions from one side of the coach-house to the other, and waving their hands to attract attention, or as a sign that they had accepted a wager. Sir John Lade, standing just in front of me, was roaring out the odds against Jim, and laying them freely with those who fancied the appearance of the unknown.

"I've seen Berks fight," said he to the Honourable Berkeley Craven. "No country hawbuck is going to knock out a man with such a record."

"He may be a country hawbuck," the other answered, "but I have been reckoned a judge of anything either on two legs or four, and I tell you, Sir John, that I never saw a man who looked better bred in my life. Are you still laying against him?"

"Three to one."

"Have you once in hundreds."

"Very good, Craven! There they go! Berks! Berks! Bravo! Berks! Bravo! I think, Craven, that I shall trouble you for that hundred."

The two men had stood up to each other, Jim as light upon his feet as a goat, with his left well out and his right thrown across the lower part of his chest, while Berks held both arms half extended and his feet almost level, so that he might lead off with either side. For an instant they looked each other over, and then Berks, ducking his head and rushing in with a handover-hand style of hitting, bored Jim down into his corner. It was a backward slip rather than a knockdown, but a thin trickle of blood was seen at the corner of Jim's mouth. In an instant the seconds had seized their men and carried them back into their corners.

"Do you mind doubling our bet?" said Berkeley Craven, who was craning his neck to get a glimpse of Jim.

"Four to one on Berks! Four to one on Berks!" cried the ringsiders.

"The odds have gone up, you see. Will you have four to one in hundreds?"

"Very good, Sir John."

"You seem to fancy him more for having been knocked down."

"He was pushed down, but he stopped every blow, and I liked the look on his face as he got up again."

"Well, it's the old stager for me. Here they come again! He's got a pretty style, and he covers his points well, but it isn't the best looking that wins."

They were at it again, and I was jumping about upon my bucket in my excitement. It was evident that Berks meant to finish the battle off-hand, whilst Jim, with two of the most experienced men in England to advise him, was quite aware that his correct tactics were to allow the ruffian to expend his strength and wind in vain. There was something horrible in the ferocious energy of Berks's hitting, every blow fetching a grunt from him as he smashed it in, and after each I gazed at Jim, as I have gazed at a stranded vessel upon the Sussex beach when wave after wave has roared over it, fearing each time that I should find it miserably mangled. But still the lamplight shone upon the lad's clear, alert face, upon his well-opened eyes and his firm-set mouth, while the blows were taken upon his forearm or allowed, by a quick duck of the head, to whistle over his shoulder. But Berks was artful as well as violent. Gradually he worked Jim back into an angle of the ropes from which there was no escape, and then, when he had him fairly penned, he sprang upon him like a tiger. What happened was so quick that I cannot set its sequence down in words, but I saw Jim make a quick stoop under the swinging arms, and at the same instant I heard a sharp, ringing smack, and there was Jim dancing about in the middle of the ring, and Berks lying upon his side on the floor, with his hand to his eye.

How they roared! Prize-fighters, Corinthians, Prince, stable-boy, and landlord were all shouting at the top of their lungs. Old Buckhorse was skipping about on a box beside me, shrieking out criticisms and advice in strange, obsolete ring-jargon, which no one could understand. His dull eyes were shining, his parchment face was quivering with excitement, and his strange musical call rang out above all the hubbub. The two men were hurried to their corners, one second sponging them down and the other flapping a towel in front of their face;

whilst they, with arms hanging down and legs extended, tried to draw all the air they could into their lungs in the brief space allowed them.

"Where's your country hawbuck now?" cried Craven, triumphantly. "Did ever you witness anything more masterly?"

"He's no Johnny Raw, certainly," said Sir John, shaking his head. "What odds are you giving on Berks, Lord Sole?"

"Two to one."

"I take you twice in hundreds."

"Here's Sir John Lade hedging!" cried my uncle, smiling back at us over his shoulder.

"Time!" said Jackson, and the two men sprang forward to the mark again.

This round was a good deal shorter than that which had preceded it. Berks's orders evidently were to close at any cost, and so make use of his extra weight and strength before the superior condition of his antagonist could have time to tell. On the other hand, Jim, after his experience in the last round, was less disposed to make any great exertion to keep him at arms' length. He led at Berks's head, as he came rushing in, and missed him, receiving a severe body blow in return, which left the imprint of four angry knuckles above his ribs. As they closed Jim caught his opponent's bullet head under his arm for an instant, and put a couple of half-arm blows in; but the prize-fighter pulled him over by his weight, and the two fell panting side by side upon the ground. Jim sprang up, however, and walked over to his corner, while Berks, distressed by his evening's dissipation, leaned one arm upon Mendoza and the other upon Dutch Sam as he made for his seat.

"Bellows to mend!" cried Jem Belcher. "Where's the four to one now?"

"Give us time to get the lid off our pepper-box," said Mendoza. "We mean to make a night of it."

"Looks like it," said Jack Harrison. "He's shut one of his eyes already. Even money that my boy wins it!"

"How much?" asked several voices.

"Two pound four and threepence," cried Harrison, counting out all his worldly wealth.

"Time!" said Jackson once more.

They were both at the mark in an instant, Jim as full of sprightly confidence as ever, and Berks with a fixed grin upon his bull-dog face and a most vicious gleam in the only eye which was of use to him. His half-minute had not enabled him to recover his breath, and his huge, hairy chest was rising and falling with a quick, loud panting like a spent hound. "Go in, boy! Bustle him!" roared Harrison and Belcher. "Get your wind, Joe; get your wind!" cried the Jews. So now we had a reversal of tactics, for it was Jim who went in to hit with all the vigour of his young strength and unimpaired energy, while it was the savage Berks who was paying his debt to Nature for the many injuries which he had done her. He gasped, he gurgled, his face grew purple in his attempts to get his breath, while with his long left arm extended and his right thrown across, he tried to screen himself from the attack of his wiry antagonist. "Drop when he hits!" cried Mendoza. "Drop and have a rest!"

But there was no shyness or shiftiness about Berks's fighting. He was always a gallant ruffian, who disdained to go down before an antagonist as long as his legs would sustain him. He propped Jim off with his long arm, and though the lad sprang lightly round him look-ing for an opening, he was held off as if a forty-inch bar of iron were between them. Every instant now was in favour of Berks, and already his breathing was easier and the bluish tinge fading from his face. Jim knew that his chance of a speedy victory was slipping away from him, and he came back again and again as swift as a flash to the attack with-out being able to get past the passive defence of the trained fighting-man. It was at such a moment that ringcraft was needed, and luckily for Jim two masters of it were at his back.

"Get your left on his mark, boy," they shouted, "then go to his head with the right."

Jim heard and acted on the instant. *Plunk!* came his left just where his antagonist's ribs curved from his breast-bone. The force of the blow was half broken by Berks's elbow, but it served its purpose of bringing forward his head. *Spank*! went the right, with the clear, crisp sound of two billiard balls clapping together, and Berks reeled, flung up his arms, spun round, and fell in a huge, fleshy heap upon the floor. His seconds were on him instantly, and propped him up in a sitting position, his head rolling helplessly from one shoulder to the other, and finally toppling backwards with his chin pointed to the ceiling. Dutch Sam thrust the brandy-bladder between his teeth, while Mendoza shook him savagely and howled insults in his ear, but neither the spirits nor the sense of injury could break into that serene insensibility. "Time!" was duly called, and the Jews, seeing that the affair was over, let their man's head fall back with a crack upon the floor, and there he lay, his huge arms and legs asprawl, whilst the Corinthians and fighting-men crowded past him to shake the hand of his conqueror.

For my part, I tried also to press through the throng, but it was no easy task for one of the smallest and weakest men in the room. On all sides of me I heard a brisk discussion from amateurs and professionals of Jim's performance and of his prospects.

"He's the best bit of new stuff that I've seen since Jem Belcher fought his first fight with Paddington Jones at Wormwood Scrubbs four years ago last April," said Berkeley Craven. "You'll see him with the belt round his waist before he's five-and-twenty, or I am no judge of a man."

"That handsome face of his has cost me a cool five hundred," grumbled Sir John Lade. "Who'd have thought he was such a punishing hitter?"

"For all that," said another, "I am confident that if Joe Berks had been sober he would have eaten him. Besides, the lad was in training, and the other would burst like an overdone potato if he were hit. I never saw a man so soft, or with his wind in such condition. Put the men in training, and it's a horse to a hen on the bruiser."

Some agreed with the last speaker and some were against him, so that a brisk argument was being carried on around me. In the midst of it the Prince took his departure, which was the signal for the greater part of the company to make for the door. In this way I was able at last to reach the corner where Jim had just finished his dressing, while Champion Harrison, with tears of joy still shining upon his cheeks, was helping him on with his overcoat.

"In four rounds!" he kept repeating in a sort of an ecstasy. "Joe Berks in four rounds! And it took Jem Belcher fourteen!"

"Well, Roddy," cried Jim, holding out his hand, "I told you that I would come to London and make my name known."

"It was splendid, Jim!"

"Dear old Roddy! I saw your white face staring at me from the corner. You are not changed, for all your grand clothes and your London friends."

"It is you who are changed, Jim," said I; "I hardly knew you when you came into the room."

"Nor I," cried the smith. "Where got you all these fine feathers, Jim? Sure I am that it was not your aunt who helped you to the first step towards the prize-ring."

"Miss Hinton has been my friend—the best friend I ever had."

"Humph! I thought as much," grumbled the smith. "Well, it is no doing of mine, Jim, and you must bear witness to that when we go home again. I don't know what—but, there, it is done, and it can't be helped. After all, she's—Now, the deuce take my clumsy tongue!"

I could not tell whether it was the wine which he had taken at supper or the excitement of Boy Jim's victory which was affecting Harrison, but his usually placid face wore a most disturbed expression, and his manner seemed to betray an alternation of exultation and embarrassment. Jim looked curiously at him, wondering evidently what it was that lay behind these abrupt sentences and sudden silences. The coach-house had in the mean time been cleared; Berks with many curses had staggered at last to his feet, and had gone off in company with two other bruisers, while Jem Belcher alone remained chatting very earnestly with my uncle.

"Very good, Belcher," I heard my uncle say.

"It would be a real pleasure to me to do it, sir," and the famous prize-fighter, as the two walked towards us.

"I wished to ask you, Jim Harrison, whether you would undertake to be my champion in the fight against Crab Wilson of Gloucester?" said my uncle.

"That is what I want, Sir Charles—to have a chance of fighting my way upwards."

"There are heavy stakes upon the event—very heavy stakes," said my uncle. "You will receive two hundred pounds, if you win. Does that satisfy you?"

"I shall fight for the honour, and because I wish to be thought worthy of being matched against Jem Belcher."

Belcher laughed good-humouredly.

"You are going the right way about it, lad," said he. "But you had a soft thing on to-night with a drunken man who was out of condition."

"I did not wish to fight him," said Jim, flushing.

"Oh, I know you have spirit enough to fight anything on two legs. I knew that the instant I clapped eyes on you; but I want you to remember that when you fight Crab Wilson, you will fight the most promising man from the west, and that the best man of the west is likely to be the best man in England. He's as quick and as long in the reach as you are, and he'll train himself to the last half-ounce of tallow. I tell you this now, d'ye see, because if I'm to have the charge of you—"

"Charge of me!"

"Yes," said my uncle. "Belcher has consented to train you for the coming battle if you are willing to enter."

"I am sure I am very much obliged to you," cried Jim, heartily. "Unless my uncle should wish to train me, there is no one I would rather have."

"Nay, Jim; I'll stay with you a few days, but Belcher knows a deal more about training than I do. Where will the quarters be?"

"I thought it would be handy for you if we fixed it at the George, at Crawley. Then, if we have choice of place, we might choose Crawley Down, for, except Molesey Hurst, and, maybe, Smitham Bottom, there isn't a spot in the country that would compare with it for a mill. Do you agree with that?"

"With all my heart," said Jim.

"Then you're my man from this hour on, d'ye see?" said Belcher. "Your food is mine, and your drink is mine, and your sleep is mine, and all you've to do is just what you are told. We haven't an hour to lose, for Wilson has been in half-training this month back. You saw his empty glass to-night."

"Jim's fit to fight for his life at the present moment," said Harrison. "But we'll both come down to Crawley to-morrow. So good night, Sir Charles."

"Good night, Roddy," said Jim. "You'll come down to Crawley and see me at my training quarters, will you not?"

And I heartily promised that I would.

"You must be more careful, nephew," said my uncle, as we rattled home in his model vis-à-vis. "*En première jeunesse* one is a little inclined to be ruled by one's heart rather than by one's reason. Jim Harrison seems to be a most respectable young fellow, but after all he is a black-smith's apprentice, and a candidate for the prize-ring. There is a vast gap between his position and that of my own blood relation, and you must let him feel that you are his superior."

"He is the oldest and dearest friend that I have in the world, sir," I answered. "We were boys together, and have never had a secret from each other. As to showing him that I am his superior, I don't know how I can do that, for I know very well that he is mine."

"Hum!" said my uncle, drily, and it was the last word that he addressed to me that night.

CHAPTER XII—THE COFFEE-ROOM OF FLADONG'S

So Boy Jim went down to the George, at Crawley, under the charge of Jim Belcher and Champion Harrison, to train for his great fight with Crab Wilson, of Gloucester, whilst every club and bar parlour of London rang with the account of how he had appeared at a supper of Corinthians, and beaten the formidable Joe Berks in four rounds. I remembered that afternoon at Friar's Oak when Jim had told me that he would make his name known, and his words had come true sooner than he could have expected it, for, go where one might, one heard of nothing but the match between Sir Lothian Hume and Sir Charles Tregellis, and the points of the two probable combatants. The betting was still steadily in favour of Wilson, for he had a number of bye-battles to set against this single victory of Jim's, and it was thought by connoisseurs who had seen him spar that the singular defensive tactics which had given him his nickname would prove very puzzling to a raw antagonist. In height, strength, and reputation for gameness there was very little to choose between them, but Wilson had been the more severely tested.

It was but a few days before the battle that my father made his promised visit to London. The seaman had no love of cities, and was happier wandering over the Downs, and turning his glass upon every topsail which showed above the horizon, than when finding his way among crowded streets, where, as he complained, it was impossible to keep a course by the sun, and hard enough by dead reckoning. Rumours of war were in the air, however, and it was necessary that he should use his influence with Lord Nelson if a vacancy were to be found either for himself or for me.

My uncle had just set forth, as was his custom of an evening, clad in his green riding-frock, his plate buttons, his Cordovan boots, and his round hat, to show himself upon his crop-tailed tit in the Mall. I had remained behind, for, indeed, I had already made up my mind that I had no calling for this fashionable life. These men, with their small waists, their gestures, and their unnatural ways, had become wearisome to me, and even my uncle, with his cold and patronizing manner, filled me with very mixed feelings. My thoughts were back in Sussex, and I was dreaming of the kindly, simple ways of the country, when there came a rat-tat at the knocker, the ring of a hearty voice, and there, in the doorway, was the smiling, weather-beaten face, with the puckered eyelids and the light blue eyes.

"Why, Roddy, you are grand indeed!" he cried. "But I had rather see you with the King's blue coat upon your back than with all these frills and ruffles."

"And I had rather wear it, father."

"It warms my heart to hear you say so. Lord Nelson has promised me that he would find a berth for you, and to-morrow we shall seek him out and remind him of it. But where is your uncle?"

"He is riding in the Mall."

A look of relief passed over my father's honest face, for he was never very easy in his brother-in-law's company. "I have been to the Admiralty," said he, "and I trust that I shall have a ship when war breaks out; by all accounts it will not be long first. Lord St. Vincent told me so with his own lips. But I am at Fladong's, Rodney, where, if you will come and sup with me, you will see some of my messmates from the Mediterranean."

When you think that in the last year of the war we had 140,000 seamen and mariners afloat, commanded by 4000 officers, and that half of these had been turned adrift when the Peace of Amiens laid their ships up in the Hamoaze or Portsdown creek, you will understand that London, as well as the dockyard towns, was full of seafarers. You could not walk the streets without catching sight of the gipsy-faced, keen-eyed men whose plain clothes told of their thin purses as plainly as their listless air showed their weariness of a life of forced and unaccustomed inaction. Amid the dark streets and brick houses there was something out of place in their appearance, as when the sea-gulls, driven by stress of weather, are seen in the Midland shires. Yet while prize-courts procrastinated, or there was a chance of an appointment by showing their sunburned faces at the Admiralty, so long they would continue to pace with their quarter-deck strut down Whitehall, or to gather of an evening to discuss the events of the last war or the chances of the next at Fladong's, in Oxford Street, which was reserved as entirely for the Navy as Slaughter's was for the Army, or Ibbetson's for the Church of England.

It did not surprise me, therefore, that we should find the large room in which we supped crowded with naval men, but I remember that what did cause me some astonishment was to observe that all these sailors, who had served under the most varying conditions in all quarters of the globe, from the Baltic to the East Indies, should have been moulded into so uniform a type that they were more like each other than brother is commonly to brother. The rules of the service insured that every face should be clean-shaven, every head powdered, and every neck covered by the little queue of natural hair tied with a black silk ribbon. Biting winds and tropical suns had combined to darken them, whilst the habit of command and the menace of ever-recurring dangers had stamped them all with the same expression of authority and of alertness. There were some jovial faces amongst them, but the older officers, with their deep-lined cheeks and their masterful noses, were, for the most part, as austere as so many weather-beaten ascetics from the desert. Lonely watches, and a discipline which cut them off from all companionship, had left their mark upon those Red Indian faces. For my part, I could hardly eat my supper for watching them. Young as I was, I knew that if there were any freedom left in Europe it was to these men that we owed it; and I seemed to read upon their grim, harsh features the record of that long ten years of struggle which had swept the tricolour from the seas.

When we had finished our supper, my father led me into the great coffee-room, where a hundred or more officers may have been assembled, drinking their wine and smoking their long clay pipes, until the air was as thick as the main-deck in a close-fought action. As we entered we found ourselves face to face with an elderly officer who was coming out. He was a man with large, thoughtful eyes, and a full, placid face—such a face as one would expect from a philosopher and a philanthropist, rather than from a fighting seaman.

"Here's Cuddie Collingwood," whispered my father.

"Halloa, Lieutenant Stone!" cried the famous admiral very cheerily. "I have scarce caught a glimpse of you since you came aboard the Excellent after St. Vincent. You had the luck to be at the Nile also, I understand?"

"I was third of the Theseus, under Millar, sir."

"It nearly broke my heart to have missed it. I have not yet outlived it. To think of such a gallant service, and I engaged in harassing the market-boats, the miserable cabbage-carriers of St. Luccars!"

"Your plight was better than mine, Sir Cuthbert," said a voice from behind us, and a large man in the full uniform of a post-captain took a step forward to include himself in our circle. His mastiff face was heavy with emotion, and he shook his head miserably as he spoke.

"Yes, yes, Troubridge, I can understand and sympathize with your feelings."

"I passed through torment that night, Collingwood. It left a mark on me that I shall never lose until I go over the ship's side in a canvas cover. To have my beautiful Culloden laid on a sandbank just out of gunshot. To hear and see the fight the whole night through, and never to pull a lanyard or take the tompions out of my guns. Twice I opened my pistol-case to blow out my brains, and it was but the thought that Nelson might have a use for me that held me back."

Collingwood shook the hand of the unfortunate captain.

"Admiral Nelson was not long in finding a use for you, Troubridge," said he. "We have all heard of your siege of Capua, and how you ran up your ship's guns without trenches or parallels, and fired point-blank through the embrasures."

The melancholy cleared away from the massive face of the big sea-man, and his deep laughter filled the room.

"I'm not clever enough or slow enough for their Z-Z fashions," said he. "We got alongside and slapped it in through their port-holes until they struck their colours. But where have you been, Sir Cuthbert?"

"With my wife and my two little lasses at Morpeth in the North Country. I have but seen them this once in ten years, and it may be ten more, for all I know, ere I see them again. I have been doing good work for the fleet up yonder."

"I had thought, sir, that it was inland," said my father.

Collingwood took a little black bag out of his pocket and shook it.

"Inland it is," said he, "and yet I have done good work for the fleet there. What do you suppose I hold in this bag?"

"Bullets," said Troubridge.

"Something that a sailor needs even more than that," answered the admiral, and turning it over he tilted a pile of acorns on to his palm. "I carry them with me in my country walks, and where I see a fruitful nook I thrust one deep with the end of my cane. My oak trees may fight those rascals over the water when I am long forgotten. Do you know, lieutenant, how many oaks go to make an eighty-gun ship?"

My father shook his head.

"Two thousand, no less. For every two-decked ship that carries the white ensign there is a grove the less in England. So how are our grandsons to beat the French if we do not give them the trees with which to build their ships?"

He replaced his bag in his pocket, and then, passing his arm through Troubridge's, they went through the door together.

"There's a man whose life might help you to trim your own course," said my father, as we took our seats at a vacant table. "He is ever the same quiet gentleman, with his thoughts busy for the comfort of his ship's company, and his heart with his wife and children whom he has so seldom seen. It is said in the fleet that an oath has never passed his lips, Rodney, though how he managed when he was first lieutenant of a raw crew is more than I can conceive. But they all love Cuddie, for they know he's an angel to fight. How d'ye do, Captain Foley? My respects, Sir Ed'ard! Why, if they could but press the company, they would man a corvette with flag officers."

"There's many a man here, Rodney," continued my father, as he glanced about him, "whose name may never find its way into any book save his own ship's log, but who in his own way has set as fine an example as any admiral of them all. We know them, and talk of them in the fleet, though they may never be bawled in the streets of London. There's as much seamanship and pluck in a good cutter action as in a line-o'-battleship fight, though you may not come by a title nor the thanks of Parliament for it. There's Hamilton, for example, the quiet, pale-faced man who is leaning against the pillar. It was he who, with six rowing-boats, cut out the 44-gun frigate Hermione from under the muzzles of two hundred shore-guns in the harbour of Puerto Cabello. No finer action was done in the whole war. There's Jaheel Brenton, with the whiskers. It was he who attacked twelve Spanish gunboats in his one little brig, and made four of them strike to him. There's Walker, of the Rose cutter, who, with thirteen men, engaged three French privateers with crews of a hundred and forty-six. He sank one, captured one, and chased the third. How are you, Captain Ball? I hope I see you well?"

Two or three of my father's acquaintances who had been sitting close by drew up their chairs to us, and soon quite a circle had formed, all talking loudly and arguing upon sea matters, shaking their long, red-tipped pipes at each other as they spoke. My father whispered in my ear that his neighbour was Captain Foley, of the Goliath, who led the van at the Nile, and that the tall, thin, foxy-haired man opposite was Lord Cochrane, the most dashing frigate captain in the Service. Even at Friar's Oak we had heard how, in the little Speedy, of fourteen small guns with fifty-four men, he had carried by boarding the Spanish frigate Gamo with her crew of three hundred. It was easy to see that he was a quick, irascible, high-blooded man, for he was talking hotly about his grievances with a flush of anger upon his freckled cheeks.

"We shall never do any good upon the ocean until we have hanged the dockyard contractors," he cried. "I'd have a dead dockyard contractor as a figure-head for every first-rate in the fleet, and a provision dealer for every frigate. I know them with their puttied seams and their devil bolts, risking five hundred lives that they may steal a few pounds' worth of copper. What became of the Chance, and of the Martin, and of the Orestes? They foundered at sea, and were never heard of more, and I say that the crews of them were murdered men."

Lord Cochrane seemed to be expressing the views of all, for a murmur of assent, with a mutter of hearty, deep-sea curses, ran round the circle.

"Those rascals over yonder manage things better," said an old one-eyed captain, with the blue-and-white riband for St. Vincent peeping out of his third buttonhole. "They sheer away their heads if they get up to any foolery. Did ever a vessel come out of Toulon as my 38-gun frigate did from Plymouth last year, with her masts rolling about until her shrouds were like iron bars on one side and hanging in festoons upon the other? The meanest sloop that ever sailed out of France would have overmatched her, and then it would be on me, and not on this Devonport bungler, that a court-martial would be called."

They loved to grumble, those old salts, for as soon as one had shot off his grievance his neighbour would follow with another, each more bitter than the last.

"Look at our sails!" cried Captain Foley. "Put a French and a British ship at anchor together, and how can you tell which is which?"

"Frenchy has his fore and maintop-gallant masts about equal," said my father.

"In the old ships, maybe, but how many of the new are laid down on the French model? No, there's no way of telling them at anchor. But let them hoist sail, and how d'you tell them then?"

"Frenchy has white sails," cried several.

"And ours are black and rotten. That's the difference. No wonder they outsail us when the wind can blow through our canvas."

"In the Speedy," said Cochrane, "the sailcloth was so thin that, when I made my observation, I always took my meridian through the fore-topsail and my horizon through the foresail."

There was a general laugh at this, and then at it they all went again, letting off into speech all those weary broodings and silent troubles which had rankled during long years of service, for an iron discipline prevented them from speaking when their feet were upon their own quarter-decks. One told of his powder, six pounds of which were needed to throw a ball a thousand yards. Another cursed the Admiralty Courts, where a prize goes in as a full-rigged ship and comes out as a schooner. The old captain spoke of the promotions by Parliamentary interest which had put many a youngster into the captain's cabin when he should have been in the gun-room. And then they came back to the difficulty of finding crews for their vessels, and they all together raised up their voices and wailed.

"What is the use of building fresh ships," cried Foley, "when even with a ten-pound bounty you can't man the ships that you have got?"

But Lord Cochrane was on the other side in this question.

"You'd have the men, sir, if you treated them well when you got them," said he. "Admiral Nelson can get his ships manned. So can Admiral Collingwood. Why? Because he has thought for the men, and so the men have thought for him. Let men and officers know and respect each other, and there's no difficulty in keeping a ship's company. It's the infernal plan of turning a crew over from ship to ship and leaving the officers behind that rots the Navy. But I have never found a difficulty, and I dare swear that if I hoist my pennant to-morrow I shall have all my old Speedies back, and as many volunteers as I care to take."

"That is very well, my lord," said the old captain, with some warmth; "when the Jacks hear that the Speedy took fifty vessels in thirteen months, they are sure to volunteer to serve with her commander. Every good cruiser can fill her complement quickly enough. But it is not the cruisers that fight the country's battles and blockade the enemy's ports. I say that all prize-money should be divided equally among the whole fleet, and until you have such a rule, the smartest men will always be found where they are of least service to any one but themselves."

This speech produced a chorus of protests from the cruiser officers and a hearty agreement from the line-of-battleship men, who seemed to be in the majority in the circle which had gathered round. From the flushed faces and angry glances it was evident that the question was one upon which there was strong feeling upon both sides.

"What the cruiser gets the cruiser earns," cried a frigate captain.

"Do you mean to say, sir," said Captain Foley, "that the duties of an officer upon a cruiser demand more care or higher professional ability than those of one who is employed upon blockade service, with a lee coast under him whenever the wind shifts to the west, and the top-masts of an enemy's squadron for ever in his sight?"

"I do not claim higher ability, sir."

"Then why should you claim higher pay? Can you deny that a seaman before the mast makes more in a fast frigate than a lieutenant can in a battleship?"

"It was only last year," said a very gentlemanly-looking officer, who might have passed for a buck upon town had his skin not been burned to copper in such sunshine as never bursts upon London—"it was only last year that I brought the old Alexander back from the Mediterranean, floating like an empty barrel and carrying nothing but honour for her cargo. In the Channel we fell in with the frigate Minerva from the Western Ocean, with her lee ports under water and her hatches bursting with the plunder which had been too valuable to trust to the prize crews. She had ingots of silver along her yards and bowsprit, and a bit of silver plate at the truck of the masts. My Jacks could have fired into her, and would, too, if they had not been held back. It made them mad to think of all they had done in the south, and then to see this saucy frigate flashing her money before their eyes."

"I cannot see their grievance, Captain Ball," said Cochrane.

"When you are promoted to a two-decker, my lord, it will possibly become clearer to you."

"You speak as if a cruiser had nothing to do but take prizes. If that is your view, you will permit me to say that you know very little of the matter. I have handled a sloop, a corvette, and a frigate, and I have found a great variety of duties in each of them. I have had to avoid the enemy's battleships and to fight his cruisers. I have had to chase and capture his privateers, and to cut them out when they run under his batteries. I have had to engage his forts, to take my men ashore, and to destroy his guns and his signal stations. All this, with convoying, reconnoitring, and risking one's own ship in order to gain a knowledge of the enemy's movements, comes under the duties of the commander of a cruiser. I make bold to say that the man who can carry these objects out with success has deserved better of the country than the officer of a battleship, tacking from Ushant to the Black Rocks and back again until she builds up a reef with her beef-bones."

"Sir," said the angry old sailor, "such an officer is at least in no danger of being mistaken for a privateersman."

"I am surprised, Captain Bulkeley," Cochran retorted hotly, "that you should venture to couple the names of privateersman and King's officer."

There was mischief brewing among these hot-headed, short-spoken salts, but Captain Foley changed the subject to discuss the new ships which were being built in the French ports. It was of interest to me to hear these men, who were spending their lives in fighting against our neighbours, discussing their character and ways. You cannot conceive—you who live in times of peace and charity—how fierce the hatred was in England at that time against the French, and above all against their great leader. It was more than a mere prejudice or dislike. It was a deep, aggressive loathing of which you may even now form some conception if you examine the papers or caricatures of the day.

The word "Frenchman" was hardly spoken without "rascal" or "scoundrel" slipping in before it. In all ranks of life and in every part of the country the feeling was the same. Even the Jacks aboard our ships fought with a viciousness against a French vessel which they would never show to Dane, Dutchman, or Spaniard.

If you ask me now, after fifty years, why it was that there should have been this virulent feeling against them, so foreign to the easy-going and tolerant British nature, I would confess that I think the real reason was fear. Not fear of them individually, of course—our foulest detractors have never called us faint-hearted—but fear of their star, fear of their future, fear of the subtle brain whose plans always seemed to go aright, and of the heavy hand which had struck nation after nation to the ground. We were but a small country, with a population which, when the war began, was not much more than half that of France. And then, France had increased by leaps and bounds, reaching out to the north into Belgium and Holland, and to the south into Italy, whilst we were weakened by deep-lying disaffection among both Catholics and Presbyterians in Ireland. The danger was imminent and plain to the least thoughtful. One could not walk the Kent coast without seeing the beacons heaped up to tell the country of the enemy's landing, and if the sun were shining on the uplands near Boulogne, one might catch the flash of its gleam upon the bayonets of manoeuvring veterans. No wonder that a fear of the French power lay deeply in the hearts of the most gallant men, and that fear should, as it always does, beget a bitter and rancorous hatred.

The seamen did not speak kindly then of their recent enemies. Their hearts loathed them, and in the fashion of our country their lips said what the heart felt. Of the French officers they could not have spoken with more chivalry, as of worthy foemen, but the nation was an abomination to them. The older men had fought against them in the American War, they had fought again for the last ten years, and the dearest wish of their hearts seemed to be that they might be called upon to do the same for the remainder of their days. Yet if I was surprised by the virulence of their animosity against the French, I was even more so to hear how highly they rated them as antagonists. The long succession of British victories which had finally made the French take to their ports and resign the struggle in despair had given all of us the idea that for some reason a Briton on the water must, in the nature of things, always have the best of it against a Frenchman. But these men who had done the fighting did not think so. They were loud in their praise of their foemen's gallantry, and precise in their reasons for his defeat. They showed how the officers of the old French Navy had nearly all been aristocrats. How the Revolution had swept them out of their ships, and the force been left with insubordinate seamen and no competent leaders. This ill-directed fleet had been hustled into port by the pressure of the well-manned and well-commanded British, who had pinned them there ever since, so that they had never had an opportunity of learning seamanship. Their harbour drill and their harbour gunnery had been of no service when sails had to be trimmed and broadsides fired on the heave of an Atlantic swell. Let one of their frigates get to sea and have a couple of years' free run in which the crew might learn their duties, and then it would be a feather in the cap of a British officer if with a ship of equal force he could bring down her colours.

Such were the views of these experienced officers, fortified by many reminiscences and examples of French gallantry, such as the way in which the crew of the L'Orient had fought her quarter-deck guns when the main-deck was in a blaze beneath them, and when they must have known that they were standing over an exploding magazine. The general hope was that the West Indian expedition since the peace might have given many of their fleet an ocean train-ing, and that they might be tempted out into mid-Channel if the war were to break out afresh. But would it break out afresh? We had spent gigantic sums and made enormous exertions to curb the power of Napoleon and to prevent him from becoming the universal despot of Europe. Would the Government try it again? Or were they appalled by the gigantic load of debt which must bend the backs of many generations unborn? Pitt was there, and surely he was not a man to leave his work half done.

And then suddenly there was a bustle at the door. Amid the grey swirl of the tobacco-smoke I could catch a glimpse of a blue coat and gold epaulettes, with a crowd gathering thickly round them, while a hoarse murmur rose from the group which thickened into a deep-chested cheer. Every one was on his feet, peering and asking each other what it might mean. And still the crowd seethed and the cheering swelled.

"What is it? What has happened?" cried a score of voices.

"Put him up! Hoist him up!" shouted somebody, and an instant later I saw Captain Troubridge appear above the shoulders of the crowd. His face was flushed, as if he were in wine, and he was waving what seemed to be a letter in the air. The cheering died away, and there was such a hush that I could hear the crackle of the paper in his hand.

"Great news, gentlemen!" he roared. "Glorious news! Rear-Admiral Collingwood has directed me to communicate it to you. The French Ambassador has received his papers to-night. Every ship on the list is to go into commission. Admiral Cornwallis is ordered out of Cawsand Bay to cruise off Ushant. A squadron is starting for the North Sea and another for the Irish Channel."

He may have had more to say, but his audience could wait no longer. How they shouted and stamped and raved in their delight! Harsh old flag-officers, grave post-captains, young lieutenants, all were roaring like schoolboys breaking up for the holidays. There was no thought now of those manifold and weary grievances to which I had listened. The foul weather was passed, and the landlocked sea-birds would be out on the foam once more. The rhythm of "God Save the King" swelled through the babel, and I heard the old lines sung in a way that made you forget their bad rhymes and their bald sentiments. I trust that you will never hear them so sung, with tears upon rugged cheeks, and catchings of the breath from strong men. Dark days will have come again before you hear such a song or see such a sight as that. Let those talk of the phlegm of our countrymen who have never seen them when the lava crust of restraint is broken, and when for an instant the strong, enduring fires of the North glow upon the surface. I saw them then, and if I do not see them now, I am not so old or so foolish as to doubt that they are there.

CHAPTER XIII—LORD NELSON

My father's appointment with Lord Nelson was an early one, and he was the more anxious to be punctual as he knew how much the Admiral's movements must be affected by the news which we had heard the night before. I had hardly breakfasted then, and my uncle had not rung for his chocolate, when he called for me at Jermyn Street. A walk of a few hundred yards brought us to the high building of discoloured brick in Piccadilly, which served the Hamiltons as a town house, and which Nelson used as his head-quarters when business or pleasure called him from Merton. A footman answered our knock, and we were ushered into a large drawing-room with sombre furniture and melancholy curtains. My father sent in his name, and there we sat, looking at the white Italian statuettes in the corners, and the picture of Vesuvius and the Bay of Naples which hung over the harpsichord. I can remember that a black clock was ticking loudly upon the mantelpiece, and that every now and then, amid the rumble of the hackney coaches, we could hear boisterous laughter from some inner chamber.

When at last the door opened, both my father and I sprang to our feet, expecting to find ourselves face to face with the greatest living Englishman. It was a very different person, however, who swept into the room.

She was a lady, tall, and, as it seemed to me, exceedingly beautiful, though, perhaps, one who was more experienced and more critical
might have thought that her charm lay in the past rather than the
present. Her queenly figure was moulded upon large and noble lines,
while her face, though already tending to become somewhat heavy
and coarse, was still remarkable for the brilliancy of the complexion,
the beauty of the large, light blue eyes, and the tinge of the dark hair
which curled over the low white forehead. She carried herself in the
most stately fashion, so that as I looked at her majestic entrance, and at
the pose which she struck as she glanced at my father, I was reminded
of the Queen of the Peruvians as, in the person of Miss Polly Hinton,
she incited Boy Jim and myself to insurrection.

"Lieutenant Anson Stone?" she asked.

"Yes, your ladyship," answered my father.

"Ah," she cried, with an affected and exaggerated start, "you know
me, then?"

"I have seen your ladyship at Naples."

"Then you have doubtless seen my poor Sir William also—my poor,
poor Sir William!" She touched her dress with her white, ring-covered
fingers, as if to draw our attention to the fact that she was in the deepest mourning.

"I heard of your ladyship's sad loss," said my father.

"We died together," she cried. "What can my life be now save a
long-drawn living death?"

She spoke in a beautiful, rich voice, with the most heart-broken thrill
in it, but I could not conceal from myself that she appeared to be one
of the most robust persons that I had ever seen, and I was surprised
to notice that she shot arch little questioning glances at me, as if the
admiration even of so insignificant a person were of some interest to
her. My father, in his blunt, sailor fashion, tried to stammer out some
commonplace condolence, but her eyes swept past his rude, weather-
beaten face to ask and reask what effect she had made upon me.

"There he hangs, the tutelary angel of this house," she cried, pointing with a grand sweeping gesture to a painting upon the wall, which

represented a very thin-faced, high-nosed gentleman with several orders upon his coat. "But enough of my private sorrow!" She dashed invisible tears from her eyes. "You have come to see Lord Nelson. He bid me say that he would be with you in an instant. You have doubtless heard that hostilities are about to reopen?"

"We heard the news last night."

"Lord Nelson is under orders to take command of the Mediterranean Fleet. You can think at such a moment—But, ah, is it not his lordship's step that I hear?"

My attention was so riveted by the lady's curious manner and by the gestures and attitudes with which she accompanied every remark, that I did not see the great admiral enter the room. When I turned he was standing close by my elbow, a small, brown man with the lithe, slim figure of a boy. He was not clad in uniform, but he wore a high-collared brown coat, with the right sleeve hanging limp and empty by his side. The expression of his face was, as I remember it, exceedingly sad and gentle, with the deep lines upon it which told of the chafing of his urgent and fiery soul. One eye was disfigured and sightless from a wound, but the other looked from my father to myself with the quickest and shrewdest of expressions. Indeed, his whole manner, with his short, sharp glance and the fine poise of the head, spoke of energy and alertness, so that he reminded me, if I may compare great things with small, of a well-bred fighting terrier, gentle and slim, but keen and ready for whatever chance might send.

"Why, Lieutenant Stone," said he, with great cordiality, holding out his left hand to my father, "I am very glad to see you. London is full of Mediterranean men, but I trust that in a week there will not be an officer amongst you all with his feet on dry land."

"I had come to ask you, sir, if you could assist me to a ship."

"You shall have one, Stone, if my word goes for anything at the Admiralty. I shall want all my old Nile men at my back. I cannot promise you a first-rate, but at least it shall be a 64-gun ship, and I can tell you that there is much to be done with a handy, well-manned, well-found 64-gun ship."

"Who could doubt it who has heard of the Agamemnon?" cried Lady Hamilton, and straightway she began to talk of the admiral and of his doings with such extravagance of praise and such a shower of compliments and of epithets, that my father and I did not know which way to look, feeling shame and sorrow for a man who was compelled to listen to such things said in his own presence. But when I ventured to glance at Lord Nelson I found, to my surprise, that, far from showing any embarrassment, he was smiling with pleasure, as if this gross flattery of her ladyship's were the dearest thing in all the world to him.

"Come, come, my dear lady," said he, "you speak vastly beyond my merits;" upon which encouragement she started again in a theatrical apostrophe to Britain's darling and Neptune's eldest son, which he endured with the same signs of gratitude and pleasure. That a man of the world, five-and-forty years of age, shrewd, honest, and acquainted with Courts, should be beguiled by such crude and coarse homage, amazed me, as it did all who knew him; but you who have seen much of life do not need to be told how often the strongest and noblest nature has its one inexplicable weakness, showing up the more obviously in contrast to the rest, as the dark stain looks the fouler upon the whitest sheet.

"You are a sea-officer of my own heart, Stone," said he, when her ladyship had exhausted her panegyric. "You are one of the old breed!" He walked up and down the room with little, impatient steps as he talked, turning with a whisk upon his heel every now and then, as if some invisible rail had brought him up. "We are getting too fine for our work with these new-fangled epaulettes and quarter-deck trimmings. When I joined the Service, you would find a lieutenant gammoning and rigging his own bowsprit, or aloft, maybe, with a marlinspike slung round his neck, showing an example to his men. Now, it's as much as he'll do to carry his own sextant up the companion. When could you join?"

"To-night, my lord."

"Right, Stone, right! That is the true spirit. They are working double tides in the yards, but I do not know when the ships will be ready. I hoist my flag on the Victory on Wednesday, and we sail at once."

"No, no; not so soon! She cannot be ready for sea," said Lady Hamilton, in a wailing voice, clasping her hands and turning up her eyes as she spoke.

"She must and she shall be ready," cried Nelson, with extraordinary vehemence. "By Heaven! if the devil stands at the door, I sail on Wednesday. Who knows what these rascals may be doing in my absence? It maddens me to think of the deviltries which they may be devising. At this very instant, dear lady, the Queen, our Queen, may be straining her eyes for the topsails of Nelson's ships."

Thinking, as I did, that he was speaking of our own old Queen Charlotte, I could make no meaning out of this; but my father told me afterwards that both Nelson and Lady Hamilton had conceived an extraordinary affection for the Queen of Naples, and that it was the interests of her little kingdom which he had so strenuously at heart. It may have been my expression of bewilderment which attracted Nelson's attention to me, for he suddenly stopped in his quick quarter-deck walk, and looked me up and down with a severe eye.

"Well, young gentleman!" said he, sharply.

"This is my only son, sir," said my father. "It is my wish that he should join the Service, if a berth can be found for him; for we have all been King's officers for many generations."

"So, you wish to come and have your bones broken?" cried Nelson, roughly, looking with much disfavour at the fine clothes which had cost my uncle and Mr. Brummel such a debate. "You will have to change that grand coat for a tarry jacket if you serve under me, sir."

I was so embarrassed by the abruptness of his manner that I could but stammer out that I hoped I should do my duty, on which his stern mouth relaxed into a good-humoured smile, and he laid his little brown hand for an instant upon my shoulder.

"I dare say that you will do very well," said he. "I can see that you have the stuff in you. But do not imagine that it is a light service which you undertake, young gentleman, when you enter His Majesty's Navy. It is a hard profession. You hear of the few who succeed, but what do you know of the hundreds who never find their way? Look at my own luck! Out of 200 who were with me in the San Juan expedition, 145 died in a single night. I have been in 180 engagements, and I have, as you see, lost my eye and my arm, and been sorely wounded besides. It chanced that I came through, and here I am flying my admiral's flag; but I remember many a man as good as me who did not come through. Yes," he added, as her ladyship broke in with a voluble protest, "many and many as good a man who has gone to the sharks or the land-crabs. But it is a useless sailor who does not risk himself every day, and the lives of all of us are in the hands of Him who best knows when to claim them."

For an instant, in his earnest gaze and reverent manner, we seemed to catch a glimpse of the deeper, truer Nelson, the man of the Eastern counties, steeped in the virile Puritanism which sent from that district the Ironsides to fashion England within, and the Pilgrim Fathers to spread it without. Here was the Nelson who declared that he saw the hand of God pressing upon the French, and who waited on his knees in the cabin of his flag-ship while she bore down upon the enemy's line. There was a human tenderness, too, in his way of speaking of his dead comrades, which made me understand why it was that he was so beloved by all who served with him, for, iron-hard as he was as seaman and fighter, there ran through his complex nature a sweet and un-English power of affectionate emotion, showing itself in tears if he were moved, and in such tender impulses as led him afterwards to ask his flag-captain to kiss him as he lay dying in the cockpit of the Victory.

My father had risen to depart, but the admiral, with that kindliness which he ever showed to the young, and which had been momentarily chilled by the unfortunate splendour of my clothes, still paced up and down in front of us, shooting out crisp little sentences of exhortation and advice.

"It is ardour that we need in the Service, young gentleman," said he. "We need red-hot men who will never rest satisfied. We had them in the Mediterranean, and we shall have them again. There was a band of brothers! When I was asked to recommend one for special service, I told the Admiralty they might take the names as they came, for the same spirit animated them all. Had we taken nineteen vessels, we should never have said it was well done while the twentieth sailed the seas. You know how it was with us, Stone. You are too old a Mediterranean man for me to tell you anything."

"I trust, my lord, that I shall be with you when next we meet them," said my father.

"Meet them we shall and must. By Heaven, I shall never rest until I have given them a shaking. The scoundrel Bonaparte wishes to humble us. Let him try, and God help the better cause!"

He spoke with such extraordinary animation that the empty sleeve flapped about in the air, giving him the strangest appearance. Seeing my eyes fixed upon it, he turned with a smile to my father.

"I can still work my fin, Stone," said he, putting his hand across to the stump of his arm. "What used they to say in the fleet about it?"

"That it was a sign, sir, that it was a bad hour to cross your hawse."

"They knew me, the rascals. You can see, young gentleman, that not a scrap of the ardour with which I serve my country has been shot away. Some day you may find that you are flying your own flag, and when that time comes you may remember that my advice to an officer is that he should have nothing to do with tame, slow measures. Lay all your stake, and if you lose through no fault of your own, the country will find you another stake as large. Never mind manoeuvres! Go for them! The only manoeuvre you need is that which will place you alongside your enemy. Always fight, and you will always be right. Give not a thought to your own ease or your own life, for from the day that you draw the blue coat over your back you have no life of your own. It is the country's, to be most freely spent if the smallest gain can come from it. How is the wind this morning, Stone?"

"East-south-east," my father answered, readily.

"Then Cornwallis is, doubtless, keeping well up to Brest, though, for my own part, I had rather tempt them out into the open sea."

"That is what every officer and man in the fleet would prefer, your lordship," said my father.

"They do not love the blockading service, and it is little wonder, since neither money nor honour is to be gained at it. You can remember how it was in the winter months before Toulon, Stone, when we had neither firing, wine, beef, pork, nor flour aboard the ships, nor a spare piece of rope, canvas, or twine. We braced the old hulks with our spare cables, and God knows there was never a Levanter that I did not expect it to send us to the bottom. But we held our grip all the same. Yet I fear that we do not get much credit for it here in England, Stone, where they light the windows for a great battle, but they do not understand that it is easier for us to fight the Nile six times over, than to keep our station all winter in the blockade. But I pray God that we may meet this new fleet of theirs and settle the matter by a pell-mell battle."

"May I be with you, my lord!" said my father, earnestly. "But we have already taken too much of your time, and so I beg to thank you for your kindness and to wish you good morning."

"Good morning, Stone!" said Nelson. "You shall have your ship, and if I can make this young gentleman one of my officers it shall be done. But I gather from his dress," he continued, running his eye over me, "that you have been more fortunate in prize-money than most of your comrades. For my own part, I never did nor could turn my thoughts to money-making."

My father explained that I had been under the charge of the famous Sir Charles Tregellis, who was my uncle, and with whom I was now residing.

"Then you need no help from me," said Nelson, with some bitterness. "If you have either guineas or interest you can climb over the heads of old sea-officers, though you may not know the poop from the galley, or a carronade from a long nine. Nevertheless—But what the deuce have we here?"

The footman had suddenly precipitated himself into the room, but stood abashed before the fierce glare of the admiral's eye.

"Your lordship told me to rush to you if it should come," he explained, holding out a large blue envelope.

"By Heaven, it is my orders!" cried Nelson, snatching it up and fumbling with it in his awkward, one-handed attempt to break the seals. Lady Hamilton ran to his assistance, but no sooner had she glanced at the paper inclosed than she burst into a shrill scream, and throwing up her hands and her eyes, she sank backwards in a swoon. I could not but observe, however, that her fall was very carefully executed, and that she was fortunate enough, in spite of her insensibility, to arrange her drapery and attitude into a graceful and classical design. But he, the honest seaman, so incapable of deceit or affectation that he could not suspect it in others, ran madly to the bell, shouting for the maid, the doctor, and the smelling-salts, with incoherent words of grief, and such passionate terms of emotion that my father thought it more discreet to twitch me by the sleeve as a signal that we should steal from the room. There we left him then in the dim-lit London drawing-room, beside himself with pity for this shallow and most artificial woman, while without, at the edge of the Piccadilly curb, there stood the high dark berline ready to start him upon that long journey which was to end in his chase of the French fleet over seven thousand miles of ocean, his meeting with it, his victory, which confined Napoleon's ambition for ever to the land, and his death, coming, as I would it might come to all of us, at the crowning moment of his life.

CHAPTER XIV—ON THE ROAD

And now the day of the great fight began to approach. Even the imminent outbreak of war and the renewed threats of Napoleon were sec-
ondary things in the eyes of the sportsmen—and the sportsmen in
those days made a large half of the population. In the club of the
patrician and the plebeian gin-shop, in the coffee-house of the merchant or the barrack of the soldier, in London or the provinces, the
same question was interesting the whole nation. Every west-country
coach brought up word of the fine condition of Crab Wilson, who
had returned to his own native air for his training, and was known to
be under the immediate care of Captain Barclay, the expert. On the
other hand, although my uncle had not yet named his man, there was
no doubt amongst the public that Jim was to be his nominee, and the
report of his physique and of his performance found him many backers. On the whole, however, the betting was in favour of Wilson, for
Bristol and the west country stood by him to a man, whilst London
opinion was divided. Three to two were to be had on Wilson at any
West End club two days before the battle.

I had twice been down to Crawley to see Jim in his training quarters, where I found him undergoing the severe regimen which was
usual. From early dawn until nightfall he was running, jumping, striking a bladder which swung upon a bar, or sparring with his formidable

trainer. His eyes shone and his skin glowed with exuberent health, and he was so confident of success that my own misgivings vanished as I watched his gallant bearing and listened to his quiet and cheerful words.

"But I wonder that you should come and see me now, Rodney," said he, when we parted, trying to laugh as he spoke. "I have become a bruiser and your uncle's paid man, whilst you are a Corinthian upon town. If you had not been the best and truest little gentleman in the world, you would have been my patron instead of my friend before now."

When I looked at this splendid fellow, with his high-bred, clean-cut face, and thought of the fine qualities and gentle, generous impulses which I knew to lie within him, it seemed so absurd that he should speak as though my friendship towards him were a condescension, that I could not help laughing aloud.

"That is all very well, Rodney," said he, looking hard into my eyes. "But what does your uncle think about it?"

This was a poser, and I could only answer lamely enough that, much as I was indebted to my uncle, I had known Jim first, and that I was surely old enough to choose my own friends.

Jim's misgivings were so far correct that my uncle did very strongly object to any intimacy between us; but there were so many other points in which he disapproved of my conduct, that it made the less difference. I fear that he was already disappointed in me. I would not develop an eccentricity, although he was good enough to point out several by which I might "come out of the ruck," as he expressed it, and so catch the attention of the strange world in which he lived.

"You are an active young fellow, nephew," said he. "Do you not think that you could engage to climb round the furniture of an ordinary room without setting foot upon the ground? Some little tour-de-force of the sort is in excellent taste. There was a captain in the Guards who attained considerable social success by doing it for a small wager. Lady Lieven, who is exceedingly exigeant, used to invite him to her evenings merely that he might exhibit it."

I had to assure him that the feat would be beyond me.

"You are just a little *difficile*," said he, shrugging his shoulders. "As my nephew, you might have taken your position by perpetuating my own delicacy of taste. If you had made bad taste your enemy, the world of fashion would willingly have looked upon you as an arbiter by virtue of your family traditions, and you might without a struggle have stepped into the position to which this young upstart Brummell aspires. But you have no instinct in that direction. You are incapable of minute attention to detail. Look at your shoes! Look at your cravat! Look at your watch-chain! Two links are enough to show. I have shown three, but it was an indiscretion. At this moment I can see no less than five of yours. I regret it, nephew, but I do not think that you are destined to attain that position which I have a right to expect from my blood relation."

"I am sorry to be a disappointment to you, sir," said I.

"It is your misfortune not to have come under my influence earlier," said he. "I might then have moulded you so as to have satisfied even my own aspirations. I had a younger brother whose case was a similar one. I did what I could for him, but he would wear ribbons in his shoes, and he publicly mistook white Burgundy for Rhine wine. Eventually the poor fellow took to books, and lived and died in a country vicarage. He was a good man, but he was commonplace, and there is no place in society for commonplace people."

"Then I fear, sir, that there is none for me," said I. "But my father has every hope that Lord Nelson will find me a position in the fleet. If I have been a failure in town, I am none the less conscious of your kindness in trying to advance my interests, and I hope that, should I receive my commission, I may be a credit to you yet."

"It is possible that you may attain the very spot which I had marked out for you, but by another road," said my uncle. "There are many men in town, such as Lord St. Vincent, Lord Hood, and others, who move in the most respectable circles, although they have nothing but their services in the Navy to recommend them."

It was on the afternoon of the day before the fight that this conversation took place between my uncle and myself in the dainty sanctum of his Jermyn-Street house. He was clad, I remember, in his flowing brocade dressing-gown, as was his custom before he set off for his club, and his foot was extended upon a stool—for Abernethy had just been in to treat him for an incipient attack of the gout. It may have been the pain, or it may have been his disappointment at my career, but his manner was more testy than was usual with him, and I fear that there was something of a sneer in his smile as he spoke of my deficiencies. For my own part I was relieved at the explanation, for my father had left London in the full conviction that a vacancy would speedily be found for us both, and the one thing which had weighed upon my mind was that I might have found it hard to leave my uncle without interfering with the plans which he had formed. I was heart-weary of this empty life, for which I was so ill-fashioned, and weary also of that intolerant talk which would make a coterie of frivolous women and foolish fops the central point of the universe. Something of my uncle's sneer may have flickered upon my lips as I heard him allude with supercilious surprise to the presence in those sacrosanct circles of the men who had stood between the country and destruction.

"By the way, nephew," said he, "gout or no gout, and whether Abernethy likes it or not, we must be down at Crawley to-night. The battle will take place upon Crawley Downs. Sir Lothian Hume and his man are at Reigate. I have reserved beds at the George for both of us. The crush will, it is said, exceed anything ever known. The smell of these country inns is always most offensive to me—*mais que voulez-vous?* Berkeley Craven was saying in the club last night that there is not a bed within twenty miles of Crawley which is not bespoke, and that they are charging three guineas for the night. I hope that your young friend, if I must describe him as such, will fulfil the promise which he has shown, for I have rather more upon the event than I care to lose. Sir Lothian has been plunging also—he made a single bye-bet of five thousand to three upon Wilson in Limmer's yesterday. From what I hear of his affairs it will be a serious matter for him if we should pull it off. Well, Lorimer?"

"A person to see you, Sir Charles," said the new valet.

"You know that I never see any one until my dressing is complete."

"He insists upon seeing you, sir. He pushed open the door."

"Pushed it open! What d'you mean, Lorimer? Why didn't you put him out?"

A smile passed over the servant's face. At the same moment there came a deep voice from the passage.

"You show me in this instant, young man, d'ye 'ear? Let me see your master, or it'll be the worse for you."

I thought that I had heard the voice before, but when, over the shoulder of the valet, I caught a glimpse of a large, fleshy, bull-face, with a flattened Michael Angelo nose in the centre of it, I knew at once that it was my neighbour at the supper party.

"It's Warr, the prizefighter, sir," said I.

"Yes, sir," said our visitor, pushing his huge form into the room. "It's Bill Warr, landlord of the One Ton public-'ouse, Jermyn Street, and the gamest man upon the list. There's only one thing that ever beat me, Sir Charles, and that was my flesh, which creeps over me that amazin' fast that I've always got four stone that 'as no business there. Why, sir, I've got enough to spare to make a feather-weight champion out of. You'd 'ardly think, to look at me, that even after Mendoza fought me I was able to jump the four-foot ropes at the ring-side just as light as a little kiddy; but if I was to chuck my castor into the ring now I'd never get it till the wind blew it out again, for blow my dicky if I could climb after. My respec's to you, young sir, and I 'ope I see you well."

My uncle's face had expressed considerable disgust at this invasion of his privacy, but it was part of his position to be on good terms with the fighting-men, so he contented himself with asking curtly what business had brought him there. For answer the huge prizefighter looked meaningly at the valet.

"It's important, Sir Charles, and between man and man," said he.

"You may go, Lorimer. Now, Warr, what is the matter?"

The bruiser very calmly seated himself astride of a chair with his arms resting upon the back of it.

"I've got information, Sir Charles," said he.

"Well, what is it?" cried my uncle, impatiently.

"Information of value."

"Out with it, then!"

"Information that's worth money," said Warr, and pursed up his lips.

"I see. You want to be paid for what you know?"

The prizefighter smiled an affirmative.

"Well, I don't buy things on trust. You should know me better than to try on such a game with me."

"I know you for what you are, Sir Charles, and that is a noble, slap-up Corinthian. But if I was to use this against you, d'ye see, it would be worth 'undreds in my pocket. But my 'eart won't let me do it, for Bill Warr's always been on the side o' good sport and fair play. If I use it for you, then I expect that you won't see me the loser."

"You can do what you like," said my uncle. "If your news is of service to me, I shall know how to treat you."

"You can't say fairer than that. We'll let it stand there, gov'nor, and you'll do the 'andsome thing, as you 'ave always 'ad the name for doin'. Well, then, your man, Jim 'Arisen, fights Crab Wilson, of Gloucester, at Crawley Down to-morrow mornin' for a stake."

"What of that?"

"Did you 'appen to know what the bettin' was yesterday?"

"It was three to two on Wilson."

"Right you are, gov'nor. Three to two was offered in my own bar-parlour. D'you know what the bettin' is to-day?"

"I have not been out yet."

"Then I'll tell you. It's seven to one against your man."

"What?"

"Seven to one, gov'nor, no less."

"You're talking nonsense, Warr! How could the betting change from three to two to seven to one?"

"I've been to Tom Owen's, and I've been to the 'Ole in the Wall, and I've been to the Waggon and 'Orses, and you can get seven to one in any of them. There's tons of money being laid against your man. It's a 'orse to a 'en in every sportin' 'ouse and boozin' ken from 'ere to Stepney."

For a moment the expression upon my uncle's face made me realize that this match was really a serious matter to him. Then he shrugged his shoulders with an incredulous smile.

"All the worse for the fools who give the odds," said he. "My man is all right. You saw him yesterday, nephew?"

"He was all right yesterday, sir."

"If anything had gone wrong I should have heard."

"But perhaps," said Warr, "it 'as not gone wrong with 'im yet."

"What d'you mean?"

"I'll tell you what I mean, sir. You remember Berks? You know that 'e ain't to be overmuch depended on at any time, and that 'e 'ad a grudge against your man 'cause 'e laid 'im out in the coach-'ouse. Well, last night about ten o'clock in 'e comes into my bar, and the three bloodiest rogues in London at 'is 'eels. There was Red Ike, 'im that was warned off the ring 'cause 'e fought a cross with Bittoon; and there was Fightin' Yussef, who would sell 'is mother for a seven-shillin'-bit; the third was Chris McCarthy, who is a fogle-snatcher by trade, with a pitch outside the 'Aymarket Theatre. You don't often see four such beauties together, and all with as much as they could carry, save only Chris, who is too leary a cove to drink when there's somethin' goin' forward. For my part, I showed 'em into the parlour, not 'cos they was worthy of it, but 'cos I knew right well they would start bashin' some of my customers, and maybe get my license into trouble if I left 'em in the bar. I served 'em with drink, and stayed with 'em just to see that they didn't lay their 'ands on the stuffed parroquet and the pictures.

"Well, gov'nor, to cut it short, they began to talk about the fight, and they all laughed at the idea that young Jim 'Arrison could win it—all except Chris, and e' kept a-nudging and a-twitchin' at the others until Joe Berks nearly gave him a wipe across the face for 'is trouble. I saw somethin' was in the wind, and it wasn't very 'ard to guess what it was—especially when Red Ike was ready to put up a fiver that Jim 'Arrison would never fight at all. So I up to get another bottle of liptrap, and I slipped round to the shutter that we pass the liquor through from the private bar into the parlour. I drew it an inch open, and I might 'ave been at the table with them, I could 'ear every word that clearly.

"There was Chris McCarthy growlin' at them for not keepin' their tongues still, and there was Joe Berks swearin' that 'e would knock 'is face in if 'e dared give 'im any of 'is lip. So Chris 'e sort of argued with them, for 'e was frightened of Berks, and 'e put it to them whether they would be fit for the job in the mornin', and whether the gov'nor would pay the money if 'e found they 'ad been drinkin' and were not to be trusted. This struck them sober, all three, an' Fighting Yussef asked what time they were to start. Chris said that as long as they were at Crawley before the George shut up they could work it. 'It's poor pay for a chance of a rope,' said Red Ike. 'Rope be damned!' cried Chris, takin' a little loaded stick out of his side pocket. 'If three of you 'old him down and I break his arm-bone with this, we've earned our money, and we don't risk more'n six months' jug.' "E'll fight,' said Berks. 'Well, it's the only fight 'e'll get,' answered Chris, and that was all I 'eard of it. This mornin' out I went, and I found as I told you afore that the money is goin' on to Wilson by the ton, and that no odds are too long for the layers. So it stands, gov'nor, and you know what the meanin' of it may be better than Bill Warr can tell you."

"Very good, Warr," said my uncle, rising. "I am very much obliged to you for telling me this, and I will see that you are not a loser by it. I put it down as the gossip of drunken ruffians, but none the less you have served me vastly by calling my attention to it. I suppose I shall see you at the Downs to-morrow?"

"Mr. Jackson 'as asked me to be one o' the beaters-out, sir."

"Very good. I hope that we shall have a fair and good fight. Good day to you, and thank you."

My uncle had preserved his jaunty demeanour as long as Warr was in the room, but the door had hardly closed upon him before he turned to me with a face which was more agitated than I had ever seen it.

"We must be off for Crawley at once, nephew," said he, ringing the bell. "There's not a moment to be lost. Lorimer, order the bays to be harnessed in the curricle. Put the toilet things in, and tell William to have it round at the door as soon as possible."

"I'll see to it, sir," said I, and away I ran to the mews in Little Ryder Street, where my uncle stabled his horses. The groom was away, and I had to send a lad in search of him, while with the help of the livery-man I dragged the curricle from the coach-house and brought the two mares out of their stalls. It was half an hour, or possibly three-quarters, before everything had been found, and Lorimer was already waiting in Jermyn Street with the inevitable baskets, whilst my uncle stood in the open door of his house, clad in his long fawn-coloured driving-coat, with no sign upon his calm pale face of the tumult of impatience which must, I was sure, be raging within.

"We shall leave you, Lorimer," said he. "We might find it hard to get a bed for you. Keep at her head, William! Jump in, nephew. Halloa, Warr, what is the matter now?"

The prizefighter was hastening towards us as fast as his bulk would allow.

"Just one word before you go, Sir Charles," he panted. "I've just 'eard in my taproom that the four men I spoke of left for Crawley at one o'clock."

"Very good, Warr," said my uncle, with his foot upon the step.

"And the odds 'ave risen to ten to one."

"Let go her head, William!"

"Just one more word, gov'nor. You'll excuse the liberty, but if I was you I'd take my pistols with me."

"Thank you; I have them."

The long thong cracked between the ears of the leader, the groom sprang for the pavement, and Jermyn Street had changed for St. James's, and that again for Whitehall with a swiftness which showed that the gallant mares were as impatient as their master. It was half-past four by the Parliament clock as we flew on to Westminster Bridge. There was the flash of water beneath us, and then we were between those two long dun-coloured lines of houses which had been the avenue which had led us to London. My uncle sat with tightened lips and a brooding brow. We had reached Streatham before he broke the silence.

"I have a good deal at stake, nephew," said he.

"So have I, sir," I answered.

"You!" he cried, in surprise.

"My friend, sir."

"Ah, yes, I had forgot. You have some eccentricities, after all, nephew. You are a faithful friend, which is a rare enough thing in our circles. I never had but one friend of my own position, and he—but you've heard me tell the story. I fear it will be dark before we reach Crawley."

"I fear that it will."

"In that case we may be too late."

"Pray God not, sir!"

"We sit behind the best cattle in England, but I fear lest we find the roads blocked before we get to Crawley. Did you observe, nephew, that these four villains spoke in Warr's hearing of the master who was behind them, and who was paying them for their infamy? Did you not understand that they were hired to cripple my man? Who, then, could have hired them? Who had an interest unless it was—I know Sir Lothian Hume to be a desperate man. I know that he has had heavy card losses at Watier's and White's. I know also that he has much at stake upon this event, and that he has plunged upon it with a rashness which made his friends think that he had some private reason for being satisfied as to the result. By Heaven, it all hangs together! If it should be so—!" He relapsed into silence, but I saw the same look of cold fierceness settle upon his features which I had marked there when he and Sir John Lade had raced wheel to wheel down the Godstone road.

The sun sank slowly towards the low Surrey hills, and the shadows crept steadily eastwards, but the whirr of the wheels and the roar of the hoofs never slackened. A fresh wind blew upon our faces, while the young leaves drooped motionless from the wayside branches. The golden edge of the sun was just sinking behind the oaks of Reigate Hill when the dripping mares drew up before the Crown at Redhill.

The landlord, an old sportsman and ringsider, ran out to greet so well-known a Corinthian as Sir Charles Tregellis.

"You know Berks, the bruiser?" asked my uncle.

"Yes, Sir Charles."

"Has he passed?"

"Yes, Sir Charles. It may have been about four o'clock, though with this crowd of folk and carriages it's hard to swear to it. There was him, and Red Ike, and Fighting Yussef the Jew, and another, with a good bit of blood betwixt the shafts. They'd been driving her hard, too, for she was all in a lather."

"That's ugly, nephew," said my uncle, when we were flying onwards towards Reigate. "If they drove so hard, it looks as though they wished to get early to work."

"Jim and Belcher would surely be a match for the four of them," I suggested.

"If Belcher were with him I should have no fear. But you cannot tell what *diablerie* they may be up to. Let us only find him safe and sound, and I'll never lose sight of him until I see him in the ring. We'll sit up on guard with our pistols, nephew, and I only trust that these villains may be indiscreet enough to attempt it. But they must have been very sure of success before they put the odds up to such a figure, and it is that which alarms me."

"But surely they have nothing to win by such villainy, sir? If they were to hurt Jim Harrison the battle could not be fought, and the bets would not be decided."

"So it would be in an ordinary prize-battle, nephew; and it is fortunate that it should be so, or the rascals who infest the ring would soon make all sport impossible. But here it is different. On the terms of the wager I lose unless I can produce a man, within the prescribed ages, who can beat Crab Wilson. You must remember that I have never named my man. *C'est dommage*, but so it is! We know who it is and so do our opponents, but the referees and stakeholder would take no notice of that. If we complain that Jim Harrison has been crippled, they would answer that they have no official knowledge that

Jim Harrison was our nominee. It's play or pay, and the villains are taking advantage of it."

My uncle's fears as to our being blocked upon the road were only too well founded, for after we passed Reigate there was such a procession of every sort of vehicle, that I believe for the whole eight miles there was not a horse whose nose was further than a few feet from the back of the curricle or barouche in front. Every road leading from London, as well as those from Guildford in the west and Tunbridge in the east, had contributed their stream of four-in-hands, gigs, and mounted sportsmen, until the whole broad Brighton highway was choked from ditch to ditch with a laughing, singing, shouting throng, all flowing in the same direction. No man who looked upon that motley crowd could deny that, for good or evil, the love of the ring was confined to no class, but was a national peculiarity, deeply seated in the English nature, and a common heritage of the young aristocrat in his drag and of the rough costers sitting six deep in their pony cart. There I saw statesmen and soldiers, noblemen and lawyers, farmers and squires, with roughs of the East End and yokels of the shires, all toiling along with the prospect of a night of discomfort before them, on the chance of seeing a fight which might, for all that they knew, be decided in a single round. A more cheery and hearty set of people could not be imagined, and the chaff flew about as thick as the dust clouds, while at every wayside inn the landlord and the drawers would be out with trays of foam-headed tankards to moisten those importunate throats. The ale-drinking, the rude good-fellowship, the heartiness, the laughter at discomforts, the craving to see the fight—all these may be set down as vulgar and trivial by those to whom they are distasteful; but to me, listening to the far-off and uncertain echoes of our distant past, they seem to have been the very bones upon which much that is most solid and virile in this ancient race was moulded.

But, alas for our chance of hastening onwards! Even my uncle's skill could not pick a passage through that moving mass. We could but fall into our places and be content to snail along from Reigate to Horley and on to Povey Cross and over Lowfield Heath, while day shaded away into twilight, and that deepened into night. At Kimberham Bridge the carriage-lamps were all lit, and it was wonderful, where the road curved downwards before us, to see this writhing serpent with the golden scales crawling before us in the darkness. And then, at last, we saw the formless mass of the huge Crawley elm looming before us in the gloom, and there was the broad village street with the glimmer of the cottage windows, and the high front of the old George Inn, glowing from every door and pane and crevice, in honour of the noble company who were to sleep within that night.

CHAPTER XV—FOUL PLAY

My uncle's impatience would not suffer him to wait for the slow rotation which would bring us to the door, but he flung the reins and a crown-piece to one of the rough fellows who thronged the side-walk, and pushing his way vigorously through the crowd, he made for the entrance. As he came within the circle of light thrown by the windows, a whisper ran round as to who this masterful gentleman with the pale face and the driving-coat might be, and a lane was formed to admit us. I had never before understood the popularity of my uncle in the sporting world, for the folk began to huzza as we passed with cries of "Hurrah for Buck Tregellis! Good luck to you and your man, Sir Charles! Clear a path for a bang-up noble Corinthian!" whilst the landlord, attracted by the shouting, came running out to greet us.

"Good evening, Sir Charles!" he cried. "I hope I see you well, sir, and I trust that you will find that your man does credit to the George."

"How is he?" asked my uncle, quickly.

"Never better, sir. Looks a picture, he does—and fit to fight for a kingdom."

My uncle gave a sigh of relief.

"Where is he?" he asked.

"He's gone to his room early, sir, seein' that he had some very partic'lar business to-morrow mornin'," said the landlord, grinning.

"Where is Belcher?"

"Here he is, in the bar parlour."

He opened a door as he spoke, and looking in we saw a score of well-dressed men, some of whose faces had become familiar to me during my short West End career, seated round a table upon which stood a steaming soup-tureen filled with punch. At the further end, very much at his ease amongst the aristocrats and exquisites who surrounded him, sat the Champion of England, his superb figure thrown back in his chair, a flush upon his handsome face, and a loose red handkerchief knotted carelessly round his throat in the picturesque fashion which was long known by his name. Half a century has passed since then, and I have seen my share of fine men. Perhaps it is because I am a slight creature myself, but it is my peculiarity that I had rather look upon a splendid man than upon any work of Nature. Yet during all that time I have never seen a finer man than Jim Belcher, and if I wish to match him in my memory, I can only turn to that other Jim whose fate and fortunes I am trying to lay before you.

There was a shout of jovial greeting when my uncle's face was seen in the doorway.

"Come in, Tregellis!" "We were expecting you!" "There's a devilled bladebone ordered." "What's the latest from London?" "What is the meaning of the long odds against your man?" "Have the folk gone mad?" "What the devil is it all about?" They were all talking at once.

"Excuse me, gentlemen," my uncle answered. "I shall be happy to give you any information in my power a little later. I have a matter of some slight importance to decide. Belcher, I would have a word with you!"

The Champion came out with us into the passage.

"Where is your man, Belcher?"

"He has gone to his room, sir. I believe that he should have a clear twelve hours' sleep before fighting."

"What sort of day has he had?"

"I did him lightly in the matter of exercise. Clubs, dumbbells, walking, and a half-hour with the mufflers. He'll do us all proud, sir, or

I'm a Dutchman! But what in the world's amiss with the betting? If I didn't know that he was as straight as a line, I'd ha' thought he was planning a cross and laying against himself."

"It's about that I've hurried down. I have good information, Belcher, that there has been a plot to cripple him, and that the rogues are so sure of success that they are prepared to lay anything against his appearance."

Belcher whistled between his teeth.

"I've seen no sign of anything of the kind, sir. No one has been near him or had speech with him, except only your nephew there and myself."

"Four villains, with Berks at their head, got the start of us by several hours. It was Warr who told me."

"What Bill Warr says is straight, and what Joe Berks does is crooked. Who were the others, sir?"

"Red Ike, Fighting Yussef, and Chris McCarthy."

"A pretty gang, too! Well, sir, the lad is safe, but it would be as well, perhaps, for one or other of us to stay in his room with him. For my own part, as long as he's my charge I'm never very far away."

"It is a pity to wake him."

"He can hardly be asleep with all this racket in the house. This way, sir, and down the passage!"

We passed along the low-roofed, devious corridors of the old-fashioned inn to the back of the house.

"This is my room, sir," said Belcher, nodding to a door upon the right. "This one upon the left is his." He threw it open as he spoke. "Here's Sir Charles Tregellis come to see you, Jim," said he; and then, "Good Lord, what is the meaning of this?"

The little chamber lay before us brightly illuminated by a brass lamp which stood upon the table. The bedclothes had not been turned down, but there was an indentation upon the counterpane which showed that some one had lain there. One-half of the lattice window was swinging on its hinge, and a cloth cap lying upon the table was the only sign of the occupant. My uncle looked round him and shook his head.

"It seems that we are too late," said he.

"That's his cap, sir. Where in the world can he have gone to with his head bare? I thought he was safe in his bed an hour ago. Jim! Jim!" he shouted.

"He has certainly gone through the window," cried my uncle. "I believe these villains have enticed him out by some devilish device of their own. Hold the lamp, nephew. Ha! I thought so. Here are his footmarks upon the flower-bed outside."

The landlord, and one or two of the Corinthians from the bar-parlour, had followed us to the back of the house. Some one had opened the side door, and we found ourselves in the kitchen garden, where, clustering upon the gravel path, we were able to hold the lamp over the soft, newly turned earth which lay between us and the window.

"That's his footmark!" said Belcher. "He wore his running boots this evening, and you can see the nails. But what's this? Some one else has been here."

"A woman!" I cried.

"By Heaven, you're right, nephew," said my uncle.

Belcher gave a hearty curse.

"He never had a word to say to any girl in the village. I took partic'lar notice of that. And to think of them coming in like this at the last moment!"

"It's clear as possible, Tregellis," said the Hon. Berkeley Craven, who was one of the company from the bar-parlour. "Whoever it was came outside the window and tapped. You see here, and here, the small feet have their toes to the house, while the others are all leading away. She came to summon him, and he followed her."

"That is perfectly certain," said my uncle. "There's not a moment to be lost. We must divide and search in different directions, unless we can get some clue as to where they have gone."

"There's only the one path out of the garden," cried the landlord, leading the way. "It opens out into this back lane, which leads up to the stables. The other end of the lane goes out into the side road."

The bright yellow glare from a stable lantern cut a ring suddenly from the darkness, and an ostler came lounging out of the yard.

"Who's that?" cried the landlord.

"It's me, master! Bill Shields."

"How long have you been there, Bill?"

"Well, master, I've been in an' out of the stables this hour back. We can't pack in another 'orse, and there's no use tryin'. I daren't 'ardly give them their feed, for, if they was to thicken out just ever so little—"

"See here, Bill. Be careful how you answer, for a mistake may cost you your place. Have you seen any one pass down the lane?"

"There was a feller in a rabbit-skin cap some time ago. 'E was loiterin' about until I asked 'im what 'is business was, for I didn't care about the looks of 'im, or the way that 'e was peepin' in at the windows. I turned the stable lantern on to 'im, but 'e ducked 'is face, an' I could only swear to 'is red 'ead."

I cast a quick glance at my uncle, and I saw that the shadow had deepened upon his face.

"What became of him?" he asked.

"'E slouched away, sir, an' I saw the last of 'im."

"You've seen no one else? You didn't, for example, see a woman and a man pass down the lane together?"

"No, sir."

"Or hear anything unusual?"

"Why, now that you mention it, sir, I did 'ear somethin'; but on a night like this, when all these London blades are in the village—"

"What was it, then?" cried my uncle, impatiently.

"Well, sir, it was a kind of a cry out yonder as if some one 'ad got 'imself into trouble. I thought, maybe, two sparks were fightin', and I took no partic'lar notice."

"Where did it come from?"

"From the side road, yonder."

"Was it distant?"

"No, sir; I should say it didn't come from more'n two hundred yards."

"A single cry?"

"Well, it was a kind of screech, sir, and then I 'eard somebody drivin' very 'ard down the road. I remember thinking that it was strange that any one should be driving away from Crawley on a great night like this."

My uncle seized the lantern from the fellow's hand, and we all trooped behind him down the lane. At the further end the road cut it across at right angles. Down this my uncle hastened, but his search was not a long one, for the glaring light fell suddenly upon something which brought a groan to my lips and a bitter curse to those of Jem Belcher. Along the white surface of the dusty highway there was drawn a long smear of crimson, while beside this ominous stain there lay a murderous little pocket-bludgeon, such as Warr had described in the morning.

CHAPTER XVI—CRAWLEY DOWNS

All through that weary night my uncle and I, with Belcher, Berkeley Craven, and a dozen of the Corinthians, searched the country side for some trace of our missing man, but save for that ill-boding splash upon the road not the slightest clue could be obtained as to what had befallen him. No one had seen or heard anything of him, and the single cry in the night of which the ostler told us was the only indication of the tragedy which had taken place. In small parties we scoured the country as far as East Grinstead and Bletchingley, and the sun had been long over the horizon before we found ourselves back at Crawley once more with heavy hearts and tired feet. My uncle, who had driven to Reigate in the hope of gaining some intelligence, did not return until past seven o'clock, and a glance at his face gave us the same black news which he gathered from ours.

We held a council round our dismal breakfast-table, to which Mr. Berkeley Craven was invited as a man of sound wisdom and large experience in matters of sport. Belcher was half frenzied by this sudden ending of all the pains which he had taken in the training, and could only rave out threats at Berks and his companions, with terrible menaces as to what he would do when he met them. My uncle sat grave and thoughtful, eating nothing and drumming his fingers upon the table, while my heart was heavy within me, and I could have sunk my face into my hands and burst into tears as I thought how power-less I was to aid my friend. Mr. Craven, a fresh-faced, alert man of the world, was the only one of us who seemed to preserve both his wits and his appetite.

"Let me see! The fight was to be at ten, was it not?" he asked.

"It was to be."

"I dare say it will be, too. Never say die, Tregellis! Your man has still three hours in which to come back."

My uncle shook his head.

"The villains have done their work too well for that, I fear," said he.

"Well, now, let us reason it out," said Berkeley Craven. "A woman comes and she coaxes this young man out of his room. Do you know any young woman who had an influence over him?"

My uncle looked at me.

"No," said I. "I know of none."

"Well, we know that she came," said Berkeley Craven. "There can be no question as to that. She brought some piteous tale, no doubt, such as a gallant young man could hardly refuse to listen to. He fell into the trap, and allowed himself to be decoyed to the place where these rascals were waiting for him. We may take all that as proved, I should fancy, Tregellis."

"I see no better explanation," said my uncle.

"Well, then, it is obviously not the interest of these men to kill him. Warr heard them say as much. They could not make sure, perhaps, of doing so tough a young fellow an injury which would certainly prevent him from fighting. Even with a broken arm he might pull the fight off, as men have done before. There was too much money on for them to run any risks. They gave him a tap on the head, therefore, to prevent his mak-ing too much resistance, and they then drove him off to some farmhouse or stable, where they will hold him a prisoner until the time for the fight is over. I warrant that you see him before to-night as well as ever he was."

This theory sounded so reasonable that it seemed to lift a little of the weight from my heart, but I could see that from my uncle's point of view it was a poor consolation.

"I dare say you are right, Craven," said he.

"I am sure that I am."

"But it won't help us to win the fight."

"That's the point, sir," cried Belcher. "By the Lord, I wish they'd let me take his place, even with my left arm strapped behind me."

"I should advise you in any case to go to the ringside," said Craven. "You should hold on until the last moment in the hope of your man turning up."

"I shall certainly do so. And I shall protest against paying the wagers under such circumstances."

Craven shrugged his shoulders.

"You remember the conditions of the match," said he. "I fear it is pay or play. No doubt the point might be submitted to the referees, but I cannot doubt that they would have to give it against you."

We had sunk into a melancholy silence, when suddenly Belcher sprang up from the table.

"Hark!" he cried. "Listen to that!"

"What is it?" we cried, all three.

"The betting! Listen again!"

Out of the babel of voices and roaring of wheels outside the window a single sentence struck sharply on our ears.

"Even money upon Sir Charles's nominee!"

"Even money!" cried my uncle. "It was seven to one against me, yesterday. What is the meaning of this?"

"Even money either way," cried the voice again.

"There's somebody knows something," said Belcher, "and there's nobody has a better right to know what it is than we. Come on, sir, and we'll get to the bottom of it."

The village street was packed with people, for they had been sleeping twelve and fifteen in a room, whilst hundreds of gentlemen had spent the night in their carriages. So thick was the throng that it was no easy matter to get out of the George. A drunken man, snoring horribly in his breathing, was curled up in the passage, absolutely oblivious to the stream of people who flowed round and occasionally over him.

"What's the betting, boys?" asked Belcher, from the steps.

"Even money, Jim," cried several voices.

"It was long odds on Wilson when last I heard."

"Yes; but there came a man who laid freely the other way, and he started others taking the odds, until now you can get even money."

"Who started it?"

"Why, that's he! The man that lies drunk in the passage. He's been pouring it down like water ever since he drove in at six o'clock, so it's no wonder he's like that."

Belcher stooped down and turned over the man's inert head so as to show his features.

"He's a stranger to me, sir."

"And to me," added my uncle.

"But not to me," I cried. "It's John Cumming, the landlord of the inn at Friar's Oak. I've known him ever since I was a boy, and I can't be mistaken."

"Well, what the devil can he know about it?" said Craven.

"Nothing at all, in all probability," answered my uncle. "He is backing young Jim because he knows him, and because he has more brandy than sense. His drunken confidence set others to do the same, and so the odds came down."

"He was as sober as a judge when he drove in here this morning," said the landlord. "He began backing Sir Charles's nominee from the moment he arrived. Some of the other boys took the office from him, and they very soon brought the odds down amongst them."

"I wish he had not brought himself down as well," said my uncle. "I beg that you will bring me a little lavender water, landlord, for the smell of this crowd is appalling. I suppose you could not get any sense from this drunken fellow, nephew, or find out what it is he knows."

It was in vain that I rocked him by the shoulder and shouted his name in his ear. Nothing could break in upon that serene intoxication.

"Well, it's a unique situation as far as my experience goes," said Berkeley Craven. "Here we are within a couple of hours of the fight, and yet you don't know whether you have a man to represent you. I hope you don't stand to lose very much, Tregellis."

My uncle shrugged his shoulders carelessly, and took a pinch of his snuff with that inimitable sweeping gesture which no man has ever ventured to imitate.

"Pretty well, my boy!" said he. "But it is time that we thought of going up to the Downs. This night journey has left me just a little *effleuré*, and I should like half an hour of privacy to arrange my toilet. If this is my last kick, it shall at least be with a well-brushed boot."

I have heard a traveller from the wilds of America say that he looked upon the Red Indian and the English gentleman as closely akin, citing the passion for sport, the aloofness and the suppression of the emotions in each. I thought of his words as I watched my uncle that morning, for I believe that no victim tied to the stake could have had a worse outlook before him. It was not merely that his own fortunes were largely at stake, but it was the dreadful position in which he would stand before this immense concourse of people, many of whom had put their money upon his judgment, if he should find himself at the last moment with an impotent excuse instead of a champion to put before them. What a situation for a man who prided himself upon his aplomb, and upon bringing all that he undertook to the very highest standard of success! I, who knew him well, could tell from his wan cheeks and his restless fingers that he was at his wit's ends what to do; but no stranger who observed his jaunty bearing, the flecking of his laced handkerchief, the handling of his quizzing glass, or the shooting of his ruffles, would ever have thought that this butterfly creature could have had a care upon earth.

It was close upon nine o'clock when we were ready to start for the Downs, and by that time my uncle's curricle was almost the only vehicle left in the village street. The night before they had lain with their wheels interlocking and their shafts under each other's bodies, as thick as they could fit, from the old church to the Crawley Elm, spanning the road five-deep for a good half-mile in length. Now the grey village street lay before us almost deserted save by a few women and children.

Men, horses, carriages—all were gone. My uncle drew on his driving-gloves and arranged his costume with punctilious neatness; but I observed that he glanced up and down the road with a haggard and yet expectant eye before he took his seat. I sat behind with Belcher, while the Hon. Berkeley Craven took the place beside him.

The road from Crawley curves gently upwards to the upland heather-clad plateau which extends for many miles in every direction. Strings of pedestrians, most of them so weary and dust-covered that it was evident that they had walked the thirty miles from London during the night, were plodding along by the sides of the road or trailing over the long mottled slopes of the moorland. A horseman, fantastically dressed in green and splendidly mounted, was waiting at the cross-roads, and as he spurred towards us I recognised the dark, handsome face and bold black eyes of Mendoza.

"I am waiting here to give the office, Sir Charles," said he. "It's down the Grinstead road, half a mile to the left."

"Very good," said my uncle, reining his mares round into the cross-road.

"You haven't got your man there," remarked Mendoza, with something of suspicion in his manner.

"What the devil is that to you?" cried Belcher, furiously.

"It's a good deal to all of us, for there are some funny stories about."

"You keep them to yourself, then, or you may wish you had never heard them."

"All right, Jem! Your breakfast don't seem to have agreed with you this morning."

"Have the others arrived?" asked my uncle, carelessly.

"Not yet, Sir Charles. But Tom Oliver is there with the ropes and stakes. Jackson drove by just now, and most of the ring-keepers are up."

"We have still an hour," remarked my uncle, as he drove on. "It is possible that the others may be late, since they have to come from Reigate."

"You take it like a man, Tregellis," said Craven. "We must keep a bold face and brazen it out until the last moment."

"Of course, sir," cried Belcher. "I'll never believe the betting would rise like that if somebody didn't know something. We'll hold on by our teeth and nails, Sir Charles, and see what comes of it."

We could hear a sound like the waves upon the beach, long before we came in sight of that mighty multitude, and then at last, on a sudden dip of the road, we saw it lying before us, a whirlpool of humanity with an open vortex in the centre. All round, the thousands of carriages and horses were dotted over the moor, and the slopes were gay with tents and booths. A spot had been chosen for the ring, where a great basin had been hollowed out in the ground, so that all round that natural amphitheatre a crowd of thirty thousand people could see very well what was going on in the centre. As we drove up a buzz of greeting came from the people upon the fringe which was nearest to us, spreading and spreading, until the whole multitude had joined in the acclamation. Then an instant later a second shout broke forth, beginning from the other side of the arena, and the faces which had been turned towards us whisked round, so that in a twinkling the whole foreground changed from white to dark.

"It's they. They are in time," said my uncle and Craven together.

Standing up on our curricle, we could see the cavalcade approaching over the Downs. In front came a huge yellow barouche, in which sat Sir Lothian Hume, Crab Wilson, and Captain Barclay, his trainer. The postillions were flying canary-yellow ribands from their caps, those being the colours under which Wilson was to fight. Behind the carriage there rode a hundred or more noblemen and gentlemen of the west country, and then a line of gigs, tilburies, and carriages wound away down the Grinstead road as far as our eyes could follow it. The big barouche came lumbering over the sward in our direction until Sir Lothian Hume caught sight of us, when he shouted to his postillions to pull up.

"Good morning, Sir Charles," said he, springing out of the carriage. "I thought I knew your scarlet curricle. We have an excellent morning for the battle."

My uncle bowed coldly, and made no answer.

"I suppose that since we are all here we may begin at once," said Sir Lothian, taking no notice of the other's manner.

"We begin at ten o'clock. Not an instant before."

"Very good, if you prefer it. By the way, Sir Charles, where is your man?"

"I would ask you that question, Sir Lothian," answered my uncle. "Where is my man?"

A look of astonishment passed over Sir Lothian's features, which, if it were not real, was most admirably affected.

"What do you mean by asking me such a question?"

"Because I wish to know."

"But how can I tell, and what business is it of mine?"

"I have reason to believe that you have made it your business."

"If you would kindly put the matter a little more clearly there would be some possibility of my understanding you."

They were both very white and cold, formal and unimpassioned in their bearing, but exchanging glances which crossed like rapier blades. I thought of Sir Lothian's murderous repute as a duellist, and I trembled for my uncle.

"Now, sir, if you imagine that you have a grievance against me, you will oblige me vastly by putting it into words."

"I will," said my uncle. "There has been a conspiracy to maim or kidnap my man, and I have every reason to believe that you are privy to it."

An ugly sneer came over Sir Lothian's saturnine face.

"I see," said he. "Your man has not come on quite as well as you had expected in his training, and you are hard put to it to invent an excuse. Still, I should have thought that you might have found a more probable one, and one which would entail less serious consequences."

"Sir," answered my uncle, "you are a liar, but how great a liar you are nobody knows save yourself."

Sir Lothian's hollow cheeks grew white with passion, and I saw for an instant in his deep-set eyes such a glare as comes from the frenzied hound rearing and ramping at the end of its chain. Then, with an effort, he became the same cold, hard, self-contained man as ever.

"It does not become our position to quarrel like two yokels at a fair," said he; "we shall go further into the matter afterwards."

"I promise you that we shall," answered my uncle, grimly.

"Meanwhile, I hold you to the terms of your wager. Unless you produce your nominee within five-and-twenty minutes, I claim the match."

"Eight-and-twenty minutes," said my uncle, looking at his watch. "You may claim it then, but not an instant before."

He was admirable at that moment, for his manner was that of a man with all sorts of hidden resources, so that I could hardly make myself realize as I looked at him that our position was really as desperate as I knew it to be. In the meantime Berkeley Craven, who had been exchanging a few words with Sir Lothian Hume, came back to our side.

"I have been asked to be sole referee in this matter," said he. "Does that meet with your wishes, Sir Charles?"

"I should be vastly obliged to you, Craven, if you will undertake the duties."

"And Jackson has been suggested as timekeeper."

"I could not wish a better one."

"Very good. That is settled."

In the meantime the last of the carriages had come up, and the horses had all been picketed upon the moor. The stragglers who had dotted the grass had closed in until the huge crowd was one unit with a single mighty voice, which was already beginning to bellow its impatience. Looking round, there was hardly a moving object upon the whole vast expanse of green and purple down. A belated gig was coming at full gallop down the road which led from the south, and a few pedestrians were still trailing up from Crawley, but nowhere was there a sign of the missing man.

"The betting keeps up for all that," said Belcher. "I've just been to the ring-side, and it is still even."

"There's a place for you at the outer ropes, Sir Charles," said Craven.

"There is no sign of my man yet. I won't come in until he arrives."

"It is my duty to tell you that only ten minutes are left."

"I make it five," cried Sir Lothian Hume.

"That is a question which lies with the referee," said Craven, firmly. "My watch makes it ten minutes, and ten it must be."

"Here's Crab Wilson!" cried Belcher, and at the same moment a shout like a thunderclap burst from the crowd. The west countryman had emerged from his dressing-tent, followed by Dutch Sam and Tom Owen, who were acting as his seconds. He was nude to the waist, with a pair of white calico drawers, white silk stockings, and running shoes. Round his middle was a canary-yellow sash, and dainty little ribbons of the same colour fluttered from the sides of his knees. He carried a high white hat in his hand, and running down the lane which had been kept open through the crowd to allow persons to reach the ring, he threw the hat high into the air, so that it fell within the staked inclosure. Then with a double spring he cleared the outer and inner line of rope, and stood with his arms folded in the centre.

I do not wonder that the people cheered. Even Belcher could not help joining in the general shout of applause. He was certainly a splendidly built young athlete, and one could not have wished to look upon a finer sight as his white skin, sleek and luminous as a panther's, gleamed in the light of the morning sun, with a beautiful liquid rippling of muscles at every movement. His arms were long and slingy, his shoulders loose and yet powerful, with the downward slant which is a surer index of power than squareness can be. He clasped his hands behind his head, threw them aloft, and swung them backwards, and at every movement some fresh expanse of his smooth, white skin became knobbed and gnarled with muscles, whilst a yell of admiration and delight from the crowd greeted each fresh exhibition. Then, folding his arms once more, he stood like a beautiful statue waiting for his antagonist.

Sir Lothian Hume had been looking impatiently at his watch, and now he shut it with a triumphant snap.

"Time's up!" he cried. "The match is forfeit."

"Time is not up," said Craven.

"I have still five minutes." My uncle looked round with despairing eyes.

"Only three, Tregellis!"

A deep angry murmur was rising from the crowd.

"It's a cross! It's a cross! It's a fake!" was the cry.

"Two minutes, Tregellis!"

"Where's your man, Sir Charles? Where's the man that we have backed?" Flushed faces began to crane over each other, and angry eyes glared up at us.

"One more minute, Tregellis! I am very sorry, but it will be my duty to declare it forfeit against you."

There was a sudden swirl in the crowd, a rush, a shout, and high up in the air there spun an old black hat, floating over the heads of the ring-siders and flickering down within the ropes.

"Saved, by the Lord!" screamed Belcher.

"I rather fancy," said my uncle, calmly, "that this must be my man."

"Too late!" cried Sir Lothian.

"No," answered the referee. "It was still twenty seconds to the hour. The fight will now proceed."

CHAPTER XVII—THE RING-SIDE

Out of the whole of that vast multitude I was one of the very few who had observed whence it was that this black hat, skimming so opportunely over the ropes, had come. I have already remarked that when we looked around us there had been a single gig travelling very rapidly upon the southern road. My uncle's eyes had rested upon it, but his attention had been drawn away by the discussion between Sir Lothian Hume and the referee upon the question of time. For my own part, I had been so struck by the furious manner in which these belated travellers were approaching, that I had continued to watch them with all sorts of vague hopes within me, which I did not dare to put into words for fear of adding to my uncle's disappointments. I had just made out that the gig contained a man and a woman, when suddenly I saw it swerve off the road, and come with a galloping horse and bounding wheels right across the moor, crashing through the gorse bushes, and sinking down to the hubs in the heather and bracken. As the driver pulled up his foam-spattered horse, he threw the reins to his companion, sprang from his seat, butted furiously into the crowd, and then an instant afterwards up went the hat which told of his challenge and defiance.

"There is no hurry now, I presume, Craven," said my uncle, as coolly as if this sudden effect had been carefully devised by him.

"Now that your man has his hat in the ring you can take as much time as you like, Sir Charles."

"Your friend has certainly cut it rather fine, nephew."

"It is not Jim, sir," I whispered. "It is some one else."

My uncle's eyebrows betrayed his astonishment.

"Some one else!" he ejaculated.

"And a good man too!" roared Belcher, slapping his thigh with a crack like a pistol-shot. "Why, blow my dickey if it ain't old Jack Harrison himself!"

Looking down at the crowd, we had seen the head and shoulders of a powerful and strenuous man moving slowly forward, and leaving behind him a long V-shaped ripple upon its surface like the wake of a swimming dog. Now, as he pushed his way through the looser fringe the head was raised, and there was the grinning, hardy face of the smith looking up at us. He had left his hat in the ring, and was enveloped in an overcoat with a blue bird's-eye handkerchief tied round his neck. As he emerged from the throng he let his great-coat fly loose, and showed that he was dressed in his full fighting kit—black drawers, chocolate stockings, and white shoes.

"I'm right sorry to be so late, Sir Charles," he cried. "I'd have been sooner, but it took me a little time to make it all straight with the missus. I couldn't convince her all at once, an' so I brought her with me, and we argued it out on the way."

Looking at the gig, I saw that it was indeed Mrs. Harrison who was seated in it. Sir Charles beckoned him up to the wheel of the curricle.

"What in the world brings you here, Harrison?" he whispered. "I am as glad to see you as ever I was to see a man in my life, but I confess that I did not expect you."

"Well, sir, you heard I was coming," said the smith.

"Indeed, I did not."

"Didn't you get a message, Sir Charles, from a man named Cumming, landlord of the Friar's Oak Inn? Mister Rodney there would know him."

"We saw him dead drunk at the George."

"There, now, if I wasn't afraid of it!" cried Harrison, angrily. "He's always like that when he's excited, and I never saw a man more off his head than he was when he heard I was going to take this job over. He brought a bag of sovereigns up with him to back me with."

"That's how the betting got turned," said my uncle. "He found others to follow his lead, it appears."

"I was so afraid that he might get upon the drink that I made him promise to go straight to you, sir, the very instant he should arrive. He had a note to deliver."

"I understand that he reached the George at six, whilst I did not return from Reigate until after seven, by which time I have no doubt that he had drunk his message to me out of his head. But where is your nephew Jim, and how did you come to know that you would be needed?"

"It is not his fault, I promise you, that you should be left in the lurch. As to me, I had my orders to take his place from the only man upon earth whose word I have never disobeyed."

"Yes, Sir Charles," said Mrs. Harrison, who had left the gig and approached us. "You can make the most of it this time, for never again shall you have my Jack—not if you were to go on your knees for him."

"She's not a patron of sport, and that's a fact," said the smith.

"Sport!" she cried, with shrill contempt and anger. "Tell me when all is over."

She hurried away, and I saw her afterwards seated amongst the bracken, her back turned towards the multitude, and her hands over her ears, cowering and wincing in an agony of apprehension.

Whilst this hurried scene had been taking place, the crowd had become more and more tumultuous, partly from their impatience at the delay, and partly from their exuberant spirits at the unexpected chance of seeing so celebrated a fighting man as Harrison. His identity had already been noised abroad, and many an elderly connoisseur plucked his long net-purse out of his fob, in order to put a few guineas upon the man who would represent the school of the past against the present. The younger men were still in favour of the west-countryman, and small odds were to be had either way in proportion to the number of the supporters of each in the different parts of the crowd.

In the mean time Sir Lothian Hume had come bustling up to the Honourable Berkeley Craven, who was still standing near our curricle.

"I beg to lodge a formal protest against these proceedings," said he.

"On what grounds, sir?"

"Because the man produced is not the original nominee of Sir Charles Tregellis."

"I never named one, as you are well aware," said my uncle.

"The betting has all been upon the understanding that young Jim Harrison was my man's opponent. Now, at the last moment, he is withdrawn and another and more formidable man put into his place."

"Sir Charles Tregellis is quite within his rights," said Craven, firmly. "He undertook to produce a man who should be within the age limits stipulated, and I understand that Harrison fulfils all the conditions. You are over five-and-thirty, Harrison?"

"Forty-one next month, master."

"Very good. I direct that the fight proceed."

But alas! there was one authority which was higher even than that of the referee, and we were destined to an experience which was the prelude, and sometimes the conclusion, also, of many an old-time fight. Across the moor there had ridden a black-coated gentleman, with buff-topped hunting-boots and a couple of grooms behind him, the little knot of horsemen showing up clearly upon the curving swells and then dipping down into the alternate hollows. Some of the more observant of the crowd had glanced suspiciously at this advancing figure, but the majority had not observed him at all until he reined up his horse upon a knoll which overlooked the amphitheatre, and in a stentorian voice announced that he represented the Custos rotulorum of His Majesty's county of Sussex, that he proclaimed this assembly to be gathered together for an illegal purpose, and that he was commissioned to disperse it by force, if necessary.

Never before had I understood that deep-seated fear and whole-some respect which many centuries of bludgeoning at the hands of the law had beaten into the fierce and turbulent natives of these islands. Here was a man with two attendants upon one side, and on the other thirty thousand very angry and disappointed people, many of them fighters by profession, and some from the roughest and most dangerous classes in the country. And yet it was the single man who appealed confidently to force, whilst the huge multitude swayed and murmured like a mutinous fierce-willed creature brought face to face with a power against which it knew that there was neither argument nor resistance. My uncle, however, with Berkeley Craven, Sir John Lade, and a dozen other lords and gentlemen, hurried across to the interrupter of the sport.

"I presume that you have a warrant, sir?" said Craven.

"Yes, sir, I have a warrant."

"Then I have a legal right to inspect it."

The magistrate handed him a blue paper which the little knot of gentlemen clustered their heads over, for they were mostly magistrates themselves, and were keenly alive to any possible flaw in the wording. At last Craven shrugged his shoulders, and handed it back.

"This seems to be correct, sir," said he.

"It is entirely correct," answered the magistrate, affably. "To prevent waste of your valuable time, gentlemen, I may say, once for all, that it is my unalterable determination that no fight shall, under any circum-stances, be brought off in the county over which I have control, and I am prepared to follow you all day in order to prevent it."

To my inexperience this appeared to bring the whole matter to a conclusion, but I had underrated the foresight of those who arrange these affairs, and also the advantages which made Crawley Down so favourite a rendezvous. There was a hurried consultation between the principals, the backers, the referee, and the timekeeper.

"It's seven miles to Hampshire border and about two to Surrey," said Jackson. The famous Master of the Ring was clad in honour of the occasion in a most resplendent scarlet coat worked in gold at the buttonholes, a white stock, a looped hat with a broad black band, buff knee-breeches, white silk stockings, and paste buckles—a costume which did justice to his magnificent figure, and especially to those famous "balustrade" calves which had helped him to be the finest runner and jumper as well as the most formidable pugilist in England. His hard, high-boned face, large piercing eyes, and immense physique made him a fitting leader for that rough and tumultuous body who had named him as their commander-in-chief.

"If I might venture to offer you a word of advice," said the affable official, "it would be to make for the Hampshire line, for Sir James Ford, on the Surrey border, has as great an objection to such assemblies as I have, whilst Mr. Merridew, of Long Hall, who is the Hampshire magistrate, has fewer scruples upon the point."

"Sir," said my uncle, raising his hat in his most impressive manner, "I am infinitely obliged to you. With the referee's permission, there is nothing for it but to shift the stakes."

In an instant a scene of the wildest animation had set in. Tom Owen and his assistant, Fogo, with the help of the ring-keepers, plucked up the stakes and ropes, and carried them off across country. Crab Wilson was enveloped in great coats, and borne away in the barouche, whilst Champion Harrison took Mr. Craven's place in our curricle. Then, off the huge crowd started, horsemen, vehicles, and pedestrians, rolling slowly over the broad face of the moorland. The carriages rocked and pitched like boats in a seaway, as they lumbered along, fifty abreast, scrambling and lurching over everything which came in their way. Sometimes, with a snap and a thud, one axle would come to the ground, whilst a wheel reeled off amidst the tussocks of heather, and roars of delight greeted the owners as they looked ruefully at the ruin. Then as the gorse clumps grew thinner, and the sward more level, those on foot began to run, the riders struck in their spurs, the drivers cracked their whips, and away they all streamed in the maddest, wildest cross-country steeplechase, the yellow barouche and the crimson curricle, which held the two champions, leading the van.

"What do you think of your chances, Harrison?" I heard my uncle ask, as the two mares picked their way over the broken ground.

"It's my last fight, Sir Charles," said the smith. "You heard the missus say that if she let me off this time I was never to ask again. I must try and make it a good one."

"But your training?"

"I'm always in training, sir. I work hard from morning to night, and I drink little else than water. I don't think that Captain Barclay can do much better with all his rules."

"He's rather long in the reach for you."

"I've fought and beat them that were longer. If it comes to a rally I should hold my own, and I should have the better of him at a throw."

"It's a match of youth against experience. Well, I would not hedge a guinea of my money. But, unless he was acting under force, I cannot forgive young Jim for having deserted me."

"He was acting under force, Sir Charles."

"You have seen him, then?"

"No, master, I have not seen him."

"You know where he is?"

"Well, it is not for me to say one way or the other. I can only tell you that he could not help himself. But here's the beak a-comin' for us again."

The ominous figure galloped up once more alongside of our curricle, but this time his mission was a more amiable one.

"My jurisdiction ends at that ditch, sir," said he. "I should fancy that you could hardly wish a better place for a mill than the sloping field beyond. I am quite sure that no one will interfere with you there."

His anxiety that the fight should be brought off was in such contrast to the zeal with which he had chased us from his county, that my uncle could not help remarking upon it.

"It is not for a magistrate to wink at the breaking of the law, sir," he answered. "But if my colleague of Hampshire has no scruples about its being brought off within his jurisdiction, I should very much like to see the fight," with which he spurred his horse up an adjacent knoll, from which he thought that he might gain the best view of the proceedings.

And now I had a view of all those points of etiquette and curious survivals of custom which are so recent, that we have not yet appreciated that they may some day be as interesting to the social historian as they then were to the sportsman. A dignity was given to the contest by a rigid code of ceremony, just as the clash of mail-clad knights was prefaced and adorned by the calling of the heralds and the showing of blazoned shields. To many in those ancient days the tourney may have seemed a bloody and brutal ordeal, but we who look at it with ample perspective see that it was a rude but gallant preparation for the conditions of life in an iron age. And so also, when the ring has become as extinct as the lists, we may understand that a broader philosophy would show that all things, which spring up so naturally and spontaneously, have a function to fulfil, and that it is a less evil that two men should, of their own free will, fight until they can fight no more than that the standard of hardihood and endurance should run the slightest risk of being lowered in a nation which depends so largely upon the individual qualities of her citizens for her defence. Do away with war, if the cursed thing can by any wit of man be avoided, but until you see your way to that, have a care in meddling with those primitive qualities to which at any moment you may have to appeal for your own protection.

Tom Owen and his singular assistant, Fogo, who combined the functions of prize-fighter and of poet, though, fortunately for himself, he could use his fists better than his pen, soon had the ring arranged according to the rules then in vogue. The white wooden posts, each with the P.C. of the pugilistic club printed upon it, were so fixed as to leave a square of 24 feet within the roped enclosure. Outside this ring an outer one was pitched, eight feet separating the two. The inner was for the combatants and for their seconds, while in the outer there were places for the referee, the timekeeper, the backers, and a few select and fortunate individuals, of whom, through being in my uncle's company, I was one. Some twenty well-known prize-fighters, including my friend Bill Warr, Black Richmond, Maddox, The Pride of Westminster, Tom Belcher, Paddington Jones, Tough Tom Blake, Symonds the ruffian, Tyne the tailor, and others, were stationed in the outer ring as beaters. These fellows all wore the high white hats which were at that time much affected by the fancy, and they were armed with horse-whips, silver-mounted, and each bearing the P.C. monogram. Did any one, be it East End rough or West End patrician, intrude within the outer ropes, this corp of guardians neither argued nor expostulated, but they fell upon the offender and laced him with their whips until he escaped back out of the forbidden ground. Even with so formidable a guard and such fierce measures, the beaters-out, who had to check the forward heaves of a maddened, straining crowd, were often as exhausted at the end of a fight as the principals themselves. In the mean time they formed up in a line of sentinels, presenting under their row of white hats every type of fighting face, from the fresh boyish countenances of Tom Belcher, Jones, and the other younger recruits, to the scarred and mutilated visages of the veteran bruisers.

Whilst the business of the fixing of the stakes and the fastening of the ropes was going forward, I from my place of vantage could hear the talk of the crowd behind me, the front two rows of which were lying upon the grass, the next two kneeling, and the others standing in serried ranks all up the side of the gently sloping hill, so that each line could just see over the shoulders of that which was in front. There were several, and those amongst the most experienced, who took the gloomiest view of Harrison's chances, and it made my heart heavy to overhear them.

"It's the old story over again," said one. "They won't bear in mind that youth will be served. They only learn wisdom when it's knocked into them."

"Ay, ay," responded another. "That's how Jack Slack thrashed Boughton, and I myself saw Hooper, the tinman, beat to pieces by the fighting oilman. They all come to it in time, and now it's Harrison's turn."

"Don't you be so sure about that!" cried a third. "I've seen Jack Harrison fight five times, and I never yet saw him have the worse of it. He's a slaughterer, and so I tell you."

"He was, you mean."

"Well, I don't see no such difference as all that comes to, and I'm putting ten guineas on my opinion."

"Why," said a loud, consequential man from immediately behind me, speaking with a broad western burr, "vrom what I've zeen of this young Gloucester lad, I doan't think Harrison could have stood bevore him for ten rounds when he vas in his prime. I vas coming up in the Bristol coach yesterday, and the guard he told me that he had vifteen thousand pound in hard gold in the boot that had been zent up to back our man."

"They'll be in luck if they see their money again," said another. "Harrison's no lady's-maid fighter, and he's blood to the bone. He'd have a shy at it if his man was as big as Carlton House."

"Tut," answered the west-countryman. "It's only in Bristol and Gloucester that you can get men to beat Bristol and Gloucester."

"It's like your damned himpudence to say so," said an angry voice from the throng behind him. "There are six men in London that would hengage to walk round the best twelve that hever came from the west."

The proceedings might have opened by an impromptu bye-battle between the indignant cockney and the gentleman from Bristol, but a prolonged roar of applause broke in upon their altercation. It was caused by the appearance in the ring of Crab Wilson, followed by Dutch Sam and Mendoza carrying the basin, sponge, brandy-bladder, and other badges of their office. As he entered Wilson pulled the canary-yellow handkerchief from his waist, and going to the corner post, he tied it to the top of it, where it remained fluttering in the breeze. He then took a bundle of smaller ribands of the same colour from his seconds, and walking round, he offered them to the noblemen and Corinthians at half-a-guinea apiece as souvenirs of the fight. His brisk trade was only brought to an end by the appearance of Harrison, who climbed in a very leisurely manner over the ropes, as befitted his more mature years and less elastic joints. The yell which greeted him was even more enthusiastic than that which had heralded Wilson, and there was a louder ring of admiration in it, for the crowd had already had their opportunity of seeing Wilson's physique, whilst Harrison's was a surprise to them.

I had often looked upon the mighty arms and neck of the smith, but I had never before seen him stripped to the waist, or understood the marvellous symmetry of development which had made him in his youth the favourite model of the London sculptors. There was none of that white sleek skin and shimmering play of sinew which made Wilson a beautiful picture, but in its stead there was a rugged grandeur of knotted and tangled muscle, as though the roots of some old tree were writhing from breast to shoulder, and from shoulder to elbow. Even in repose the sun threw shadows from the curves of his skin, but when he exerted himself every muscle bunched itself up, distinct and hard, breaking his whole trunk into gnarled knots of sinew. His skin, on face and body, was darker and harsher than that of his youthful antagonist, but he looked tougher and harder, an effect which was increased by the sombre colour of his stockings and breeches. He entered the ring, sucking a lemon, with Jim Belcher and Caleb Baldwin, the coster, at his heels. Strolling across to the post, he tied his blue bird's-eye handkerchief over the west-countryman's yellow, and then walked to his opponent with his hand out.

"I hope I see you well, Wilson," said he.

"Pretty tidy, I thank you," answered the other. "We'll speak to each other in a different vashion, I 'spects, afore we part."

"But no ill-feeling," said the smith, and the two fighting men grinned at each other as they took their own corners.

"May I ask, Mr. Referee, whether these two men have been weighed?" asked Sir Lothian Hume, standing up in the outer ring.

"Their weight has just been taken under my supervision, sir," answered Mr. Craven. "Your man brought the scale down at thirteen-three, and Harrison at thirteen-eight."

"He's a fifteen-stoner from the loins upwards," cried Dutch Sam, from his corner.

"We'll get some of it off him before we finish."

"You'll get more off him than ever you bargained for," answered Jim Belcher, and the crowd laughed at the rough chaff.

CHAPTER XVIII—THE SMITH'S LAST BATTLE

"Clear the outer ring!" cried Jackson, standing up beside the ropes with a big silver watch in his hand.

Ss–whack! ss–whack! ss–whack! went the horse-whips—for a number of the spectators, either driven onwards by the pressure behind or willing to risk some physical pain on the chance of getting a better view, had crept under the ropes and formed a ragged fringe within the outer ring. Now, amidst roars of laughter from the crowd and a shower of blows from the beaters-out, they dived madly back, with the ungainly haste of frightened sheep blundering through a gap in their hurdles. Their case was a hard one, for the folk in front refused to yield an inch of their places—but the arguments from the rear prevailed over everything else, and presently every frantic fugitive had been absorbed, whilst the beaters-out took their stands along the edge at regular intervals, with their whips held down by their thighs.

"Gentlemen," cried Jackson, again, "I am requested to inform you that Sir Charles Tregellis's nominee is Jack Harrison, fighting at thirteen-eight, and Sir Lothian Hume's is Crab Wilson, at thirteen-three. No person can be allowed at the inner ropes save the referee and the timekeeper. I have only to beg that, if the occasion should require it, you will all give me your assistance to keep the ground clear, to prevent confusion, and to have a fair fight. All ready?"

"All ready!" from both corners.

"Time!"

There was a breathless hush as Harrison, Wilson, Belcher, and Dutch Sam walked very briskly into the centre of the ring. The two men shook hands, whilst their seconds did the same, the four hands crossing each other. Then the seconds dropped back, and the two champions stood toe to toe, with their hands up.

It was a magnificent sight to any one who had not lost his sense of appreciation of the noblest of all the works of Nature. Both men fulfilled that requisite of the powerful athlete that they should look larger without their clothes than with them. In ring slang, they buffed well. And each showed up the other's points on account of the extreme contrast between them: the long, loose-limbed, deer-footed youngster, and the square-set, rugged veteran with his trunk like the stump of an oak. The betting began to rise upon the younger man from the instant that they were put face to face, for his advantages were obvious, whilst those qualities which had brought Harrison to the top in his youth were only a memory in the minds of the older men. All could see the three inches extra of height and two of reach which Wilson possessed, and a glance at the quick, cat-like motions of his feet, and the perfect poise of his body upon his legs, showed how swiftly he could spring either in or out from his slower adversary. But it took a subtler insight to read the grim smile which flickered over the smith's mouth, or the smouldering fire which shone in his grey eyes, and it was only the old-timers who knew that, with his mighty heart and his iron frame, he was a perilous man to lay odds against.

Wilson stood in the position from which he had derived his nick-name, his left hand and left foot well to the front, his body sloped very far back from his loins, and his guard thrown across his chest, but held well forward in a way which made him exceedingly hard to get at. The smith, on the other hand, assumed the obsolete attitude which Humphries and Mendoza introduced, but which had not for ten years been seen in a first-class battle. Both his knees were slightly bent, he stood square to his opponent, and his two big brown fists were held over his mark so that he could lead equally with either. Wilson's hands, which moved incessantly in and out, had been stained with some astringent juice with the purpose of preventing them from puffing, and so great was the contrast between them and his white forearms, that I imagined that he was wearing dark, close-fitting gloves until my uncle explained the matter in a whisper. So they stood in a quiver of eagerness and expectation, whilst that huge multitude hung so silently and breathlessly upon every motion that they might have believed themselves to be alone, man to man, in the centre of some primeval solitude.

It was evident from the beginning that Crab Wilson meant to throw no chance away, and that he would trust to his lightness of foot and quickness of hand until he should see something of the tactics of this rough-looking antagonist. He paced swiftly round several times, with little, elastic, menacing steps, whilst the smith pivoted slowly to correspond. Then, as Wilson took a backward step to induce Harrison to break his ground and follow him, the older man grinned and shook his head.

"You must come to me, lad," said he. "I'm too old to scamper round the ring after you. But we have the day before us, and I'll wait."

He may not have expected his invitation to be so promptly answered; but in an instant, with a panther spring, the west-countryman was on him. *Smack! smack! smack! Thud! thud!* The first three were on Harrison's face, the last two were heavy counters upon Wilson's body. Back danced the youngster, disengaging himself in beautiful style, but with two angry red blotches over the lower line of his ribs. "Blood for Wilson!" yelled the crowd, and as the smith faced round to follow the movements of his nimble adversary, I saw with a thrill that his chin was crimson and dripping. In came Wilson again with a feint at the mark and a flush hit on Harrison's cheek; then, breaking the force of the smith's ponderous right counter, he brought the round to a conclusion by slipping down upon the grass.

"First knock-down for Harrison!" roared a thousand voices, for ten times as many pounds would change hands upon the point.

"I appeal to the referee!" cried Sir Lothian Hume. "It was a slip, and not a knock-down."

"I give it a slip," said Berkeley Craven, and the men walked to their corners, amidst a general shout of applause for a spirited and well-contested opening round. Harrison fumbled in his mouth with his finger and thumb, and then with a sharp half-turn he wrenched out a tooth, which he threw into the basin. "Quite like old times," said he to Belcher.

"Have a care, Jack!" whispered the anxious second. "You got rather more than you gave."

"Maybe I can carry more, too," said he serenely, whilst Caleb Baldwin mopped the big sponge over his face, and the shining bottom of the tin basin ceased suddenly to glimmer through the water.

I could gather from the comments of the experienced Corinthians around me, and from the remarks of the crowd behind, that Harrison's chance was thought to have been lessened by this round.

"I've seen his old faults and I haven't seen his old merits," said Sir John Lade, our opponent of the Brighton Road. "He's as slow on his feet and with his guard as ever. Wilson hit him as he liked."

"Wilson may hit him three times to his once, but his one is worth Wilson's three," remarked my uncle. "He's a natural fighter and the other an excellent sparrer, but I don't hedge a guinea."

A sudden hush announced that the men were on their feet again, and so skilfully had the seconds done their work, that neither looked a jot the worse for what had passed. Wilson led viciously with his left, but misjudged his distance, receiving a smashing counter on the mark in reply which sent him reeling and gasping to the ropes. "Hurrah for the old one!" yelled the mob, and my uncle laughed and nudged Sir John Lade. The west-countryman smiled, and shook himself like a dog from the water as with a stealthy step he came back to the centre of the ring, where his man was still standing. Bang came Harrison's right upon the mark once more, but Crab broke the blow with his elbow, and jumped laughing away. Both men were a little winded, and their quick, high breathing, with the light patter of their feet as they danced round each other, blended into one continuous, long-drawn sound. Two simultaneous exchanges with the left made a clap like a pistol-shot, and then as Harrison rushed in for a fall, Wilson slipped him, and over went my old friend upon his face, partly from the impetus of his own futile attack, and partly from a swinging half-arm blow which the west-countryman brought home upon his ear as he passed.

"Knock-down for Wilson," cried the referee, and the answering roar was like the broadside of a seventy-four. Up went hundreds of curly brimmed Corinthian hats into the air, and the slope before us was a bank of flushed and yelling faces. My heart was cramped with my fears, and I winced at every blow, yet I was conscious also of an abso-lute fascination, with a wild thrill of fierce joy and a certain exultation in our common human nature which could rise above pain and fear in its straining after the very humblest form of fame.

Belcher and Baldwin had pounced upon their man, and had him up and in his corner in an instant, but, in spite of the coolness with which the hardy smith took his punishment, there was immense exultation amongst the west-countrymen.

"We've got him! He's beat! He's beat!" shouted the two Jew seconds. "It's a hundred to a tizzy on Gloucester!"

"Beat, is he?" answered Belcher. "You'll need to rent this field before you can beat him, for he'll stand a month of that kind of fly-flappin'." He was swinging a towel in front of Harrison as he spoke, whilst Baldwin mopped him with the sponge.

"How is it with you, Harrison?" asked my uncle.

"Hearty as a buck, sir. It's as right as the day."

The cheery answer came with so merry a ring that the clouds cleared from my uncle's face.

"You should recommend your man to lead more, Tregellis," said Sir John Lade. "He'll never win it unless he leads."

"He knows more about the game than you or I do, Lade. I'll let him take his own way."

"The betting is three to one against him now," said a gentleman, whose grizzled moustache showed that he was an officer of the late war.

"Very true, General Fitzpatrick. But you'll observe that it is the raw young bloods who are giving the odds, and the Sheenies who are taking them. I still stick to my opinion."

The two men came briskly up to the scratch at the call of time, the smith a little lumpy on one side of his head, but with the same good-humoured and yet menacing smile upon his lips. As to Wilson, he was exactly as he had begun in appearance, but twice I saw him close his lips sharply as if he were in a sudden spasm of pain, and the blotches over his ribs were darkening from scarlet to a sullen purple. He held his guard somewhat lower to screen this vulnerable point, and he danced round his opponent with a lightness which showed that his wind had not been impaired by the body-blows, whilst the smith still adopted the impassive tactics with which he had commenced.

Many rumours had come up to us from the west as to Crab Wilson's fine science and the quickness of his hitting, but the truth surpassed what had been expected of him. In this round and the two which followed he showed a swiftness and accuracy which old ringsiders declared that Mendoza in his prime had never surpassed. He was in and out like lightning, and his blows were heard and felt rather than seen. But Harrison still took them all with the same dogged smile, occasionally getting in a hard body-blow in return, for his adversary's height and his position combined to keep his face out of danger. At the end of the fifth round the odds were four to one, and the west-countrymen were riotous in their exultation.

"What think you now?" cried the west-countryman behind me, and in his excitement he could get no further save to repeat over and over again, "What think you now?" When in the sixth round the smith was peppered twice without getting in a counter, and had the worst of the fall as well, the fellow became inarticulate altogether, and could only huzza wildly in his delight. Sir Lothian Hume was smiling and nodding his head, whilst my uncle was coldly impassive, though I was sure that his heart was as heavy as mine.

"This won't do, Tregellis," said General Fitzpatrick. "My money is on the old one, but the other is the finer boxer."

"My man is *un peu passé*, but he will come through all right," answered my uncle.

I saw that both Belcher and Baldwin were looking grave, and I knew that we must have a change of some sort, or the old tale of youth and age would be told once more.

The seventh round, however, showed the reserve strength of the hardy old fighter, and lengthened the faces of those layers of odds who had imagined that the fight was practically over, and that a few finishing rounds would have given the smith his coup-de-grâce. It was clear when the two men faced each other that Wilson had made himself up for mischief, and meant to force the fighting and maintain the lead which he had gained, but that grey gleam was not quenched yet in the veteran's eyes, and still the same smile played over his grim face. He had become more jaunty, too, in the swing of his shoulders and the poise of his head, and it brought my confidence back to see the brisk way in which he squared up to his man.

Wilson led with his left, but was short, and he only just avoided a dangerous right-hander which whistled in at his ribs. "Bravo, old 'un, one of those will be a dose of laudanum if you get it home," cried Belcher. There was a pause of shuffling feet and hard breathing, broken by the thud of a tremendous body blow from Wilson, which the smith stopped with the utmost coolness. Then again a few seconds of silent tension, when Wilson led viciously at the head, but Harrison took it on his forearm, smiling and nodding at his opponent. "Get the pepper-box open!" yelled Mendoza, and Wilson sprang in to carry out his instructions, but was hit out again by a heavy drive on the chest. "Now's the time! Follow it up!" cried Belcher, and in rushed the smith, pelting in his half-arm blows, and taking the returns without a wince, until Crab Wilson went down exhausted in the corner. Both men had their marks to show, but Harrison had all the best of the rally, so it was our turn to throw our hats into the air and to shout ourselves hoarse, whilst the seconds clapped their man upon his broad back as they hurried him to his corner.

"What think you now?" shouted all the neighbours of the west-countryman, repeating his own refrain.

"Why, Dutch Sam never put in a better rally," cried Sir John Lade. "What's the betting now, Sir Lothian?"

"I have laid all that I intend; but I don't think my man can lose it." For all that, the smile had faded from his face, and I observed that he glanced continually over his shoulder into the crowd behind him.

A sullen purple cloud had been drifting slowly up from the south-west—though I dare say that out of thirty thousand folk there were very few who had spared the time or attention to mark it. Now it suddenly made its presence apparent by a few heavy drops of rain, thickening rapidly into a sharp shower, which filled the air with its hiss, and rattled noisily upon the high, hard hats of the Corinthians. Coat-collars were turned up and handkerchiefs tied round. necks, whilst the skins of the two men glistened with the moisture as they stood up to each other once more. I noticed that Belcher whispered very earnestly into Harrison's ear as he rose from his knee, and that the smith nodded his head curtly, with the air of a man who understands and approves of his orders.

And what those orders were was instantly apparent. Harrison was to be turned from the defender into the attacker. The result of the rally in the last round had convinced his seconds that when it came to give-and-take hitting, their hardy and powerful man was likely to have the better of it. And then on the top of this came the rain. With the slippery grass the superior activity of Wilson would be neutralized, and he would find it harder to avoid the rushes of his opponent. It was in taking advantage of such circumstances that the art of ringcraft lay, and many a shrewd and vigilant second had won a losing battle for his man. "Go in, then! Go in!" whooped the two prize-fighters, while every backer in the crowd took up the roar.

And Harrison went in, in such fashion that no man who saw him do it will ever forget it. Crab Wilson, as game as a pebble, met him with a flush hit every time, but no human strength or human science seemed capable of stopping the terrible onslaught of this iron man.

Round after round he scrambled his way in, slap-bang, right and left, every hit tremendously sent home. Sometimes he covered his own face with his left, and sometimes he disdained to use any guard at all, but his springing hits were irresistible. The rain lashed down upon them, pouring from their faces and running in crimson trickles over their bodies, but neither gave any heed to it save to manoeuvre always with the view of bringing it in to each other's eyes. But round after round the west-countryman fell, and round after round the betting rose, until the odds were higher in our favour than ever they had been against us. With a sinking heart, filled with pity and admiration for these two gallant men, I longed that every bout might be the last, and yet the "Time!" was hardly out of Jackson's mouth before they had both sprung from their second's knees, with laughter upon their mutilated faces and chaffing words upon their bleeding lips. It may have been a humble object-lesson, but I give you my word that many a time in my life I have braced myself to a hard task by the remembrance of that morning upon Crawley Downs, asking myself if my manhood were so weak that I would not do for my country, or for those whom I loved, as much as these two would endure for a paltry stake and for their own credit amongst their fellows. Such a spectacle may brutalize those who are brutal, but I say that there is a spiritual side to it also, and that the sight of the utmost human limit of endurance and courage is one which bears a lesson of its own.

But if the ring can breed bright virtues, it is but a partisan who can deny that it can be the mother of black vices also, and we were destined that morning to have a sight of each. It so chanced that, as the battle went against his man, my eyes stole round very often to note the expression upon Sir Lothian Hume's face, for I knew how fearlessly he had laid the odds, and I understood that his fortunes as well as his champion were going down before the smashing blows of the old bruiser. The confident smile with which he had watched the opening rounds had long vanished from his lips, and his cheeks had turned of a sallow pallor, whilst his small, fierce grey eyes looked furtively from under his craggy brows, and more than once he burst into savage

imprecations when Wilson was beaten to the ground. But especially
I noticed that his chin was always coming round to his shoulder, and
that at the end of every round he sent keen little glances flying backwards into the crowd. For some time, amidst the immense hillside
of faces which banked themselves up on the slope behind us, I was
unable to pick out the exact point at which his gaze was directed.
But at last I succeeded in following it. A very tall man, who showed a
pair of broad, bottle-green shoulders high above his neighbours, was
looking very hard in our direction, and I assured myself that a quick
exchange of almost imperceptible signals was going on between him
and the Corinthian baronet. I became conscious, also, as I watched
this stranger, that the cluster of men around him were the roughest
elements of the whole assembly: fierce, vicious-looking fellows, with
cruel, debauched faces, who howled like a pack of wolves at every blow,
and yelled execrations at Harrison whenever he walked across to his
corner. So turbulent were they that I saw the ringkeepers whisper
together and glance up in their direction, as if preparing for trouble in
store, but none of them had realized how near it was to breaking out,
or how dangerous it might prove.

Thirty rounds had been fought in an hour and twenty-five minutes, and the rain was pelting down harder than ever. A thick steam
rose from the two fighters, and the ring was a pool of mud. Repeated
falls had turned the men brown, with a horrible mottling of crimson
blotches. Round after round had ended by Crab Wilson going down,
and it was evident, even to my inexperienced eyes, that he was weak-
ening rapidly. He leaned heavily upon the two Jews when they led
him to his corner, and he reeled when their support was withdrawn.
Yet his science had, through long practice, become an automatic thing
with him, so that he stopped and hit with less power, but with as great
accuracy as ever. Even now a casual observer might have thought that
he had the best of the battle, for the smith was far the more terribly
marked, but there was a wild stare in the west-countryman's eyes, and
a strange catch in his breathing, which told us that it is not the most
dangerous blow which shows upon the surface. A heavy cross-buttock

at the end of the thirty-first round shook the breath from his body, and he came up for the thirty-second with the same jaunty gallantry as ever, but with the dazed expression of a man whose wind has been utterly smashed.

"He's got the roly-polies," cried Belcher. "You have it your own way now!"

"I'll vight for a week yet," gasped Wilson.

"Damme, I like his style," cried Sir John Lade. "No shifting, nothing shy, no hugging nor hauling. It's a shame to let him fight. Take the brave fellow away!"

"Take him away! Take him away!" echoed a hundred voices.

"I won't be taken away! Who dares say so?" cried Wilson, who was back, after another fall, upon his second's knee.

"His heart won't suffer him to cry enough," said General Fitzpatrick. "As his patron, Sir Lothian, you should direct the sponge to be thrown up."

"You think he can't win it?"

"He is hopelessly beat, sir."

"You don't know him. He's a glutton of the first water."

"A gamer man never pulled his shirt off; but the other is too strong for him."

"Well, sir, I believe that he can fight another ten rounds." He half turned as he spoke, and I saw him throw up his left arm with a singular gesture into the air.

"Cut the ropes! Fair play! Wait till the rain stops!" roared a stentorian voice behind me, and I saw that it came from the big man with the bottle-green coat. His cry was a signal, for, like a thunderclap, there came a hundred hoarse voices shouting together: "Fair play for Gloucester! Break the ring! Break the ring!"

Jackson had called "Time," and the two mud-plastered men were already upon their feet, but the interest had suddenly changed from the fight to the audience. A succession of heaves from the back of the crowd had sent a series of long ripples running through it, all the heads swaying rhythmically in the one direction like a wheatfield in a squall. With every impulsion the oscillation increased, those in front trying vainly to steady themselves against the rushes from behind, until suddenly there came a sharp snap, two white stakes with earth clinging to their points flew into the outer ring, and a spray of people, dashed from the solid wave behind, were thrown against the line of the beaters-out. Down came the long horse-whips, swayed by the most vigorous arms in England; but the wincing and shouting victims had no sooner scrambled back a few yards from the merciless cuts, before a fresh charge from the rear hurled them once more into the arms of the prize-fighters. Many threw themselves down upon the turf and allowed successive waves to pass over their bodies, whilst others, driven wild by the blows, returned them with their hunting-crops and walking-canes. And then, as half the crowd strained to the left and half to the right to avoid the pressure from behind, the vast mass was suddenly reft in twain, and through the gap surged the rough fellows from behind, all armed with loaded sticks and yelling for "Fair play and Gloucester!" Their determined rush carried the prize-fighters before them, the inner ropes snapped like threads, and in an instant the ring was a swirling, seething mass of figures, whips and sticks falling and clattering, whilst, face to face, in the middle of it all, so wedged that they could neither advance nor retreat, the smith and the west-countryman continued their long-drawn battle as oblivious of the chaos raging round them as two bulldogs would have been who had got each other by the throat. The driving rain, the cursing and screams of pain, the swish of the blows, the yelling of orders and advice, the heavy smell of the damp cloth—every incident of that scene of my early youth comes back to me now in my old age as clearly as if it had been but yesterday.

It was not easy for us to observe anything at the time, however, for we were ourselves in the midst of the frantic crowd, swaying about and carried occasionally quite off our feet, but endeavouring to keep our places behind Jackson and Berkeley Craven, who, with sticks and whips meeting over their heads, were still calling the rounds and superintending the fight.

"The ring's broken!" shouted Sir Lothian Hume. "I appeal to the referee! The fight is null and void."

"You villain!" cried my uncle, hotly; "this is your doing."

"You have already an account to answer for with me," said Hume, with his sinister sneer, and as he spoke he was swept by the rush of the crowd into my uncle's very arms. The two men's faces were not more than a few inches apart, and Sir Lothian's bold eyes had to sink before the imperious scorn which gleamed coldly in those of my uncle.

"We will settle our accounts, never fear, though I degrade myself in meeting such a blackleg. What is it, Craven?"

"We shall have to declare a draw, Tregellis."

"My man has the fight in hand."

"I cannot help it. I cannot attend to my duties when every moment I am cut over with a whip or a stick."

Jackson suddenly made a wild dash into the crowd, but returned with empty hands and a rueful face.

"They've stolen my timekeeper's watch," he cried. "A little cove snatched it out of my hand."

My uncle clapped his hand to his fob.

"Mine has gone also!" he cried.

"Draw it at once, or your man will get hurt," said Jackson, and we saw that as the undaunted smith stood up to Wilson for another round, a dozen rough fellows were clustering round him with bludgeons.

"Do you consent to a draw, Sir Lothian Hume?"

"I do."

"And you, Sir Charles?"

"Certainly not."

"The ring is gone."

"That is no fault of mine."

"Well, I see no help for it. As referee I order that the men be withdrawn, and that the stakes be returned to their owners."

"A draw! A draw!" shrieked every one, and the crowd in an instant dispersed in every direction, the pedestrians running to get a good lead upon the London road, and the Corinthians in search of their horses and carriages. Harrison ran over to Wilson's corner and shook him by the hand.

"I hope I have not hurt you much."

"I'm hard put to it to stand. How are you?"

"My head's singin' like a kettle. It was the rain that helped me."

"Yes, I thought I had you beat one time. I never wish a better battle."

"Nor me either. Good-bye."

And so those two brave-hearted fellows made their way amidst the yelping roughs, like two wounded lions amidst a pack of wolves and jackals. I say again that, if the ring has fallen low, it is not in the main the fault of the men who have done the fighting, but it lies at the door of the vile crew of ring-side parasites and ruffians, who are as far below the honest pugilist as the welsher and the blackleg are below the noble racehorse which serves them as a pretext for their villainies.

CHAPTER XIX—CLIFFE ROYAL

My uncle was humanely anxious to get Harrison to bed as soon as possible, for the smith, although he laughed at his own injuries, had none the less been severely punished.

"Don't you dare ever to ask my leave to fight again, Jack Harrison," said his wife, as she looked ruefully at his battered face. "Why, it's worse than when you beat Black Baruk; and if it weren't for your top-coat, I couldn't swear you were the man who led me to the altar! If the King of England ask you, I'll never let you do it more."

"Well, old lass, I give my davy that I never will. It's best that I leave fightin' before fightin' leaves me." He screwed up his face as he took a sup from Sir Charles's brandy flask. "It's fine liquor, sir, but it gets into my cut lips most cruel. Why, here's John Cummings of the Friars' Oak Inn, as I'm a sinner, and seekin' for a mad doctor, to judge by the look of him!"

It was certainly a most singular figure who was approaching us over the moor. With the flushed, dazed face of a man who is just recovering from recent intoxication, the landlord was tearing madly about, his hat gone, and his hair and beard flying in the wind. He ran in little zigzags from one knot of people to another, whilst his peculiar appearance drew a running fire of witticisms as he went, so that he reminded me irresistibly of a snipe skimming along through a line of guns. We saw him stop for an instant by the yellow barouche, and hand something to Sir Lothian Hume. Then on he came again, until at last, catching sight of us, he gave a cry of joy, and ran for us full speed with a note held out at arm's length.

"You're a nice cove, too, John Cummings," said Harrison, reproachfully. "Didn't I tell you not to let a drop pass your lips until you had given your message to Sir Charles?"

"I ought to be pole-axed, I ought," he cried in bitter repentance. "I asked for you, Sir Charles, as I'm a livin' man, I did, but you weren't there, and what with bein' so pleased at gettin' such odds when I knew Harrison was goin' to fight, an' what with the landlord at the George wantin' me to try his own specials, I let my senses go clean away from me. And now it's only after the fight is over that I see you, Sir Charles, an' if you lay that whip over my back, it's only what I deserve."

But my uncle was paying no attention whatever to the voluble self-reproaches of the landlord. He had opened the note, and was reading it with a slight raising of the eyebrows, which was almost the very highest note in his limited emotional gamut.

"What make you of this, nephew?" he asked, handing it to me.

This was what I read—

"SIR CHARLES TREGELLIS,
"For God's sake, come at once, when this reaches you, to Cliffe Royal, and tarry as little as possible upon the way. You will see me there, and you will hear much which concerns you deeply. I pray you to come as soon as may be; and until then I remain him whom you knew as
"JAMES HARRISON."

"Well, nephew?" asked my uncle.

"Why, sir, I cannot tell what it may mean."

"Who gave it to you, sirrah?"

"It was young Jim Harrison himself, sir," said the landlord, "though indeed I scarce knew him at first, for he looked like his own ghost. He was so eager that it should reach you that he would not leave me until the horse was harnessed and I started upon my way. There was one note for you and one for Sir Lothian Hume, and I wish to God he had chosen a better messenger!"

"This is a mystery indeed," said my uncle, bending his brows over the note. "What should he be doing at that house of ill-omen? And why does he sign himself 'him whom you knew as Jim Harrison?' By what other style should I know him? Harrison, you can throw a light upon this. You, Mrs. Harrison; I see by your face that you understand it."

"Maybe we do, Sir Charles; but we are plain folk, my Jack and I, and we go as far as we see our way, and when we don't see our way any longer, we just stop. We've been goin' this twenty year, but now we'll draw aside and let our betters get to the front; so if you wish to find what that note means, I can only advise you to do what you are asked, and to drive over to Cliffe Royal, where you will find out."

My uncle put the note into his pocket.

"I don't move until I have seen you safely in the hands of the surgeon, Harrison."

"Never mind for me, sir. The missus and me can drive down to Crawley in the gig, and a yard of stickin' plaster and a raw steak will soon set me to rights."

But my uncle was by no means to be persuaded, and he drove the pair into Crawley, where the smith was left under the charge of his wife in the very best quarters which money could procure. Then, after a hasty luncheon, we turned the mares' heads for the south.

"This ends my connection with the ring, nephew," said my uncle. "I perceive that there is no possible means by which it can be kept pure from roguery. I have been cheated and befooled; but a man learns wisdom at last, and never again do I give countenance to a prize-fight."

Had I been older or he less formidable, I might have said what was in my heart, and begged him to give up other things also—to come out from those shallow circles in which he lived, and to find some work that was worthy of his strong brain and his good heart. But the thought had hardly formed itself in my mind before he had dropped his serious vein, and was chatting away about some new silver-mounted harness which he intended to spring upon the Mall, and about the match for a thousand guineas which he meant to make between his filly Ethelberta and Lord Doncaster's famous three-year-old Aurelius.

We had got as far as Whiteman's Green, which is rather more than midway between Crawley Down and Friars' Oak, when, looking backwards, I saw far down the road the gleam of the sun upon a high yellow carriage. Sir Lothian Hume was following us.

"He has had the same summons as we, and is bound for the same destination," said my uncle, glancing over his shoulder at the distant barouche. "We are both wanted at Cliffe Royal—we, the two survivors of that black business. And it is Jim Harrison of all people who calls us there. Nephew, I have had an eventful life, but I feel as if the very strangest scene of it were waiting for me among those trees."

He whipped up the mares, and now from the curve of the road we could see the high dark pinnacles of the old Manor-house shooting up above the ancient oaks which ring it round. The sight of it, with its bloodstained and ghost-blasted reputation, would in itself have been enough to send a thrill through my nerves; but when the words of my uncle made me suddenly realize that this strange summons was indeed for the two men who were concerned in that old-world tragedy, and that it was the playmate of my youth who had sent it, I caught my breath as I seemed vaguely to catch a glimpse of some portentous thing forming itself in front of us. The rusted gates between the crumbling heraldic pillars were folded back, and my uncle flicked the mares impatiently as we flew up the weed-grown avenue, until he pulled them on their haunches before the time-blotched steps. The front door was open, and Boy Jim was waiting there to meet us.

But it was a different Boy Jim from him whom I had known and loved. There was a change in him somewhere, a change so marked that it was the first thing that I noticed, and yet so subtle that I could not put words to it. He was not better dressed than of old, for I well knew the old brown suit that he wore.

He was not less comely, for his training had left him the very model of what a man should be. And yet there was a change, a touch of dignity in the expression, a suggestion of confidence in the bearing which seemed, now that it was supplied, to be the one thing which had been needed to give him harmony and finish.

Somehow, in spite of his prowess, his old school name of "Boy" had clung very naturally to him, until that instant when I saw him standing in his self-contained and magnificent manhood in the doorway of the ancient house. A woman stood beside him, her hand resting upon his shoulder, and I saw that it was Miss Hinton of Anstey Cross.

"You remember me, Sir Charles Tregellis," said she, coming forward, as we sprang down from the curricle.

My uncle looked hard at her with a puzzled face.

"I do not think that I have the privilege, madame. And yet—"

"Polly Hinton, of the Haymarket. You surely cannot have forgotten Polly Hinton."

"Forgotten! Why, we have mourned for you in Fops' Alley for more years than I care to think of. But what in the name of wonder—"

"I was privately married, and I retired from the stage. I want you to forgive me for taking Jim away from you last night."

"It was you, then?"

"I had a stronger claim even than you could have. You were his patron; I was his mother." She drew his head down to hers as she spoke, and there, with their cheeks together, were the two faces, the one stamped with the waning beauty of womanhood, the other with the waxing strength of man, and yet so alike in the dark eyes, the blue-black hair and the broad white brow, that I marvelled that I had never read her secret on the first days that I had seen them together. "Yes," she cried, "he is my own boy, and he saved me from what is worse than death, as your nephew Rodney could tell you. Yet my lips were sealed, and it was only last night that I could tell him that it was his mother whom he had brought back by his gentleness and his patience into the sweetness of life."

"Hush, mother!" said Jim, turning his lips to her cheek. "There are some things which are between ourselves. But tell me, Sir Charles, how went the fight?"

"Your uncle would have won it, but the roughs broke the ring."

"He is no uncle of mine, Sir Charles, but he has been the best and truest friend, both to me and to my father, that ever the world could offer. I only know one as true," he continued, taking me by the hand, "and dear old Rodney Stone is his name. But I trust he was not much hurt?"

"A week or two will set him right. But I cannot pretend to understand how this matter stands, and you must allow me to say that I have not heard you advance anything yet which seems to me to justify you in abandoning your engagements at a moment's notice."

"Come in, Sir Charles, and I am convinced that you will acknowledge that I could not have done otherwise. But here, if I mistake not, is Sir Lothian Hume."

The yellow barouche had swung into the avenue, and a few moments later the weary, panting horses had pulled up behind our curricle. Sir Lothian sprang out, looking as black as a thunder-cloud.

"Stay where you are, Corcoran," said he; and I caught a glimpse of a bottle-green coat which told me who was his travelling companion. "Well," he continued, looking round him with an insolent stare, "I should vastly like to know who has had the insolence to give me so pressing an invitation to visit my own house, and what in the devil you mean by daring to trespass upon my grounds?"

"I promise you that you will understand this and a good deal more before we part, Sir Lothian," said Jim, with a curious smile playing over his face. "If you will follow me, I will endeavour to make it all clear to you."

With his mother's hand in his own, he led us into that ill-omened room where the cards were still heaped upon the sideboard, and the dark shadow lurked in the corner of the ceiling.

"Now, sirrah, your explanation!" cried Sir Lothian, standing with his arms folded by the door.

"My first explanations I owe to you, Sir Charles," said Jim; and as I listened to his voice and noted his manner, I could not but admire the effect which the company of her whom he now knew to be his mother had had upon a rude country lad. "I wish to tell you what occurred last night."

"I will tell it for you, Jim," said his mother. "You must know, Sir Charles, that though my son knew nothing of his parents, we were both alive, and had never lost sight of him. For my part, I let him have his own way in going to London and in taking up this challenge. It was only yesterday that it came to the ears of his father, who would have none of it. He was in the weakest health, and his wishes were not to be gainsayed. He ordered me to go at once and to bring his son to his side. I was at my wit's end, for I was sure that Jim would never come unless a substitute were provided for him. I went to the kind, good couple who had brought him up, and I told them how matters stood. Mrs. Harrison loved Jim as if he had been her own son, and her husband loved mine, so they came to my help, and may God bless them for their kindness to a distracted wife and mother! Harrison would take Jim's place if Jim would go to his father. Then I drove to Crawley. I found out which was Jim's room, and I spoke to him through the window, for I was sure that those who had backed him would not let him go. I told him that I was his mother. I told him who was his father. I said that I had my phaeton ready, and that he might, for all I knew, be only in time to receive the dying blessing of that parent whom he had never known. Still the boy would not go until he had my assurance that Harrison would take his place."

"Why did he not leave a message with Belcher?"

"My head was in a whirl, Sir Charles. To find a father and a mother, a new name and a new rank in a few minutes might turn a stronger brain than ever mine was. My mother begged me to come with her, and I went. The phaeton was waiting, but we had scarcely started when some fellow seized the horses' heads, and a couple of ruffians attacked us. One of them I beat over the head with the butt of the whip, so that he dropped the cudgel with which he was about to strike me; then lashing the horse, I shook off the others and got safely away. I cannot imagine who they were or why they should molest us."

"Perhaps Sir Lothian Hume could tell you," said my uncle.

Our enemy said nothing; but his little grey eyes slid round with a most murderous glance in our direction.

"After I had come here and seen my father I went down—"

My uncle stopped him with a cry of astonishment.

"What did you say, young man? You came here and you saw your father—here at Cliffe Royal?"

"Yes, sir."

My uncle had turned very pale.

"In God's name, then, tell us who your father is!"

Jim made no answer save to point over our shoulders, and glancing round, we became aware that two people had entered the room through the door which led to the bedroom stair. The one I recognized in an instant. That impassive, mask-like face and demure manner could only belong to Ambrose, the former valet of my uncle. The other was a very different and even more singular figure. He was a tall man, clad in a dark dressing-gown, and leaning heavily upon a stick. His long, bloodless countenance was so thin and so white that it gave the strangest illusion of transparency. Only within the folds of a shroud have I ever seen so wan a face. The brindled hair and the rounded back gave the impression of advanced age, and it was only the dark brows and the bright alert eyes glancing out from beneath them which made me doubt whether it was really an old man who stood before us.

There was an instant of silence, broken by a deep oath from Sir Lothian Hume—

"Lord Avon, by God!" he cried.

"Very much at your service, gentlemen," answered the strange figure in the dressing-gown.

CHAPTER XX—LORD AVON

My uncle was an impassive man by nature and had become more so by the tradition of the society in which he lived. He could have turned a card upon which his fortune depended without the twitch of a muscle, and I had seen him myself driving to imminent death on the Godstone Road with as calm a face as if he were out for his daily airing in the Mall. But now the shock which had come upon him was so great that he could only stand with white cheeks and staring, incredulous eyes. Twice I saw him open his lips, and twice he put his hand up to his throat, as though a barrier had risen betwixt himself and his utterance. Finally, he took a sudden little run forward with both his hands thrown out in greeting.

"Ned!" he cried.

But the strange man who stood before him folded his arms over his breast.

"No Charles," said he.

My uncle stopped and looked at him in amazement.

"Surely, Ned, you have a greeting for me after all these years?"

"You believed me to have done this deed, Charles. I read it in your eyes and in your manner on that terrible morning. You never asked me for an explanation. You never considered how impossible such a crime must be for a man of my character. At the first breath of suspicion you, my intimate friend, the man who knew me best, set me down as a thief and a murderer."

"No, no, Ned."

"You did, Charles; I read it in your eyes. And so it was that when I wished to leave that which was most precious to me in safe hands I had to pass you over and to place him in the charge of the one man who from the first never doubted my innocence. Better a thousand times that my son should be brought up in a humble station and in ignorance of his unfortunate father, than that he should learn to share the doubts and suspicions of his equals."

"Then he is really your son!" cried my uncle, staring at Jim in amazement.

For answer the man stretched out his long withered arm, and placed a gaunt hand upon the shoulder of the actress, whilst she looked up at him with love in her eyes.

"I married, Charles, and I kept it secret from my friends, for I had chosen my wife outside our own circles. You know the foolish pride which has always been the strongest part of my nature. I could not bear to avow that which I had done. It was this neglect upon my part which led to an estrangement between us, and drove her into habits for which it is I who am to blame and not she. Yet on account of these same habits I took the child from her and gave her an allowance on condition that she did not interfere with it. I had feared that the boy might receive evil from her, and had never dreamed in my blindness that she might get good from him. But I have learned in my miserable life, Charles, that there is a power which fashions things for us, though we may strive to thwart it, and that we are in truth driven by an unseen current towards a certain goal, however much we may deceive ourselves into thinking that it is our own sails and oars which are speeding us upon our way."

My eyes had been upon the face of my uncle as he listened, but now as I turned them from him they fell once more upon the thin, wolfish face of Sir Lothian Hume. He stood near the window, his grey silhouette thrown up against the square of dusty glass; and I have never seen such a play of evil passions, of anger, of jealousy, of disappointed greed upon a human face before.

"Am I to understand," said he, in a loud, harsh voice, "that this young man claims to be the heir of the peerage of Avon?"

"He is my lawful son."

"I knew you fairly well, sir, in our youth; but you will allow me to observe that neither I nor any friend of yours ever heard of a wife or a son. I defy Sir Charles Tregellis to say that he ever dreamed that there was any heir except myself."

"I have already explained, Sir Lothian, why I kept my marriage secret."

"You have explained, sir; but it is for others in another place to say if that explanation is satisfactory."

Two blazing dark eyes flashed out of the pale haggard face with as strange and sudden an effect as if a stream of light were to beat through the windows of a shattered and ruined house.

"You dare to doubt my word?"

"I demand a proof."

"My word is proof to those who know me."

"Excuse me, Lord Avon; but I know you, and I see no reason why I should accept your statement."

It was a brutal speech, and brutally delivered. Lord Avon staggered forward, and it was only his son on one aide and his wife on the other who kept his quivering hands from the throat of his insulter. Sir Lothian recoiled from the pale fierce face with the black brows, but he still glared angrily about the room.

"A very pretty conspiracy this," he cried, "with a criminal, an actress, and a prize-fighter all playing their parts. Sir Charles Tregellis, you shall hear from me again! And you also, my lord!" He turned upon his heel and strode from the room.

"He has gone to denounce me," said Lord Avon, a spasm of wounded pride distorting his features.

"Shall I bring him back?" cried Boy Jim.

"No, no, let him go. It is as well, for I have already made up my mind that my duty to you, my son, outweighs that which I owe, and have at such bitter cost fulfilled, to my brother and my family."

"You did me an injustice, Ned," said my uncle, "if you thought that I had forgotten you, or that I had judged you unkindly. If ever I have thought that you had done this deed—and how could I doubt the evidence of my own eyes—I have always believed that it was at a time when your mind was unhinged, and when you knew no more of what you were about than the man who is walking in his sleep."

"What do you mean when you talk about the evidence of your own eyes?" asked Lord Avon, looking hard at my uncle.

"I saw you, Ned, upon that accursed night."

"Saw me? Where?"

"In the passage."

"And doing what?"

"You were coming from your brother's room. I had heard his voice raised in anger and pain only an instant before. You carried in your hand a bag full of money, and your face betrayed the utmost agitation. If you can but explain to me, Ned, how you came to be there, you will take from my heart a weight which has pressed upon it for all these years."

No one now would have recognized in my uncle the man who was the leader of all the fops of London. In the presence of this old friend and of the tragedy which girt him round, the veil of triviality and affectation had been rent, and I felt all my gratitude towards him deepening for the first time into affection whilst I watched his pale, anxious face, and the eager hops which shone in his eyes as he awaited his friend's explanation. Lord Avon sank his face in his hands, and for a few moments there was silence in the dim grey room.

"I do not wonder now that you were shaken," said he at last. "My God, what a net was cast round me! Had this vile charge been brought against me, you, my dearest friend, would have been compelled to tear away the last doubt as to my guilt. And yet, in spite of what you have seen, Charles, I am as innocent in the matter as you are."

"I thank God that I hear you say so."

"But you are not satisfied, Charles. I can read it on your face. You wish to know why an innocent man should conceal himself for all these years."

"Your word is enough for me, Ned; but the world will wish this other question answered also."

"It was to save the family honour, Charles. You know how dear it was to me. I could not clear myself without proving my brother to have been guilty of the foulest crime which a gentleman could commit. For eighteen years I have screened him at the expense of everything which a man could sacrifice. I have lived a living death which has left me an old and shattered man when I am but in my fortieth year. But now when I am faced with the alternative of telling the facts about my brother, or of wronging my son, I can only act in one fashion, and the more so since I have reason to hope that a way may be found by which what I am now about to disclose to you need never come to the public ear."

He rose from his chair, and leaning heavily upon his two supporters, he tottered across the room to the dust-covered sideboard. There, in the centre of it, was lying that ill-boding pile of time-stained, mildewed cards, just as Boy Jim and I had seen them years before. Lord Avon turned them over with trembling fingers, and then picking up half a dozen, he brought them to my uncle.

"Place your finger and thumb upon the left-hand bottom corner of this card, Charles," said he. "Pass them lightly backwards and forwards, and tell me what you feel."

"It has been pricked with a pin."

"Precisely. What is the card?"

My uncle turned it over.

"It is the king of clubs."

"Try the bottom corner of this one."

"It is quite smooth."

"And the card is?"

"The three of spades."

"And this one?"

"It has been pricked. It is the ace of hearts." Lord Avon hurled them down upon the floor.

"There you have the whole accursed story!" he cried. "Need I go further where every word is an agony?"

"I see something, but not all. You must continue, Ned."

The frail figure stiffened itself, as though he were visibly bracing himself for an effort.

"I will tell it you, then, once and for ever. Never again, I trust, will it be necessary for me to open my lips about the miserable business. You remember our game. You remember how we lost. You remember how you all retired, and left me sitting in this very room, and at that very table. Far from being tired, I was exceedingly wakeful, and I remained here for an hour or more thinking over the incidents of the game and the changes which it promised to bring about in my fortunes. I had, as you will recollect, lost heavily, and my only consolation was that my own brother had won. I knew that, owing to his reckless mode of life, he was firmly in the clutches of the Jews, and I hoped that that which had shaken my position might have the effect of restoring his. As I sat there, fingering the cards in an abstracted way, some chance led me to observe the small needle-pricks which you have just felt. I went over the packs, and found, to my unspeakable horror, that any one who was in the secret could hold them in dealing in such a way as to be able to count the exact number of high cards which fell to each of his opponents. And then, with such a flush of shame and disgust as I had never known, I remembered how my attention had been drawn to my brother's mode of dealing, its slowness, and the way in which he held each card by the lower corner.

"I did not condemn him precipitately. I sat for a long time calling to mind every incident which could tell one way or the other. Alas! it all went to confirm me in my first horrible suspicion, and to turn it into a certainty. My brother had ordered the packs from Ledbury's, in Bond

Street. They had been for some hours in his chambers. He had played throughout with a decision which had surprised us at the time. Above all, I could not conceal from myself that his past life was not such as to make even so abominable a crime as this impossible to him. Tingling with anger and shame, I went straight up that stair, the cards in my hand, and I taxed him with this lowest and meanest of all the crimes to which a villain could descend.

"He had not retired to rest, and his ill-gotten gains were spread out upon the dressing-table. I hardly know what I said to him, but the facts were so deadly that he did not attempt to deny his guilt. You will remember, as the only mitigation of his crime, that he was not yet one and twenty years of age. My words overwhelmed him. He went on his knees to me, imploring me to spare him. I told him that out of consideration for our family I should make no public exposure of him, but that he must never again in his life lay his hand upon a card, and that the money which he had won must be returned next morning with an explanation. It would be social ruin, he protested. I answered that he must take the consequence of his own deed. Then and there I burned the papers which he had won from me, and I replaced in a canvas bag which lay upon the table all the gold pieces. I would have left the room without another word, but he clung to me, and tore the ruffle from my wrist in his attempt to hold me back, and to prevail upon me to promise to say nothing to you or Sir Lothian Hume. It was his despairing cry, when he found that I was proof against all his entreaties, which reached your ears, Charles, and caused you to open your chamber door and to see me as I returned to my room."

My uncle drew a long sigh of relief.

"Nothing could be clearer!" he murmured.

"In the morning I came, as you remember, to your room, and I returned your money. I did the same to Sir Lothian Hume. I said nothing of my reasons for doing so, for I found that I could not bring myself to confess our disgrace to you. Then came the horrible discovery which has darkened my life, and which was as great a mystery to me as it has been to you. I saw that I was suspected, and I saw, also, that even if I were to clear myself, it could only be done by a public confession of the infamy of my brother. I shrank from it, Charles. Any personal suffering seemed to me to be better than to bring public shame upon a family which has held an untarnished record through so many centuries. I fled from my trial, therefore, and disappeared from the world.

"But, first of all, it was necessary that I should make arrangements for the wife and the son, of whose existence you and my other friends were ignorant. It is with shame, Mary, that I confess it, and I acknowledge to you that the blame of all the consequences rests with me rather than with you. At the time there were reasons, now happily long gone past, which made me determine that the son was better apart from the mother, whose absence at that age he would not miss. I would have taken you into my confidence, Charles, had it not been that your suspicions had wounded me deeply—for I did not at that time understand how strong the reasons were which had prejudiced you against me.

"On the evening after the tragedy I fled to London, and arranged that my wife should have a fitting allowance on condition that she did not interfere with the child. I had, as you remember, had much to do with Harrison, the prize-fighter, and I had often had occasion to admire his simple and honest nature. I took my boy to him now, and I found him, as I expected, incredulous as to my guilt, and ready to assist me in any way. At his wife's entreaty he had just retired from the ring, and was uncertain how he should employ himself. I was able to fit him up as a smith, on condition that he should ply his trade at the village of Friar's Oak. My agreement was that James was to be brought up as their nephew, and that he should know nothing of his unhappy parents.

"You will ask me why I selected Friar's Oak. It was because I had already chosen my place of concealment; and if I could not see my boy, it was, at least, some consolation to know that he was near me. You are aware that this mansion is one of the oldest in England; but you are not aware that it has been built with a very special eye to concealment, that there are no less than two habitable secret chambers, and that the outer or thicker walls are tunnelled into passages. The existence of these rooms has always been a family secret, though it was one which I valued so little that it was only the chance of my seldom using the house which had prevented me from pointing them out to some friend. Now I found that a secure retreat was provided for me in my extremity. I stole down to my own mansion, entered it at night, and, leaving all that was dear to me behind, I crept like a rat behind the wainscot, to live out the remainder of my weary life in solitude and misery. In this worn face, Charles, and in this grizzled hair, you may read the diary of my most miserable existence.

"Once a week Harrison used to bring me up provisions, passing them through the pantry window, which I left open for the purpose. Sometimes I would steal out at night and walk under the stars once more, with the cool breeze upon my forehead; but this I had at last to stop, for I was seen by the rustics, and rumours of a spirit at Cliffe Royal began to get about. One night two ghost-hunters—"

"It was I, father," cried Boy Jim; "I and my friend, Rodney Stone."

"I know it was. Harrison told me so the same night. I was proud, James, to see that you had the spirit of the Barringtons, and that I had an heir whose gallantry might redeem the family blot which I have striven so hard to cover over. Then came the day when your mother's kindness—her mistaken kindness—gave you the means of escaping to London."

"Ah, Edward," cried his wife, "if you had seen our boy, like a caged eagle, beating against the bars, you would have helped to give him even so short a flight as this."

"I do not blame you, Mary. It is possible that I should have done so. He went to London, and he tried to open a career for himself by his own strength and courage. How many of our ancestors have done the same, save only that a sword-hilt lay in their closed hands; but of them all I do not know that any have carried themselves more gallantly!"

"That I dare swear," said my uncle, heartily.

"And then, when Harrison at last returned, I learned that my son was actually matched to fight in a public prize-battle. That would not do, Charles! It was one thing to fight as you and I have fought in our youth, and it was another to compete for a purse of gold."

"My dear friend, I would not for the world—"

"Of course you would not, Charles. You chose the best man, and how could you do otherwise? But it would not do! I determined that the time had come when I should reveal myself to my son, the more so as there were many signs that my most unnatural existence had seriously weakened my health. Chance, or shall I not rather say Providence, had at last made clear all that had been dark, and given me the means of establishing my innocence. My wife went yesterday to bring my boy at last to the side of his unfortunate father."

There was silence for some time, and then it was my uncle's voice which broke it.

"You've been the most ill-used man in the world, Ned," said he. "Please God we shall have many years yet in which to make up to you for it. But, after all, it seems to me that we are as far as ever from learning how your unfortunate brother met his death."

"For eighteen years it was as much a mystery to me as to you, Charles. But now at last the guilt is manifest. Stand forward, Ambrose, and tell your story as frankly and as fully as you have told it to me."

CHAPTER XXI—THE VALET'S STORY

The valet had shrunk into the dark corner of the room, and had remained so motionless that we had forgotten his presence until, upon this appeal from his former master, he took a step forward into the light, turning his sallow face in our direction. His usually impassive features were in a state of painful agitation, and he spoke slowly and with hesitation, as though his trembling lips could hardly frame the words. And yet, so strong is habit, that, even in this extremity of emotion he assumed the deferential air of the high-class valet, and his sentences formed themselves in the sonorous fashion which had struck my attention upon that first day when the curricle of my uncle had stopped outside my father's door.

"My Lady Avon and gentlemen," said he, "if I have sinned in this matter, and I freely confess that I have done so, I only know one way in which I can atone for it, and that is by making the full and complete confession which my noble master, Lord Avon, has demanded. I assure you, then, that what I am about to tell you, surprising as it may seem, is the absolute and undeniable truth concerning the mysterious death of Captain Barrington.

"It may seem impossible to you that one in my humble walk of life should bear a deadly and implacable hatred against a man in the position of Captain Barrington. You think that the gulf between is too wide. I can tell you, gentlemen, that the gulf which can be bridged by unlawful love can be spanned also by an unlawful hatred, and that upon the day when this young man stole from me all that made my life worth living, I vowed to Heaven that I should take from him that foul life of his, though the deed would cover but the tiniest fraction of the debt which he owed me. I see that you look askance at me, Sir Charles Tregellis, but you should pray to God, sir, that you may never have the chance of finding out what you would yourself be capable of in the same position."

It was a wonder to all of us to see this man's fiery nature breaking suddenly through the artificial constraints with which he held it in check. His short dark hair seemed to bristle upwards, his eyes glowed with the intensity of his passion, and his face expressed a malignity of hatred which neither the death of his enemy nor the lapse of years could mitigate. The demure servant was gone, and there stood in his place a deep and dangerous man, one who might be an ardent lover or a most vindictive foe.

"We were about to be married, she and I, when some black chance threw him across our path. I do not know by what base deceptions he lured her away from me. I have heard that she was only one of many, and that he was an adept at the art. It was done before ever I knew the danger, and she was left with her broken heart and her ruined life to return to that home into which she had brought disgrace and misery. I only saw her once. She told me that her seducer had burst out a-laughing when she had reproached him for his perfidy, and I swore to her that his heart's blood should pay me for that laugh.

"I was a valet at the time, but I was not yet in the service of Lord Avon. I applied for and gained that position with the one idea that it might give me an opportunity of settling my accounts with his younger brother. And yet my chance was a terribly long time coming, for many months had passed before the visit to Cliffe Royal gave me the opportunity which I longed for by day and dreamed of by night. When it did come, however, it came in a fashion which was more favourable to my plans than anything that I had ever ventured to hope for.

"Lord Avon was of opinion that no one but himself knew of the secret passages in Cliffe Royal. In this he was mistaken. I knew of them—or, at least, I knew enough of them to serve my purpose. I need not tell you how, one day, when preparing the chambers for the guests, an accidental pressure upon part of the fittings caused a panel to gape in the woodwork, and showed me a narrow opening in the wall. Making my way down this, I found that another panel led into a larger bedroom beyond. That was all I knew, but it was all that was needed for my purpose. The disposal of the rooms had been left in my hands, and I arranged that Captain Barrington should sleep in the larger and I in the smaller. I could come upon him when I wished, and no one would be the wiser.

"And then he arrived. How can I describe to you the fever of impatience in which I lived until the moment should come for which I had waited and planned. For a night and a day they gambled, and for a night and a day I counted the minutes which brought me nearer to my man. They might ring for fresh wine at what hour they liked, they always found me waiting and ready, so that this young captain hiccoughed out that I was the model of all valets. My master advised me to go to bed. He had noticed my flushed cheek and my bright eyes, and he set me down as being in a fever. So I was, but it was a fever which only one medicine could assuage.

"Then at last, very early in the morning, I heard them push back their chairs, and I knew that their game had at last come to an end. When I entered the room to receive my orders, I found that Captain Barrington had already stumbled off to bed. The others had also retired, and my master was sitting alone at the table, with his empty bottle and the scattered cards in front of him. He ordered me angrily to my room, and this time I obeyed him.

"My first care was to provide myself with a weapon. I knew that if I were face to face with him I could tear his throat out, but I must so arrange that the fashion of his death should be a noiseless one. There was a hunting trophy in the hall, and from it I took a straight heavy knife which I sharpened upon my boot. Then I stole to my room, and sat waiting upon the side of my bed. I had made up my mind what I should do. There would be little satisfaction in killing him if he was not to know whose hand had struck the blow, or which of his sins it came to avenge. Could I but bind him and gag him in his drunken sleep, then a prick or two of my dagger would arouse him to listen to what I had to say to him. I pictured the look in his eyes as the haze of sleep cleared slowly away from them, the look of anger turning suddenly to stark horror as he understood who I was and what I had come for. It would be the supreme moment of my life.

"I waited as it seemed to me for at least an hour; but I had no watch, and my impatience was such that I dare say it really was little more than a quarter of that time. Then I rose, removed my shoes, took my knife, and having opened the panel, slipped silently through. It was not more than thirty feet that I had to go, but I went inch by inch, for the old rotten boards snapped like breaking twigs if a sudden weight was placed upon them. It was, of course, pitch dark, and very, very slowly I felt my way along. At last I saw a yellow seam of light glimmering in front of me, and I knew that it came from the other panel. I was too soon, then, since he had not extinguished his candles. I had waited many months, and I could afford to wait another hour, for I did not wish to do anything precipitately or in a hurry.

"It was very necessary to move silently now, since I was within a few feet of my man, with only the thin wooden partition between. Age had warped and cracked the boards, so that when I had at last very stealthily crept my way as far as the sliding-panel, I found that I could, without any difficulty, see into the room. Captain Barrington was standing by the dressing-table with his coat and vest off. A large pile of sovereigns, and several slips of paper were lying before him, and he was counting over his gambling gains. His face was flushed, and he was heavy from want of sleep and from wine. It rejoiced me to see it, for it meant that his slumber would be deep, and that all would be made easy for me.

"I was still watching him, when of a sudden I saw him start, and a terrible expression come upon his face. For an instant my heart stood still, for I feared that he had in some way divined my presence. And then I heard the voice of my master within. I could not see the door by which he had entered, nor could I see him where he stood, but I heard all that he had to say. As I watched the captain's face flush fiery-red, and then turn to a livid white as he listened to those bitter words which told him of his infamy, my revenge was sweeter—far sweeter—than my most pleasant dreams had ever pictured it. I saw my master approach the dressing-table, hold the papers in the flame of the candle, throw their charred ashes into the grate, and sweep the golden pieces into a small brown canvas bag. Then, as he turned to leave the room, the captain seized him by the wrist, imploring him, by the memory of their mother, to have mercy upon him; and I loved my master as I saw him drag his sleeve from the grasp of the clutching fingers, and leave the stricken wretch grovelling upon the floor.

"And now I was left with a difficult point to settle, for it was hard for me to say whether it was better that I should do that which I had come for, or whether, by holding this man's guilty secret, I might not have in my hand a keener and more deadly weapon than my master's hunting-knife. I was sure that Lord Avon could not and would not expose him. I knew your sense of family pride too well, my lord, and I was certain that his secret was safe in your hands. But I both could and would; and then, when his life had been blasted, and he had been hounded from his regiment and from his clubs, it would be time, perhaps, for me to deal in some other way with him."

"Ambrose, you are a black villain," said my uncle.

"We all have our own feelings, Sir Charles; and you will permit me to say that a serving-man may resent an injury as much as a gentleman, though the redress of the duel is denied to him. But I am telling you frankly, at Lord Avon's request, all that I thought and did upon that night, and I shall continue to do so, even if I am not fortunate enough to win your approval.

"When Lord Avon had left him, the captain remained for some time in a kneeling attitude, with his face sunk upon a chair. Then he rose, and paced slowly up and down the room, his chin sunk upon his breast. Every now and then he would pluck at his hair, or shake his clenched hands in the air; and I saw the moisture glisten upon his brow. For a time I lost sight of him, and I heard him opening drawer after drawer, as though he were in search of something. Then he stood over by his dressing-table again, with his back turned to me. His head was thrown a little back, and he had both hands up to the collar of his shirt, as though he were striving to undo it. And then there was a gush as if a ewer had been upset, and down he sank upon the ground, with his head in the corner, twisted round at so strange an angle to his shoulders that one glimpse of it told me that my man was slipping swiftly from the clutch in which I had fancied that I held him. I slid my panel, and was in the room in an instant. His eyelids still quivered, and it seemed to me, as my gaze met his glazing eyes, that I could read both recognition and surprise in them. I laid my knife upon the floor, and I stretched myself out beside him, that I might whisper in his ear one or two little things of which I wished to remind him; but even as I did so, he gave a gasp and was gone.

"It is singular that I, who had never feared him in life, should be frightened at him now, and yet when I looked at him, and saw that all was motionless save the creeping stain upon the carpet, I was seized with a sudden foolish spasm of terror, and, catching up my knife, I fled swiftly and silently back to my own room, closing the panels behind me. It was only when I had reached it that I found that in my mad haste I had carried away, not the hunting-knife which I had taken with me, but the bloody razor which had dropped from the dead man's hand. This I concealed where no one has ever discovered it; but my fears would not allow me to go back for the other, as I might perhaps have done, had I foreseen how terribly its presence might tell against my master. And that, Lady Avon and gentlemen, is an exact and honest account of how Captain Barrington came by his end."

"And how was it," asked my uncle, angrily, "that you have allowed an innocent man to be persecuted all these years, when a word from you might have saved him?"

"Because I had every reason to believe, Sir Charles, that that would be most unwelcome to Lord Avon. How could I tell all this without revealing the family scandal which he was so anxious to conceal? I confess that at the beginning I did not tell him what I had seen, and my excuse must be that he disappeared before I had time to determine what I should do. For many a year, however—ever since I have been in your service, Sir Charles—my conscience tormented me, and I swore that if ever I should find my old master, I should reveal everything to him. The chance of my overhearing a story told by young Mr. Stone here, which showed me that some one was using the secret chambers of Cliffe Royal, convinced me that Lord Avon was in hiding there, and I lost no time in seeking him out and offering to do him all the justice in my power."

"What he says is true," said his master; "but it would have been strange indeed if I had hesitated to sacrifice a frail life and failing health in a cause for which I freely surrendered all that youth had to offer. But new considerations have at last compelled me to alter my resolution. My son, through ignorance of his true position, was drifting into a course of life which accorded with his strength and spirit, but not with the traditions of his house. Again, I reflected that many of those who knew my brother had passed away, that all the facts need not come out, and that my death whilst under the suspicion of such a crime would cast a deeper stain upon our name than the sin which he had so terribly expiated. For these reasons—"

The tramp of several heavy footsteps reverberating through the old house broke in suddenly upon Lord Avon's words. His wan face turned even a shade greyer as he heard it, and he looked piteously to his wife and son.

"They will arrest me!" he cried. "I must submit to the degradation of an arrest."

"This way, Sir James; this way," said the harsh tones of Sir Lothian Hume from without.

"I do not need to be shown the way in a house where I have drunk many a bottle of good claret," cried a deep voice in reply; and there in the doorway stood the broad figure of Squire Ovington in his buck-skins and top-boots, a riding-crop in his hand. Sir Lothian Hume was at his elbow, and I saw the faces of two country constables peeping over his shoulders.

"Lord Avon," said the squire, "as a magistrate of the county of Sussex, it is my duty to tell you that a warrant is held against you for the wilful murder of your brother, Captain Barrington, in the year 1786."

"I am ready to answer the charge."

"This I tell you as a magistrate. But as a man, and the Squire of Rougham Grange, I'm right glad to see you, Ned, and here's my hand on it, and never will I believe that a good Tory like yourself, and a man who could show his horse's tail to any field in the whole Down county, would ever be capable of so vile an act."

"You do me justice, James," said Lord Avon, clasping the broad, brown hand which the country squire had held out to him. "I am as innocent as you are; and I can prove it."

"Damned glad I am to hear it, Ned! That is to say, Lord Avon, that any defence which you may have to make will be decided upon by your peers and by the laws of your country."

"Until which time," added Sir Lothian Hume, "a stout door and a good lock will be the best guarantee that Lord Avon will be there when called for."

The squire's weather-stained face flushed to a deeper red as he turned upon the Londoner.

"Are you the magistrate of a county, sir?"

"I have not the honour, Sir James."

"Then how dare you advise a man who has sat on the bench for nigh twenty years! When I am in doubt, sir, the law provides me with a clerk with whom I may confer, and I ask no other assistance."

"You take too high a tone in this matter, Sir James. I am not accus-tomed to be taken to task so sharply."

"Nor am I accustomed, sir, to be interfered with in my official duties. I speak as a magistrate, Sir Lothian, but I am always ready to sustain my opinions as a man."

Sir Lothian bowed.

"You will allow me to observe, sir, that I have personal interests of the highest importance involved in this matter, I have every reason to believe that there is a conspiracy afoot which will affect my position as heir to Lord Avon's titles and estates. I desire his safe custody in order that this matter may be cleared up, and I call upon you, as a magistrate, to execute your warrant."

"Plague take it, Ned!" cried the squire, "I would that my clerk Johnson were here, for I would deal as kindly by you as the law allows; and yet I am, as you hear, called upon to secure your person."

"Permit me to suggest, sir," said my uncle, "that so long as he is under the personal supervision of the magistrate, he may be said to be under the care of the law, and that this condition will be fulfilled if he is under the roof of Rougham Grange."

"Nothing could be better," cried the squire, heartily. "You will stay with me, Ned, until this matter blows over. In other words, Lord Avon, I make myself responsible, as the representative of the law, that you are held in safe custody until your person may be required of me."

"Yours is a true heart, James."

"Tut, tut! it is the due process of the law. I trust, Sir Lothian Hume, that you find nothing to object to in it?"

Sir Lothian shrugged his shoulders, and looked blackly at the magistrate. Then he turned to my uncle.

"There is a small matter still open between us," said he. "Would you kindly give me the name of a friend? Mr. Corcoran, who is outside in my barouche, would act for me, and we might meet to-morrow morning."

"With pleasure," answered my uncle. "I dare say your father would act for me, nephew? Your friend may call upon Lieutenant Stone, of Friar's Oak, and the sooner the better."

And so this strange conference ended. As for me, I had sprung to the side of the old friend of my boyhood, and was trying to tell him my joy at his good fortune, and listening to his assurance that nothing that could ever befall him could weaken the love that he bore me. My uncle touched me on the shoulder, and we were about to leave, when Ambrose, whose bronze mask had been drawn down once more over his fiery passions, came demurely towards him.

"Beg your pardon, Sir Charles," said he; "but it shocks me very much to see your cravat."

"You are right, Ambrose," my uncle answered. "Lorimer does his best, but I have never been able to fill your place."

"I should be proud to serve you, sir; but you must acknowledge that Lord Avon has the prior claim. If he will release me—"

"You may go, Ambrose; you may go!" cried Lord Avon. "You are an excellent servant, but your presence has become painful to me."

"Thank you, Ned," said my uncle. "But you must not leave me so suddenly again, Ambrose."

"Permit me to explain the reason, sir. I had determined to give you notice when we reached Brighton; but as we drove from the village that day, I caught a glimpse of a lady passing in a phaeton between whom and Lord Avon I was well aware there was a close intimacy, although I was not certain that she was actually his wife. Her presence there confirmed me in my opinion that he was in hiding at Cliffe Royal, and I dropped from your curricle and followed her at once, in order to lay the matter before her, and explain how very necessary it was that Lord Avon should see me."

"Well, I forgive you for your desertion, Ambrose," said my uncle; "and," he added, "I should be vastly obliged to you if you would re-arrange my tie."

CHAPTER XXII—THE END

Sir James Ovington's carriage was waiting without, and in it the Avon family, so tragically separated and so strangely re-united, were borne away to the squire's hospitable home. When they had gone, my uncle mounted his curricle, and drove Ambrose and myself to the village.

"We had best see your father at once, nephew," said he. "Sir Lothian and his man started some time ago. I should be sorry if there should be any hitch in our meeting."

For my part, I was thinking of our opponent's deadly reputation as a duellist, and I suppose that my features must have betrayed my feelings, for my uncle began to laugh.

"Why, nephew," said he, "you look as if you were walking behind my coffin. It is not my first affair, and I dare bet that it will not be my last. When I fight near town I usually fire a hundred or so in Manton's back shop, but I dare say I can find my way to his waistcoat. But I confess that I am somewhat *accablé*, by all that has befallen us. To think of my dear old friend being not only alive, but innocent as well! And that he should have such a strapping son and heir to carry on the race of Avon! This will be the last blow to Hume, for I know that the Jews have given him rope on the score of his expectations. And you, Ambrose, that you should break out in such a way!"

Of all the amazing things which had happened, this seemed to have impressed my uncle most, and he recurred to it again and again. That a man whom he had come to regard as a machine for tying cravats and brewing chocolate should suddenly develop fiery human passions was indeed a prodigy. If his silver razor-heater had taken to evil ways he could not have been more astounded.

We were still a hundred yards from the cottage when I saw the tall, green-coated Mr. Corcoran striding down the garden path. My father was waiting for us at the door with an expression of subdued delight upon his face.

"Happy to serve you in any way, Sir Charles," said he. "We've arranged it for to-morrow at seven on Ditching Common."

"I wish these things could be brought off a little later in the day," said my uncle. "One has either to rise at a perfectly absurd hour, or else to neglect one's toilet."

"They are stopping across the road at the Friar's Oak inn, and if you would wish it later—"

"No, no; I shall make the effort. Ambrose, you will bring up the *batteris de toilette* at five."

"I don't know whether you would care to use my barkers," said my father. "I've had 'em in fourteen actions, and up to thirty yards you couldn't wish a better tool."

"Thank you, I have my duelling pistols under the seat. See that the triggers are oiled, Ambrose, for I love a light pull. Ah, sister Mary, I have brought your boy back to you, none the worse, I hope, for the dissipations of town."

I need not tell you how my dear mother wept over me and fondled me, for you who have mothers will know for yourselves, and you who have not will never understand how warm and snug the home nest can be. How I had chafed and longed for the wonders of town, and yet, now that I had seen more than my wildest dreams had ever deemed possible, my eyes had rested upon nothing which was so sweet and so restful as our own little sitting-room, with its terra-cotta-coloured walls, and those trifles which are so insignificant in themselves, and yet so rich in memories—the blow-fish from the Moluccas, the narwhal's horn from the Arctic, and the picture of the Ca Ira, with Lord Hotham in chase! How cheery, too, to see at one side of the shining grate my father with his pipe and his merry red face, and on the other my mother with her fingers ever turning and darting with her knitting-needles! As I looked at them I marvelled that I could ever have longed to leave them, or that I could bring myself to leave them again.

But leave them I must, and that speedily, as I learned amidst the boisterous congratulations of my father and the tears of my mother. He had himself been appointed to the Cato, 64, with post rank, whilst a note had come from Lord Nelson at Portsmouth to say that a vacancy was open for me if I should present myself at once.

"And your mother has your sea-chest all ready, my lad, and you can travel down with me to-morrow; for if you are to be one of Nelson's men, you must show him that you are worthy of it."

"All the Stones have been in the sea-service," said my mother, apologetically to my uncle, "and it is a great chance that he should enter under Lord Nelson's own patronage. But we can never forget your kindness, Charles, in showing our dear Rodney something of the world."

"On the contrary, sister Mary," said my uncle, graciously, "your son has been an excellent companion to me—so much so that I fear that I am open to the charge of having neglected my dear Fidelio. I trust that I bring him back somewhat more polished than I found him. It would be folly to call him *distingué*, but he is at least unobjectionable. Nature has denied him the highest gifts, and I find him adverse to employing the compensating advantages of art; but, at least, I have shown him something of life, and I have taught him a few lessons in finesse and deportment which may appear to be wasted upon him at present, but which, none the less, may come back to him in his more mature years. If his career in town has been a disappointment to me, the reason lies mainly in the fact that I am foolish enough to measure others by the standard which I have myself set. I am well disposed towards him, however, and I consider him eminently adapted for the profession which he is about to adopt."

He held out his sacred snuff-box to me as he spoke, as a solemn pledge of his goodwill, and, as I look back at him, there is no moment at which I see him more plainly than that with the old mischievous light dancing once more in his large intolerant eyes, one thumb in the armpit of his vest, and the little shining box held out upon his snow-white palm. He was a type and leader of a strange breed of men which has vanished away from England—the full-blooded, virile buck, exquisite in his dress, narrow in his thoughts, coarse in his amusements, and eccentric in his habits. They walk across the bright stage of English history with their finicky step, their preposterous cravats, their high collars, their dangling seals, and they vanish into those dark wings from which there is no return. The world has outgrown them, and there is no place now for their strange fashions, their practical jokes, and carefully cultivated eccentricities. And yet behind this outer veiling of folly, with which they so carefully draped themselves, they were often men of strong character and robust personality. The languid loungers of St. James's were also the yachtsmen of the Solent, the fine riders of the shires, and the hardy fighters in many a wayside battle and many a morning frolic. Wellington picked his best officers from amongst them. They condescended occasionally to poetry or oratory; and Byron, Charles James Fox, Sheridan, and Castlereagh, preserved some reputation amongst them, in spite of their publicity. I cannot think how the historian of the future can hope to understand them, when I, who knew one of them so well, and bore his blood in my veins, could never quite tell how much of him was real, and how much was due to the affectations which he had cultivated so long that they had ceased to deserve the name. Through the chinks of that armour of folly I have sometimes thought that I had caught a glimpse of a good and true man within, and it pleases me to hope that I was right.

It was destined that the exciting incidents of that day were even now not at an end. I had retired early to rest, but it was impossible for me to sleep, for my mind would turn to Boy Jim and to the extraordinary change in his position and prospects. I was still turning and tossing when I heard the sound of flying hoofs coming down the London Road, and immediately afterwards the grating of wheels as they pulled up in front of the inn. My window chanced to be open, for it was a fresh spring night, and I heard the creak of the inn door, and a voice asking whether Sir Lothian Hume was within. At the name I sprang from my bed, and I was in time to see three men, who had alighted from the carriage, file into the lighted hall. The two horses were left standing, with the glare of the open door falling upon their brown shoulders and patient heads.

Ten minutes may have passed, and then I heard the clatter of many steps, and a knot of men came clustering through the door.

"You need not employ violence," said a harsh, clear voice. "On whose suit is it?"

"Several suits, sir. They 'eld over in the 'opes that you'd pull off the fight this mornin'. Total amounts is twelve thousand pound."

"Look here, my man, I have a very important appointment for seven o'clock to-morrow. I'll give you fifty pounds if you will leave me until then."

"Couldn't do it, sir, really. It's more than our places as sheriff's officers is worth."

In the yellow glare of the carriage-lamp I saw the baronet look up at our windows, and if hatred could have killed, his eyes would have been as deadly as his pistol.

"I can't mount the carriage unless you free my hands," said he.

"Old 'ard, Bill, for 'e looks vicious. Let go o' one arm at a time! Ah, would you then?"

"Corcoran! Corcoran!" screamed a voice, and I saw a plunge, a struggle, and one frantic figure breaking its way from the rest. Then came a heavy blow, and down he fell in the middle of the moonlit road, flapping and jumping among the dust like a trout new landed.

"He's napped it this time! Get 'im by the wrists, Jim! Now, all together!"

He was hoisted up like a bag of flour, and fell with a brutal thud into the bottom of the carriage. The three men sprang in after him, a whip whistled in the darkness, and I had seen the last that I or any one else, save some charitable visitor to a debtors' gaol, was ever again destined to see of Sir Lothian Hume, the once fashionable Corinthian.

Lord Avon lived for two years longer—long enough, with the help of Ambrose, to fully establish his innocence of the horrible crime, in the shadow of which he had lived so long. What he could not clear away, however, was the effect of those years of morbid and unnatural life spent in the hidden chambers of the old house; and it was only the devotion of his wife and of his son which kept the thin and flickering flame of his life alight. She whom I had known as the play actress of Anstey Cross became the dowager Lady Avon; whilst Boy Jim, as dear to me now as when we harried birds' nests and tickled trout together, is now Lord Avon, beloved by his tenantry, the finest sportsman and the most popular man from the north of the Weald to the Channel. He was married to the second daughter of Sir James Ovington; and as I have seen three of his grandchildren within the week, I fancy that if any of Sir Lothian's descendants have their eye upon the property, they are likely to be as disappointed as their ancestor was before them. The old house of Cliffe Royal has been pulled down, owing to the terrible family associations which hung round it, and a beautiful modern building sprang up in its place. The lodge which stood by the Brighton Road was so dainty with its trellis-work and its rose bushes that I was not the only visitor who declared that I had rather be the owner of it than of the great house amongst the trees. There for many years in a happy and peaceful old age lived Jack Harrison and his wife, receiving back in the sunset of their lives the loving care which they had themselves bestowed. Never again did Champion Harrison throw his leg over the ropes of a twenty-four-foot ring; but the story of the great battle between the smith and the West Countryman is still familiar to old ring-goers, and nothing pleased him better than to re-fight it all, round by round, as he sat in the sunshine under his rose-girt porch. But if he heard the tap of his wife's stick approaching him, his talk would break off at once into the garden and its prospects, for she was still haunted by the fear that he would some day go back to the ring, and she never missed the old man for an hour without being convinced that he had hobbled off to wrest the belt from the latest upstart champion. It was at his own very earnest request that they inscribed "He fought the good fight" upon his tombstone, and though I cannot doubt that he had Black Bank and Crab Wilson in his mind when he asked it, yet none who knew him would grudge its spiritual meaning as a summing up of his clean and manly life.

Sir Charles Tregellis continued for some years to show his scarlet and gold at Newmarket, and his inimitable coats in St. James's. It was he who invented buttons and loops at the ends of dress pantaloons, and who broke fresh ground by his investigation of the comparative merits of isinglass and of starch in the preparation of shirt-fronts. There are old fops still lurking in the corners of Arthur's or of White's who can remember Tregellis's dictum, that a cravat should be so stiffened that three parts of the length could be raised by one corner, and the painful schism which followed when Lord Alvanley and his school contended that a half was sufficient. Then came the supremacy of Brummell, and the open breach upon the subject of velvet collars, in which the town followed the lead of the younger man. My uncle, who was not born to be second to any one, retired instantly to St. Albans, and announced that he would make it the centre of fashion and of society, instead of degenerate London. It chanced, however, that the mayor and corporation waited upon him with an address of thanks for his good intentions towards the town, and that the burgesses, having ordered new coats from London for the occasion, were all arrayed in velvet collars, which so preyed upon my uncle's spirits that he took to his bed, and never showed his face in public again. His money, which had ruined what might have been a great life, was divided amongst many bequests, an annuity to his valet, Ambrose, being amongst them; but enough has come to his sister, my dear mother, to help to make her old age as sunny and as pleasant as even I could wish.

And as for me—the poor string upon which these beads are strung—I dare scarce say another word about myself, lest this, which I had meant to be the last word of a chapter, should grow into the first words of a new one. Had I not taken up my pen to tell you a story of the land, I might, perchance, have made a better one of the sea; but the one frame cannot hold two opposite pictures. The day may come when I shall write down all that I remember of the greatest battle ever fought upon salt water, and how my father's gallant life was brought to an end as, with his paint rubbing against a French eighty-gun ship on one side and a Spanish seventy-four upon the other he stood eating an apple in the break of his poop. I saw the smoke banks on that October evening swirl slowly up over the Atlantic swell, and rise, and rise, until they had shredded into thinnest air, and lost themselves in the infinite blue of heaven. And with them rose the cloud which had hung over the country; and it also thinned and thinned, until God's own sun of peace and security was shining once more upon us, never more, we hope, to be bedimmed.